TRUE COLORS

AMY KNUPP

CHAPTER ONE

You better not be late picking up my sister.

Drake North grinned at the hint of a threat in the text message from his best friend as he walked—okay, damn near jogged—out of the short-term lot toward the Nashville airport terminal. Late, of course.

Got it under control, he typed as he entered the building.

The plane landed three minutes ago, Ezra texted.

Drake was fully aware of the time. He might have a rep for being fashionably late—he crammed a lot into every day, by design—but he wasn't going to let Ezra down.

Yep, Drake replied. *You can quit stalking the airline app now. It doesn't really ease your guilty conscience anyway, does it?* He couldn't resist the jab, even though he was more than a little familiar with Ezra's lifelong protectiveness toward his younger sister, Mackenzie.

As Drake made his way toward the security cutoff, keeping an eye on the scattering of arriving passengers who passed him, his phone vibrated with a phone call. He laughed when he saw it was Ez.

"Kinda busy here," Drake answered facetiously.

"Are you even to the airport yet?" his friend demanded from the other side of the globe.

"Relax. I'm in the terminal, watching for her. Her plane hasn't unloaded yet." This part of the airport was relatively calm at the moment, probably because it was nearing ten p.m. on a Wednesday.

Ez released a breath over the line, as if finally relaxing. "Thanks for doing this. I'm sorry to drag you away from whatever you had going on. I'm sure there was a woman involved somehow."

"There was," Drake said, "but not the way you think. Here's a question for you. Who's the North brother least likely to get hitched?"

"You," Ez said without hesitation, and Drake grinned because that was tough to argue with.

"Besides me. Try Cole. He proposed tonight. Popped the question on camera while Sierra was recording an episode of the remodeling show. The whole family was there watching. We went to celebrate afterward. I had to show my face for that."

"I guess you did." Ezra's surprise was evident. "Damn. One of the eternal-bachelor North brothers goes down."

"He's happy. Like I've never seen him. *Cole* and *happy* are two words you don't often hear in the same sentence. Anyway, I dragged myself away just for you."

"For Mackenzie," Ez corrected.

"You do know she's a grown woman who's been on her own in LA for years?" Drake asked. He did the math in his head to figure she must be twenty-five now, four years younger than the two of them.

"She could handle it on her own, no question, but it'd be nice if she didn't have to. And moving sucks no matter how old you are."

"That it does, but tonight'll be easy. It hardly counts as moving."

From what Drake understood, Mackenzie's move back to Nashville, where she'd grown up, was because of her job. She'd apparently sold her car, packed her bags, and had already signed a lease on an apartment here in town.

"Still, I appreciate it," Ezra said, his tone going serious. "Big-brother fail on my part. And not the first one."

Not surprising considering Ezra's demanding career, the very type Drake had always managed to avoid. As a consultant in technology, Ez often had to put the job first, drop everything, and jet to some other part of the world with little or no notice. His friend was still beating himself up because he'd promised Mackenzie he'd meet her in Nashville to help her settle in and then his schedule had changed last minute, taking him from Europe to Australia instead of back to the States.

"I've got you covered, bro. I'll get her to her apartment, make sure it looks okay, see that she has what she needs until her stuff shows up. I'll take care of her for you. You go back to doing your technology-whisperer thing."

It really was no big deal, just a couple of hours of Drake's time before he met some friends out at a bar later, and he'd do anything for his best friend. Ez had been there for him at some of the toughest times of his life.

"Gotta go," Drake said as passengers started appearing from the direction of Mackenzie's gate. "They're deplaning. I assume I'll recognize her."

"I emailed you a photo from the last time I visited her," Ez said.

"I must've missed it."

"Check your email. Dinner's on me next time I'm in town."

"Get your ass here soon. It's been a while."

They said goodbye as Drake scanned the people exiting the secured part of the airport. Not seeing her, he went to his inbox on his phone and scanned the senders until he found Ezra's name. He opened it to see Ezra and Mackenzie in a selfie on the beach. As he zoomed in on her face, it struck him as it hadn't before that she was all grown up. She looked happy and confident and attractive. As a kid, she'd always had indistinctive medium-brown hair, but there were a few copper highlights now. Her brown eyes sparkled with an indescribable something, and he could see how a guy could be drawn in by them.

Confident he could recognize her, he shoved his phone into his pocket and skimmed his gaze over the cluster of people who approached. Then he spotted a head of tousled hair the right color a few steps behind the pack, pointed downward so he couldn't see the face. As they got closer, the group in front of her dispersed, allowing him to see that, yes, this was Mackenzie. He was fairly sure of it even with her head down, as she focused on stuffing something in an oversized bag on her shoulder and rolled a carry-on behind her, and then her step stuttered as the bag rolled into her ankle, and that sealed it. Mackenzie had always been the clumsiest human he knew.

Drake stepped closer, waiting impatiently for her to look up and notice him. She was tall—she'd always been tall for a female and skinny—but the feminine curves on her were new to him. She wore jeans, a simple V-neck T-shirt, and a light-blue-and-white-plaid flannel shirt tied around her waist that highlighted the dip inward from her hips. On her feet were flat-soled sandals with copper beadwork that showed off a toe ring and wine-colored toenails. With her face still pointed down, his gaze was drawn to her collarbone, partially revealed by the wide vee of her shirt, and something about it got his attention as a man instead of as her brother's friend.

He shook himself out of that right quick, and then finally she pulled her attention from her bag and looked up. It was as if someone had zapped him with a Taser as a strange combination of familiarity and shock hit him. Familiarity because that smile and the spark in her eyes were his friend's little sister through and through and took him back to when he was a teenager and she was a busybody brat he'd affectionately called Shawlet. Shock because...*damn*. Mackenzie Shaw had grown up spectacularly. The picture Ez had sent did not do her justice.

"Drake," she said in a melodic voice that was fuller than the teenage version he remembered, "you're here."

The surprise in her tone gave away a hint of vulnerability, as if she hadn't believed he'd make it, and that waver of insecurity took him back to the time when he and Ezra had been determined to protect her from an eighth-grade putz who'd broken her naive seventh-grade heart. He and Ez had picked her up at the middle school for a week straight just to intimidate the little prick who'd kissed her after a basketball game and then ghosted her. Their intimidation had been limited to big-brother don't-fuck-with-my-sister stares, as they'd had the advantage in size, brains, and muscles and it wouldn't have been a fair fight.

Without thought, he stepped forward, wrapped her in a brief hug, and kissed the top of her head. "It sounds like you didn't think I'd show."

"Ez said you might be late." She beamed up at him, and his nostalgia was shoved aside by a surge of desire. "Thanks for picking me up."

"Welcome back," he said, more than a little rattled by his reaction to her.

Mackenzie inhaled deeply, causing her chest to rise, sexy collarbone, intriguing breasts, and all. "It feels good to be back," she said as her gaze roved over him. "Really good."

Hell. He needed a moment. Or a kick in the ass, which Ez would readily provide if he knew the thoughts firing through Drake's head.

The thought of Ezra was enough to bring him to his senses. "Let's put your brother's mind at ease," Drake said, pulling his phone back out and sidling up next to Mackenzie for a selfie. "Smile pretty. He's got his tighty-whiteys in a bunch, thinking I'll let you down."

"It's always fun to prove my brother wrong."

Drake clicked, and without inspecting the photo, he reopened the app they used to text internationally and sent it on its way. Ignoring, the whole while, the hint of Mackenzie's feminine floral scent that affected him on an elemental level.

MACKENZIE HAD DONE HER HOMEWORK.

Well, as well as she could. It wasn't easy to get the lowdown on a guy who didn't do much on social media. He had accounts —she'd found Drake on three different platforms—but he didn't post much. The content on his accounts consisted mostly of photos he was tagged in by other people. Females. Always females. Pretty, happy females draping themselves all over the youngest North brother.

Mackenzie couldn't blame them.

Drake was drape-worthy. He always had been.

He reached over and took the handle of the rolling bag from her and pulled it behind him. "Do you have another bag?" he asked as they walked in the general direction of the baggage claim area.

She laughed. "I had to check three." And paid for extra weight on two of them. Still the cheapest way to get the things she needed most immediately to Nashville.

"It might be tough to fit those on my bike."

Mackenzie halted in her tracks and peered over at him, narrowing her eyes, assessing if he could possibly be serious.

On the one hand, the thought of this mouthwatering man on a motorcycle—she assumed he wasn't talking about a Schwinn—was all kinds of distracting. On the other, surely he couldn't be that dense, could he?

No. The Drake she remembered was not stupid.

"You're bullshitting," she said as she resumed their path toward the escalator.

With an irresistible boyish grin, he said, "Got me. I switched it out for the Jeep just for you."

Between those arresting sky-blue eyes with their spark of mischief, the just-right amount of toffee-brown scruff on his jaw, and that sexy tone in his voice that made the words sound more intimate than they were, it was evident he still oozed charm the way most guys oozed sweat during a pickup game of basketball on a ninety-degree afternoon.

She could fully, privately admit to a raging crush on him back in the day, when—she could acknowledge it now—she was too young for him. Drake North had plunged her right into puberty, though he hadn't been aware of his role in her immature fantasies. Thank God.

She hadn't seen him in person for close to ten years, when he'd gone off to college. She'd thought of him on and off throughout the years, had heard vague reports of him from Ezra, and yes, had checked out his social media, but one thing she'd not been doing was pining away. She'd been living life full tilt in Los Angeles, first dipping her toes into college and then building a career she loved, meeting scores of people for both business and fun, and trying to find her place in life, like the seven billion other people on the planet.

Though the move back to Nashville had come up suddenly, it was key to her long-term plan. Living in this city she loved would enable her to put down roots. She had a down payment for a home saved, one that would buy her something decent in this part of the country, unlike on the West Coast, and once she got her bearings and laid the foundation for the new Nashville office of To the Stars, house hunting was her priority. If things went as planned, she'd be cozied up in her very own home in less than six months.

Her phone dinged from the depths of her travel bag, signaling a text, and she assumed it was Cora, her boss and friend, finally responding to Mackenzie's *I made it* text, which she'd sent as they taxied in. Now that Drake had her carry-on, it was easier to handle the oversized bag that enabled her to throw in pretty much everything except the kitchen sink—and liquids over three ounces.

The message had a local number but no name. She unlocked her phone as they got on the escalator and read the text.

This is Nadine from Hillside Haven Apartments. I realize you might already be on your way here, so I wanted to give you a heads-up. There's a problem with your apartment and I'm still assessing the extent. We can discuss details and a plan of action when you get here, but I wanted to warn you because it's a little bit shocking. We're working to remedy things at this moment. See you soon.

"You've got to be kidding me," Mackenzie said out loud, her stomach dipping. Then she scrolled up and read the message a second time before they reached the bottom of the escalator. She missed the end of the escalator, her head buried in her phone, and stumbled slightly, then righted herself. She stepped to the side and stopped. Read the text for a third time, her shoulders drooping.

"Problem?" Drake asked. He'd been behind her on the escalator and paused at her side now as he sized up the row of baggage carousels.

"There's an issue with my apartment." The apartment with the short-term lease that was crucial for her plans to work out.

"What kind of an issue?" he asked, turning his focus to her.

Mackenzie held out her phone so he could read it himself, absently glancing toward the carousels and not really seeing them. She was fighting off a host of negative thoughts, reminding herself that, as fast as she'd put all the pieces of this move into place, there were bound to be some hiccups. She would work through them.

"Let's get your bags and then we can go check it out," he said.

She let Drake figure out which carousel while she followed, typing to Nadine, asking her for more information.

By the time they had all of her suitcases lined up in front of them and Drake had ribbed her for packing like a girl, there was still no response from Nadine.

"I guess we'll go see for ourselves," Drake said. He threw a quick arm around her from the side, tugging her into him briefly.

As uneasy as she was about her apartment, all of that took a backseat as she caught the masculine scent of him, momentarily felt the heat of his solid, delectable body pressing up against her side, and thought for an instant about letting herself lean into him. Then she put a hard brake on her reaction, because that had been more of a big-brother move than a man-woman move, and she needed to keep it big-brother in her mind.

For the first time, she had a plan to get her life together, make it what she wanted and needed, and mooning over an unavailable guy, regardless of how tempting he was, was not the way to make it happen.

CHAPTER TWO

ackenzie believed you could tell a lot about a person from their vehicle. What brand was it? How old? How clean? What color? Especially in Hollywood, did the owner drive it himself or have a driver? What extras were on it? Though she didn't often get in a car with her clients, she frequently saw what they arrived in or, in some cases when she met with people at their home, could see into their eight-car garages.

The twelve-year-old, two-hundred-thousand-mile-plus white Camry she'd hocked for two thousand bucks before leaving LA likely conveyed practicality, perseverance, and determination, plus working class and either not worried about appearances or not having the budget to worry about appearances. She was in the latter group. In her job, appearances were important because of who her clients were, but she had to focus her energy on what she could afford—namely, her clothes, accessories, and hair.

Drake, on the other hand…

The shiny, new-looking black Jeep Wrangler Rubicon that he started remotely when they were still thirty feet away spoke volumes. He liked to drive and maybe off-road. He liked to impress. And he liked to play. Though the doors and roof were intact, she was pretty sure they could be removed and he could showboat to his heart's content while basking in the sun and letting the wind whip through his short dark hair. His vehicle screamed *carefree*.

He refused to let Mackenzie lift any of the suitcases into the back, and she had to admit the hint of chivalry was hot. She was all about equal rights for women and doing for herself, but she was travel weary and exhausted from packing to move for the past week, and there was no getting around it—Drake made a pretty picture with his long-sleeve tee that couldn't hide those significant biceps as they flexed with the effort. She stood back and watched him. She might not be officially mooning over him, but she would always appreciate an enticing view.

The man had filled out stupendously well.

The high school version of the star first baseman had been a treat to look at, but this version was even better. He was tall, over six feet, and his shoulders were wide, hips narrow, arms and chest nicely sculpted. And that butt... Was there anything more beautiful than a just-right baseball player's ass?

"No U-Haul necessary," Drake said with a sparkle in his eyes as he closed the back and led her to the front passenger door.

Mackenzie climbed inside and took in top-of-the-line every-thing, from the sound system to the stitched leather seats to the features. *Carefree and not hurting for money*, she amended in her mind.

"Where to?" he asked as he slid into the driver's seat.

Mackenzie swiped at her phone and pasted the address from her email into her map app. She said, "Head toward 40," then told him the address and the area of town.

"That's a decent neighborhood to live in," he said. "Older but well-maintained and safe."

"I know the area well though I haven't seen the apartment in person. It's owned by the father of one of Ez's friends. The main selling point is that he agreed to do a short-term lease without charging me higher rent." Because of that, she would make it would work, in spite of whatever problem it had tonight.

Drake touched the dash screen a couple of times, and she real-ized he'd connected it to her phone via Bluetooth as he pulled up the map and address. Her ancient Camry hadn't even had a backup camera.

"Why short-term?" he asked as he backed out of the spot and headed for the toll booth. "I was under the impression you were moving back for good."

"The plan is to buy a house in three to six months."

His brows went up on his forehead. "Big commitment."

"It is," she said with an exhale. "I'm so unbelievably ready. I've moved more times than a military kid in my life, and I just want a place that's mine for good."

"You guys did move a lot."

"It was my mom," Mackenzie said, and the sadness that always came with thoughts of her mother surfaced, diminished with the years but never gone. "Bless her, but she was not a stay-in-one-place kind of person at all." Though she had, thankfully, kept them in Nashville for every move while they were kids.

"I was sorry to hear about her death. I felt awful that I missed everything."

Her mom had died in a boating accident in the Bahamas, where she'd lived, when Mackenzie was nineteen. Drake had been on a remote trek somewhere, she vaguely remembered.

"Thank you. We were okay. I know she loved us, but Ez and I weren't super-close to her, you know? She was the type who was always searching for something better, happier, whatever. Better man, better job, better apartment." Mackenzie said it without any bitterness or anger. She'd made peace long ago with her mother's weaknesses and took comfort that she'd apparently died doing something she enjoyed, in a place she'd raved about, with a man she loved.

"Growing up, it got to the point I was almost afraid to unpack." She frowned, wishing she was exaggerating. By Mackenzie's eighteenth birthday, her mom had moved them nine times. "In LA, I wanted to stay put while I saved a down payment, but I've moved eight times in the last seven years."

"That's a lot even for someone like me who likes to shake things up frequently."

"There were solid reasons every single time, but it's been a little crazy."

"So you're ready to settle down," he said as he pulled onto the freeway entrance ramp.

"I'm ready for some stability," Mackenzie said, making a point to distinguish between that and *settling down*, because *settling down* made it sound like she wanted a husband and a puppy and a kid or two, and those were not on her list, not in the immediate future. She didn't equate the man part to stability in the least. "It kills me to have to spend three to six months in an apartment, but this move back happened so fast there was no way I could buy a house beforehand."

"Now you'll have time to look," Drake said.

"It's a priority."

Drake un-synced the climate control and set his side a couple of degrees cooler than hers. "Feel free to adjust this to whatever you need, and there's a button on the side by the door if you want the seat heater on. It's probably colder than California here."

It was. Even though she'd pulled her flannel shirt over her tee, the March wind chilled her, and she was grateful for the heat, which she felt within a few seconds of flipping the switch. Buying a car was also on her to-do list in the very near future, and she wondered if she could afford heated seats. She might have to prioritize them.

"The family business must be doing well," she said with a grin. "These are some nice wheels."

"I assume it is," he said, shrugging as he turned onto the entrance ramp to the interstate.

"You do work for North Brothers Sports, right?" Had Ezra told her that or had she assumed?

As Drake merged with traffic, he couldn't be more nonchalant when he said, "I don't work in the corporate office."

"What do you do?"

"I'm in retail. Right now I'm in the golf department, but I'm thinking I'll move to outdoor in the next couple of months to keep it interesting."

She stared at him, processing, trying to come up with a response. Drake North, who she was pretty sure had graduated from college, whose family had founded North Brothers Sports, sold golf gloves and clubs? And he drove a new Jeep that had to have cost a pretty penny.

Okay. He'd always been a people person, she guessed. To each his own. "So…full-time retail?"

He shook his head. "I'm also a personal trainer. I currently work at a gym a buddy of mine owns."

That made more sense. "You studied exercise science," she now remembered. "How long have you been doing that?"

He seemed to be calculating in his head as he zipped into the left lane and sped up when he found a big enough gap in traffic. "Close to seven months this time. I did the same job at a couple of different gyms when I first graduated. Spent some years coaching high school baseball in between."

"You've had a lot of jobs," she said.

"A few," he said with a megawatt smile. "I like to stay busy and mix it up often. Job, apartment, vehicles." He shrugged. "Variety's a good thing."

"So you're basically on the bottom of the family business? And you're fine with that?"

"It's by choice. I love my family's company and will probably always work there. I like the freedom to rotate through the departments at will. I get some privileges that allow me to bounce around, like full benefits and a share of profits. My dad took care of us all, and I'm grateful for that."

She wasn't judging, just trying to understand. She tended to give her all to her job and had worked her way up to being the owners' right-hand employee. She hoped to work at her company for many more years. It was hard to imagine such a laid-back attitude toward her career. And yet clearly Drake was happy with his life and his variety—and his lack of commitment to anything. Obviously, he had enough money to do what he wanted—she was pretty sure Ezra, at some point, had referred to each of the North brothers having loads of it thanks to those owners' shares.

"What about you?" Drake asked. "Ez said you're moving here for your job, but he didn't say what you do."

"I'm a honeymoon planner. I work for a company called To the Stars," she said. "We plan high-end niche honeymoons for the uber-rich." With a laugh, she added, "You could probably be a customer. Any wedding bells in your near future?"

He sent her a *get serious* glance and gave an exaggerated shudder as he turned his attention back to the road.

She laughed again, not thinking too hard about the flash of satisfaction at learning he didn't have a serious girlfriend. Of course he didn't. He was the type that basically screamed commitment-phobe. "I've seen a lot of your type who've succumbed."

"What's my type?"

"The guy everyone loves, who goes out all the time, with a different woman each night, likes to have a good time but keeps it light with everybody." It was an educated guess based on his reaction and the tags on his social media, and he didn't deny it, which told her she'd guessed right. "Those are the guys who fall the hardest."

"So, uber-rich in LA," he said, blatantly ignoring her assessment. "You work with any famous people?"

"Celebrities are a large percentage of my clients," she said. "Actors, musicians, producers, in addition to businesspeople and entrepreneurs."

"Anyone I've heard of?"

She listed some of the biggest Hollywood names she'd worked with, and Drake whistled.

"How'd you get into that?" he asked.

"It was a right time, right place, knowing the right person kinda thing."

"What time, place, and person would that be?"

Mackenzie leaned back and let the heated leather seat cradle her tired body, closing her eyes. "When I was a freshman, my roommate's older sister had recently started To the Stars, and she was looking for cheap part-time help. I fell in love with the job and, over the next two years, started spending more and more time working, building up referrals from happy customers. It was my dream job that I didn't know existed."

"You must be good at it."

"I can hold my own," she said. "By junior year, I was making more money than I'd make in the field I was studying, so I quit school."

"What were you studying?"

"Journalism. I was a celebrity freak growing up, and my goal was to write about famous people. But planning honeymoons, working with Hollywood stars in that capacity, I saw there's an adversarial feeling toward the press, even the writers from reputable companies that they had a good relationship with. My job makes me a valued partner instead of someone who intrudes on their privacy."

"You offer them a service they need."

"During one of the most exciting times in their lives," she agreed. "I lucked into it and I can't imagine doing anything else."

"That's a pretty cool gig," Drake said. "So why are you moving away from your clients?"

"I'm opening up a Nashville branch. I have two clients here currently, and on a trip back to meet with them, the idea struck me. I know this city and love it, and there's a lot of potential here. I put together a proposal, and Cora and Kent, the owners, jumped on it."

"And houses are easier to buy here."

"Based on what I've seen online, a lot easier."

"So who are your local clients?" he asked.

"Tomorrow I'm meeting with a brand-new one. Ellie Grant. She's marrying—"

"Thomas Maywood," Drake finished for her.

"You keep up on Nashville celebrity news," she said.

"It's hard not to know about two of the biggest country stars getting hitched. Isn't the guy supposed to plan the honeymoon?"

"I've worked with brides, grooms, couples, even friends and relatives who were paying for the honeymoon as a gift. I'll work with whoever wants a dream honeymoon."

"You get some weird requests?" he asked.

"It's never boring."

"Like what? Tell me some of the stranger ones."

While she never revealed specifics of who did what, she could tell countless anonymous stories from the past. "I had an older gentleman, a billionaire CEO with a much younger bride, who wanted goat's milk, honey, and rose water added to their bathwater each night, saying it had aphrodisiac powers. Plus bowls of shelled pistachios—they had to be imported from Turkey—scattered around the suite. Also a sex-drive booster."

"But only if they're from Turkey?" he asked as he exited the interstate.

"All pistachios are supposedly aphrodisiacs, but the Turkish ones taste superior, or so I'm told."

"So you arranged those details?"

"Yes, sir. With a smile. That was an easy one."

"I bet you have tons of good stories."

"You wouldn't believe some of them if I told you," she said as she checked the map on the dash screen. "We're getting close to my apartment."

"What do you think we'll find?"

She took her phone out to make sure she hadn't missed a text from Nadine. She hadn't. "Maybe a plumbing emergency. That would suck."

"I was thinking a roach infestation."

"Don't even go there."

"Maybe a dead mouse in the walls, stinking up the place."

"Roof blew off in a storm?" she said, making it a game while hoping everything they said was worse than reality.

"Lead paint in the bedroom," Drake said, grinning. "Don't lick the walls."

What they saw when they pulled up minutes later, though, had them shocked into silence as they both gaped with their jaws dropping.

CHAPTER THREE

"Your destination is on the right."

Mackenzie barely noticed the message from the map app that rang out over the Jeep's premium sound system. She was too caught up on the tow truck, the fire truck, two police cars, and— Was that car really sticking out of the side of the building?

A dozen or so onlookers were clustered along the sidewalk in the distance, looking casual, not too concerned, but to her, the scene was concerning. Especially if that was *her* apartment that had the Buick jutting out of it.

As soon as Drake stopped the Jeep alongside the curb, half a block down from the action, she pushed the door open and slid to the ground and gawked. There was no other word for it.

Two cops stood to the side, engrossed in conversation, their arms crossed, expressions relaxed, as if the emergency was over. The tow truck driver came around the Buick, looking like he'd pulled a car out of a building a thousand times, and spoke to the cops.

Drake came up alongside her. "Looks like you won't be moving in tonight."

"Probably not tomorrow either," she said, thinking humor was better than letting her tired body crumple to the grass and break into tears the way she wanted to. One of her suitcases had an air mattress in it and a pump and brand-new sheets, and she'd been counting the minutes until she could set up her makeshift bed in her new home and collapse in contented exhaustion.

The front right corner of the car had gone through the sliding glass door. It wasn't very far into the building, but the glass from the sliding door was shattered, and one of the posts supporting the second-story balcony, where she'd planned to put a comfy outdoor chair and table, had been taken out.

"I hope everyone's okay," she said as she skimmed her gaze from one emergency worker to the next, looking for the best person to approach. Before she could head toward the two officers, she heard her name being called.

She turned to the right to see a short blond forty-something woman approaching them in a jog. "Are you Mackenzie?"

"Yes. Nadine?"

The woman offered her hand. "That's me. It's nice to meet you, though I wish the circumstances were different."

"Looks like you've had an eventful evening," Drake said.

"Well, hello." Nadine's attention snapped to Drake, and her words came out like a purr as she peered up at him. "Eventful is one word for it, for sure. And you are...?"

"Drake." In spite of the chaotic scene around them, Mackenzie didn't miss the friendliness in the appraising look he gave Nadine. Mackenzie mentally rolled her eyes. She would swear flirting was hardwired in his veins.

"Pleasure. I manage the property and live in that end unit," Nadine said, pointing, her gaze lingering on him for an extra second, and Mackenzie had to wonder if there was, indeed, a hint of invitation in that statement or if she was just overtired and imagining it.

"It's nice to meet you, Nadine from the end unit. What the heck happened here?" Drake said, nodding toward the car.

"Was anyone hurt?" Mackenzie asked.

"I'm happy to say everyone's okay. It was a classic case of texting and driving. The driver happened to be texting Shelly, who lives in that end apartment right there"—Nadine pointed at the end opposite from hers, which looked to be just two units away from the one with the Buick lawn ornament—"asking for the best place to park, when a dog darted by and startled her so badly she hit the wrong pedal. She popped up the curb, across the few feet of grass, and, well, the rest is plainly visible."

"Teenager?" Drake asked.

"Senior," Nadine answered. "As in citizen. Shelly's grandmother. She'd just arrived after driving all the way from Alabama."

"That's awful," Mackenzie said. "But she wasn't injured?"

"A little shaken and a lot embarrassed. Once the police had what they needed from the woman, Shelly took her to the twenty-four-hour donut and coffee shop a couple of blocks away to aid recovery." Nadine shook her head as all three of them watched the tow truck driver stride to his truck, apparently ready to move in and take the car away. "Needless to say, your apartment won't be ready for a few days."

"A few days?" Drake said, frowning. "That doesn't look like it'll be done in a few days."

Mackenzie could see his point, but she wanted to believe they'd prioritize repairing it. It didn't look like the damage extended much beyond the exterior and mostly just the door.

"It looks worse from here than it is," Nadine said. "They're saying the sturdy brick wall helped stop the car and prevented a lot more damage. We'll have an engineer here first thing tomorrow to assess, but unless he unearths some surprises, we should have everything fixed quickly. And"—she turned to Mackenzie directly—"I just got off the phone with the owner as you arrived. We'd like to offer you a month of free rent to make up for the inconvenience."

"That would help," Mackenzie said, her mind already spinning through how this would affect her pending house-hunting plans. She was fending off the thought, not altogether successfully, that once again, her living situation had veered out of her control.

"Two months would help even more," Drake said, managing to pull it off with that charming grin that—she glanced at Nadine —yep, seemed to work like magic. The woman's eyes had widened and she was gazing at him thoughtfully, as if considering it.

"No," Mackenzie said in a rush. "One month is much appreciated."

"They're breaking the terms of the lease, Mackenzie. It'd be easier to find a new place to live. Why not see if Nadine can work something out for you?"

Judging by the look on Nadine's face, she wanted to work a different something out with Drake, but then who wouldn't?

"Really," Mackenzie said firmly. She tossed a warm smile at the property manager. "One month free is wonderful. If it takes longer than expected to repair the place, then we can revisit it." She shot Drake a look that warned him to cease and desist.

"You've got a deal," Nadine said, looking relieved. "And now I need to see what the police officer wants." She gestured toward the cop who was striding in their direction with purpose. She hurried off, clearly in her element.

As soon as Nadine was out of earshot, Mackenzie opened her mouth to scold Drake, but he preempted her.

"I bet I could've gotten at least six weeks out of her," he said.

"I bet you could've gotten a lot more than that," Mackenzie said dryly. "Mr. Lester, the owner, has already bent over backwards for me by giving me a short-term lease and not charging extra rent for it. I don't want to take advantage of his kindness or put Ez or his friend in a bad situation. One month of free rent will cover several nights in a hotel. That's all I need."

"You're not staying in a hotel."

She froze, again about to argue, and narrowed her eyes at him. Was he suggesting…?

"I told your brother I'd take care of you," he said. "That doesn't mean dumping you off at the Sheraton."

"Ezra's approximately half a planet away. He has no say." The argument came out automatically, because she didn't want to impose and she had to give him an out. But the thought of staying at Drake's… She quietly sucked in a shaky breath. If she had a bucket list, sleeping under the same roof as Drake North would be on it.

Nadine was making her way back to them, her attention on her phone as she swiped a few times. "I've got to get my maintenance guy here to put some boards up overnight. Are you doing okay?" she asked, as if she feared Mackenzie might try to bail on the apartment altogether.

"I am." If you didn't count the exhaustion from traveling and the serious disappointment that she wouldn't be "home" tonight. "I'd like the lease modified to show the month of free rent, if you don't mind. Could you email that to me tomorrow?"

"Of course," Nadine said, typing something in on her phone. "I can't let you in to see your unit for safety reasons, but each apartment is identical in layout and you're welcome to look at mine if you'd like to see one in person before you go."

"That's kind of you, but I still have all the photos you sent. I know I'll love it. Besides, I'm betting my chauffeur here has plans tonight, so I should let him get to them." She glanced at Drake when she said it and couldn't miss the *busted* look on his face that confirmed her guess. "But thanks for offering."

"You're more than welcome. If you change your mind, the offer stands," Nadine said. "I'm so sorry for everything."

"I'm sorry for Shelly and her grandmother. Although donuts can make just about everything seem okay for a while." Mackenzie realized she hadn't eaten since a late lunch, but right now she'd choose sleep over food—even donuts. "I'll watch for the revised lease in my email, and you'll keep me posted on the timeline?"

"Absolutely. Welcome to Nashville, Mackenzie." Nadine shook her hand, then turned to Drake, who was tapping away at a message on his phone. "Drake, I get the impression you live in town already?"

"For twenty-nine years and counting," he said, shoving his phone in his pocket and shaking her offered hand. "Thanks for taking care of Mackenzie. We'll check on progress in a couple of days."

"You're welcome anytime," she said smoothly, and Mackenzie was sure now she wasn't just talking about checking up on repairs.

As Mackenzie and Drake walked back to the Jeep, one of the police cars pulled away, and most of the onlookers had left as well. He let her into the passenger side in silence, which suited her fine, as she'd slipped into recalculating mode, thinking about how this twist in her plans was going to affect the next few days. She'd organized every detail of her move to a fault—she'd had to in order to make it work out on such a tight timeline—and she needed to wrap her head around the changes.

"So you're staying at my place?" Drake said as soon as he was in and had shut the driver's-side door. He started the engine but didn't make any move toward leaving.

"You have plans. Just take me to a hotel."

"I canceled them." He held his phone up as if that proved it.

She hadn't expected that. "You need to think it through, Drake. I have to work, starting tomorrow morning, and I mostly work at 'home.' Which means I'd be there all the time."

"I'm rarely there, so it'll be like having your own place."

"What if it takes them two weeks to fix my apartment?"

"Then it's two weeks. It's not a problem, Shawlet." He raised his brows, as if waiting for her to concede.

She expelled a breath. "You're really sure I wouldn't annoy you?"

He shot her a smile that grabbed her in the gut—she'd bet he practiced that grin in front of the mirror every night—and said, "Far from it."

She could swear she saw a flash of heat in his eyes…but that was crazy. Part of his charmer act, she knew.

"And you wouldn't expect me to cook?" she asked, mostly joking.

"Not for me, but you're welcome to use the kitchen for whatever you want. Except a date with another guy." The smile dropped from his face.

"Dating is not on my radar," she said, and then another thought hit her. "What about you? You wouldn't have slumber parties while I'm there, would you?"

He feigned a look of shock. "What kind of guy do you think I am?"

Remembering the photos on his social media accounts, she said, "Not a celibate one."

"I can be celibate. For a couple of weeks."

"I'm not asking you to be celibate. Just... I wouldn't want to have to listen to it."

"No slumber parties at my place. We'll make it a rule for both of us."

She laughed, because he gave her a lot more credit than she deserved if he thought she was going to meet someone and get to know him well enough to sleep with him within a week or two. Guys were so far down on her list right now that they didn't even register. Generally speaking. Drake would likely always *register* with her on some level. "That seems ridiculous."

While she was keeping it lighthearted—and trying not to think too hard about Drake and slumber parties—he'd gone serious. "Mackenzie, I have an extra room just sitting there, empty. Your brother crashes there whenever he's in town, so it's already known as the Shaw Suite." He put the vehicle into gear but sat there, not pulling out of the parking space, waiting for her answer.

She exhaled audibly, ignored the niggling suspicion that she might be asking for trouble, and said, "Well, if it has my name on it, then who am I to refuse?"

CHAPTER FOUR

*D*rake was reasonably certain that lace and silk had the power to start and end world conflicts. Especially lace and silk of the deepest, darkest eggplant purple.

He was walking down the hallway of his apartment, on his way from the main door to the kitchen Thursday midmorning after an early gym session, breakfast, and a visit to his mom's house. When he'd left at dawn, Mackenzie's bedroom door had been closed and she hadn't been up yet. Now it was wide open. He'd glanced in as he was passing, and the tiny scraps of purple material caught his eye.

Of course he stopped. On a damn dime.

He craned his head in, staring at the pile of what he recognized as Mackenzie's clothing from last night—jeans, tee, flannel, purple lace and silk. Dropped right where she must have shed it before falling into bed, as if it was of no consequence. For Drake, who had a thing for ladies' lingerie, especially when there was a beautiful lady in it, it wasn't of no consequence.

It got his imagination revving. Got the erotic images started up as if someone had plugged in an old-fashioned slide projector and shined it on his brain.

Respectfully, he didn't go in the room, but he did stare, and he did get caught up in thoughts that he would be better off not entertaining. Thoughts he'd worked like the devil to shove away from the time they'd arrived at his apartment last night. He'd been prepared to cook a late-night snack for Mackenzie, would've taken her out for a drink or sat on the balcony catching up if she'd wanted, but after a brief tour of his eleventh-floor apartment, she'd pled exhaustion and had gone to bed. Leaving him with his thoughts.

He'd gone out after all, to a pub about a block away, just for a couple of hours, meeting up with the people he'd canceled on earlier, Cassie, Belle, and Shawna. Fun girls. Funny. Belle, a cute redhead with legs that went on for miles, had invited him to come home with her. He'd surprised everyone—himself included—when he declined, using his houseguest as an excuse and making his way home uncharacteristically alone.

Now, when the apartment door behind him whisked open as he still gawked at the lingerie, he jumped guiltily. There was no hiding that he was standing by her bedroom, so he turned around and faced Mackenzie and gave her one of his special smiles.

"Not even twenty-four hours and it looks like a hurricane hit in there," he teased. It wasn't just the clothes in the pile. There were multiple outfits strewn on the unmade bed, one suitcase open on the floor with items all around, as if it'd exploded, and at least three pairs of shoes scattered.

Mackenzie dipped her head and said, "I'm a lot of amazing things, but neat isn't on the list."

Drake shrugged and headed to the kitchen with her following. "No skin off my back. It just caught my attention as I walked by."

To put it mildly.

He took a glass down from the cupboard and poured some water from the filtered spigot on the fridge.

"I'll keep the door closed." She went around to the opposite side of the island and settled onto one of the stools.

"Want some?" he asked, holding up the glass.

She shook her head. "Here." She slid a paper cup from Carlotta's Coffee, which was on the ground floor of his building, across the island to him, knocking a paper bag he hadn't previously noticed to the floor. She bent down and picked it up. "Straight black coffee, Guatemalan roast. And"—she opened the bag and took out a muffin—"one banana oat protein muffin." She looked unsure for an instant as she held it out to him. "Carlotta said that was your standard order."

"Carlotta knows," Drake said, deciding not to mention he'd already been to a post-workout breakfast with his brother Gabe at the gym's cafe. He happily took the muffin from her. He could always eat, especially when it was a muffin from Carlotta's. And coffee was exactly what he needed, as he'd gone for a green juice with his veggie and egg scramble and smoked salmon. "Thank you."

"She seems to know you well," Mackenzie said as she took out a cherry pastry for herself, pulled a chunk of it off, popped it in her mouth, and eyed him curiously. "Are you guys a thing?"

He laughed. "If we were, I imagine her badass husband, Jimmy, would have something to say about it."

"I should probably warn you that you might need to do damage control," she said.

"With Carlotta?"

"I'm pretty sure she got the wrong idea when I said I stayed at your place last night. And when I explained that you're my brother's friend and were doing me a favor, I don't think that persuaded her otherwise."

Probably because the coffeehouse owner did know him well and understood that when a female came out of Drake's apartment in the morning, it was usually exactly what it looked like.

"I'll talk to her," he said, not because he gave half a shit what Carlotta or anyone thought of him but rather because he didn't want anyone to think Mackenzie had done something she hadn't. He ignored the way that idea tried to root into his mind and took a large bite of muffin.

He walked around the island to sit next to her and got his first real look at her for the day. She was looking all the hell grown up, professional, and put together, from her ankle-high boots to her professional pants and jacket over a feminine shirt with a multi-strand necklace of silver and some kind of whitish stones. "Looking good, Shawlet. Very woman with a mission."

"Thanks. I am on a mission. Several of them." She opened the lid of her own coffee and breathed it in, as if the caffeine could be absorbed through her nose.

"Your meeting with Ellie Grant is today," he remembered.

"Was. At eight a.m. All done."

"You've already been? How'd you get there?"

"Uber." Mackenzie took another bite of her pastry, the first bite with sweet cherry filling, and her eyes rolled back into her head in ecstasy. Drake endeavored not to imagine what else could make her look like that.

"You should've said something," he said. "I have spare vehicles."

She laughed. "That you do." She'd seen both his Porsche 911 and his motorcycle last night when he'd parked the Jeep in the spot between the two in the building's underground garage. She'd made a not-too-original joke about boys and their toys. "You'd let me drive the Porsche?"

"Whoa. No one drives the Porsche but me. But the Jeep is yours for as long as you need it."

"No one?" she repeated. "Not even your brothers?"

"Especially not my brothers."

"Not even Zane?" she asked of his twin.

"He's more interested in fighter jets than sports cars. The 911 might be too slow for him." He saw no need to explain how they weren't really "twin close" anymore, not since Zane had put distance between them when he'd abandoned their long-standing plans to go to college together—the two of them plus Ezra—and chosen the military route instead.

Mackenzie laughed, as he'd intended, and he liked the light, feminine sound of it. "If you're sure, I would happily 'settle' for the Jeep. I have a long to-do list. First up is finding a place to store my stuff until my apartment is ready." She pulled out her phone, unlocked it, and tapped and swiped and tapped some more.

"I'll ask my mom if you can keep it at her house," Drake said.

"She's got a big garage and only one car in there. I'm sure she wouldn't mind."

"She doesn't even know me."

"She knows Ezra. Knows of you."

Mackenzie shook her head. "I'm already imposing on you. I don't want to do that to a woman I've never met."

"Then meet her. You need to network and meet people anyway, right? Come with me to dinner Sunday at my mom's house. My brothers will all be there. Weekly thing, no big deal."

Mackenzie seemed to consider it, tilting her head and ceasing with the phone swipes.

"Yes?" he said.

Grinning, she said, "Why do I get the impression you're used to getting whatever you want?"

"Because I am?" he said, then shrugged. His mom liked to say he could charm the skin off a snake, and he didn't apologize for it. "My brothers would say it's because I'm the youngest and I'm spoiled. I'd say it's because I'm irresistible."

"And humble too," she said. "I'll go if you're sure your family won't mind. I'd love to meet them."

"That's settled. I'll text her about your belongings and dinner."

"Are any of your brothers, by chance, in the market for an exotic honeymoon?"

A sound came out of him, a cross between a laugh and a scoff. "North brothers are *not* the marrying type," he said. "Well, except for our black sheep, Cole. He got engaged just last night, right before I picked you up. So you might hit him up. He's only recently accepted his share of money from the family business, though, so something extravagant might be a hard sell."

"I love a challenge. How can you be sure your brothers aren't the marrying type, especially if one of them just went down?"

"Put it this way," Drake said. "I can't remember the last time any of them had more than a handful of dates with one person, let alone a girlfriend."

"Yourself included?"

"Myself especially." Drake loved women, loved flirting with

them, talking to them, sleeping with them, but actual long-term relationships? Not his thing.

"It's almost like you're daring the universe. Tempting fate," she said with a smirk. She popped the last bit of her pastry into her mouth, chewed and swallowed it, then washed it down with steaming java from her Carlotta's cup. "So tell me about your personal training," she said out of nowhere.

He wondered if she was considering joining the gym he worked at and working out with him. Out of habit, he eyed her surreptitiously, trying to size up her physical strengths and weaknesses. Of course, you couldn't tell the whole story from looking, but Mackenzie didn't appear to have an ounce of fat on her body. She didn't need to lose weight, but that said nothing of her muscle strength or overall fitness. He suspected, for starters, she had a hard-core sugar habit.

He hopped off the stool and busied himself sweeping the crumbs from the counter. "What do you want to know?"

"The basics. Do you only do it at the gym or do you have clients outside of it?"

"Only at the gym," he said, opening the freezer and searching for something to thaw for dinner.

"Have you ever thought of expanding? Going out on your own? Meeting clients in their home?"

"No," he said without hesitation as he took out a package of grass-fed sirloin and set it on the counter. Oh, he'd considered it for about twenty seconds when he was getting ready to graduate, and only because one of his buddies in the sequence was doing it, but just getting set up for it was a lot of work and details. If you were going to go to that trouble, you needed to stick to it for a long time to make it worthwhile. Just like with women, Drake made a conscious effort to avoid long-term job commitments. Because, from what he'd seen, as soon as you got comfortable, something could come along and change everything in a heartbeat, take everything away. He wasn't a fan of that kind of loss, to put it mildly, and in fact did everything he could to avoid it.

"Ellie Grant is looking to hire a trainer to come to her house. I told her I might know someone."

There was a millisecond when Drake's interest was piqued. The thought of working with someone high-profile like Ellie Grant… Intriguing. But not practical.

"I've got plenty to keep me busy between North Brothers and the gym," he said, a note of regret in his voice. "Besides, I'm not set up to do that."

"You could get set up."

"I could," he repeated. "But there's zero chance of it. Sorry, Shawlet."

Mackenzie looked pensive and semi-defeated for a moment, then she straightened again. "Do you work today?" she asked.

"I've got a shift at the gym. Four p.m."

"What about tomorrow?"

"Eight to two. And before you ask, I've got the early-morning shift at the gym Saturday, and I'll be at North Brothers both Saturday and Sunday all day."

"Could you meet Ellie tomorrow afternoon?"

Drake laughed as he picked up the empty pastry bag and threw it in the trash can under the sink. "I can see why you're good at your job."

"It's just that she's unsure, needs some help outfitting her gym, but she doesn't want to buy a bunch of equipment she doesn't know how to use or won't like. She's never had a personal trainer, wants to set up the gym at her home—and by home I mean estate, compound, mansion, that kind of thing— and has the money but not the know-how. It seems like you have the knowledge she needs—"

"I do," Drake said with zero lack of confidence. "But I can't just wake up one morning and decide to branch out on my own. There's a lot to get into place. Liability insurance, pricing, policies, contracts…" Just the thought made him itchy.

Mackenzie nodded slowly, her lips pursed as she seemed to be lost in thought again. "I understand. Could you maybe just meet with her and hear her out about what she's looking for, then give her some input on what to buy and who she could call?" She was leaning her elbows on the island, her chin propped up on one fist as she implored him with those pretty brown eyes that sparkled with so much life and persuasion. And then she issued the clincher. "Please? For me?"

Drake studied her across the island, his palms flat on the countertop, as his internal arguments ceased and he was sucked in by that sparkle. "Okay," he finally said. "I'll meet with her one time. Only to advise. For you."

It was becoming obvious that Ezra's little sister was damn hard to resist, and if her apartment wasn't ready soon, Drake could very easily find himself in hot water.

CHAPTER FIVE

There was a certain level of confidence in a man, one that didn't verge too far toward unjustified cockiness, that was sexy and alluring. Drake had that in spades, Mackenzie thought as she watched him talk to Ellie Grant as if he'd known her for half his life. He had his "charm" setting on high, seemingly naturally, but his "flirt" button was off and he was all business and enthusiasm.

The powerhouse country singer was five feet and one inch of charisma, bluntness, and determination. Mackenzie had been able to tell within thirty seconds of meeting her yesterday that she funneled every last bit of her sixty-one inches into everything she did, and that, no doubt, was part of the reason she was an entertainment giant. At the same time, she had a warmth and genuineness about her that made Mackenzie think, if they were in a different situation, they could become close friends.

She and Drake had arrived nearly an hour ago at Ellie's estate, checking in with the gatekeeper at the end of the long, winding driveway and then being greeted by Ellie herself at the house. Ellie had asked him to sign a confidentiality agreement, as Mackenzie had done the day before, and made it seem as normal as taking their shoes off at the door, which they hadn't done, because they were meeting on a sprawling heated patio next to the pool.

They'd spent the first fifteen minutes with Mackenzie going over a folder of five exotic honeymoon locations—Bali, Bora Bora, Seychelles, Fiji, and Sri Lanka—just a general overview of each, along with bits of feedback from her previous clients, so that Ellie and Thomas could look them over and point her in a direction, whether they chose one of these locales or not. Ellie had bubbled over with enthusiasm and promised to talk to her fiancé as soon as possible.

Since then, Mackenzie had sat back and let Drake do his thing, and he did his thing well. She would never guess this was his first time. There was no question he knew what he was talking about. He was well-versed in the topic of home gyms and fitness goals and motivation and even safety, and though it was easy to forget because of his carefree party-guy persona, it was obvious he was an intelligent man.

"Come with me," Ellie said, standing. "I'll show you the space I have in mind for the gym."

Drake had been jotting notes on his phone for the past half hour as Ellie answered his questions about what exercise programs she'd done in the past, what she liked and disliked, what her goals were, and what her fiancé would consider important as well. Now he stood and slid his phone into his pocket and waited for Mackenzie as she also rose, banging her hip into the table in the process. He held a hand out toward her and she wondered if he was going to touch her waist or her back again, like he had two nights ago at the airport. He didn't quite come into contact with her body, though, as she walked in front of him as directed, and it hit her that she wanted to feel the pressure and heat of his hand on her. Wanted it more than a little.

"The pool house might not be the most conventional place, but we currently get no use out of it," Ellie said, leading them toward the structure on the other side of the pool that looked like a mini southern estate in and of itself, with tall columns in front, one wall full of windowed doors, and even a hexagonal cupola on top.

"This is incredible," Mackenzie said as soon as she entered, ahead of Drake. It appeared to be one large room centered in the building and a couple of small rooms off to the sides. The ceiling was high, with vaults and arches and the underside of the cupola stretching above them. There were two seating clusters of thick-cushioned sofas and armchairs as well as a game table for four, with leather captain's chairs surrounding it and a chess board on top.

"We never use it," Ellie said. "It's a cryin' shame. Which is why I want to turn it into the workout room."

Mackenzie turned toward Drake and saw the moment when he took in the space and the possibilities. His face lit up, eyes sparked, brows rose, and he said, simply, "Oh, yeah."

"You think it could work?" Ellie asked hopefully.

"This could be a dream of a gym for both you and Thomas." He wandered to the far wall, sizing up the space, his brow furrowing as if he was imagining what would fit where. "What are the other rooms?"

Ellie showed them each side, one a kitchen area and the other a roomy bath and shower room. "We could knock down walls if we need to—"

"No need," he said. "The bath can be a changing room, with enough space to add a hot tub. The kitchen space is good for storing cold drinks, but you could reconfigure this space," he said, gesturing to one end of the long, narrow room, "to a sauna."

"Ooh, I love that idea." Ellie clasped her hands together. "And you think this main area is big enough for the actual workin'-out space?"

Drake sprang into animated action, outlining with his hands different sections of the main room where he would create stations—one for cardio equipment, one for Thomas's weight machines, one for yoga and stretching, and one for free weights, exercise balls, and whatever other handheld equipment they ended up buying. Before Ellie could get a word in edgewise, Drake was swiping his phone and jotting down ideas as he talked an enthusiastic mile a minute. Mackenzie stopped listening to details at the mention of stationary bikes and air rowers and other torture machines and instead homed her attention in on his body language.

He loved this. And she loved watching him so deeply into it.

It was another half hour later when they emerged from the pool house, having delved into details about what, exactly, would serve Ellie and Thomas's purposes best. Mackenzie was on the fringes of all of it and totally fine with that, as the scenery was more than pleasant. She thrived on helping people solve problems, from the best way to get to a private island in the Galapagos to how to find an expert on fitness when you wanted to get fit but couldn't work out in public because of the stir it might cause, but she could easily admit this was not her area of interest or expertise.

It was clear Drake and Ellie had hit it off, and Mackenzie couldn't understand his hesitation to become Ellie's trainer. Sure, he'd explained the practical obstacles that would have to be overcome to go into business for himself, but none of it would be difficult if he really wanted to do it. And judging by his engagement, part of him really wanted to do it, at least on some level. Something was holding him back.

"You're really good at this," Ellie was saying as they paused next to the outdoor table they'd previously sat at. "You figured out exactly what we need. So my question is, how can I convince you to help me with the actual purchasing? Thomas might know more than me, but he's in New York for the next week for appearances. How do I know where to buy this stuff? Which brands and models to get? Lord, I don't have a clue about any of it. So what do you say, Drake? Help a girl out?"

"It's hard to say no to a beautiful lady," he said, his flirtatious nature finally popping up. "For you, I'd be happy to help select the right pieces and get them ordered. Let me do some research and I'll get the specifics together for you. We can meet again and figure out the logistics. Then I can hook you up with a trainer who can work with you in your new home gym. How's that sound?"

"God yes. Thank you, Drake. I can't wait to do this."

"The shopping or the working out?" Mackenzie asked, and Ellie laughed as Drake looked momentarily confused and then cracked a grin as he shook his head.

"Both, of course," Ellie said with a wink.

As the three of them said goodbye, Ellie pulled Mackenzie into a hug and told her she and Thomas would check out the honeymoon options as soon as he got back in town—or maybe sooner if he could find the time. Mackenzie reveled in the gesture, loved that she'd connected with Ellie, relished the dynamic woman's acceptance and trust. Whether hooking her up with Drake had helped with that, Mackenzie didn't know and didn't care. She was more intrigued by the things she'd learned about her brother's best friend today—and the things she still wanted to figure out.

CHAPTER SIX

The more Drake updated Ezra on his sister, the better Drake would remember why he couldn't suggest he and Mackenzie blow off the slumber party ban and the separate bedrooms and cozy up together in his bed.

Or that's what he hoped anyway.

As he and Mackenzie walked up the front path to his mom's home Sunday evening, where Drake and his brothers had grown up, he typed a message to let Ez know he was introducing her to his family so that she could start networking and broadening her social and business circles. He closed the app without receiving a response, belatedly calculating that it was fifteen hours later in Sydney, so the start of the business week for Ezra. It didn't matter. The point of the message was not to start a conversation.

It's your guilty conscience, you jerk-off.

He'd spent several hours today working side by side with Mackenzie at the kitchen bar in his apartment, each with their laptop and their own objectives. She'd been corresponding with someone in Cambodia regarding the upcoming honeymoon of one of her LA clients, trying to get a guarantee that the resort in Siem Reap did, indeed, have a place where the groom's favorite sushi chef could work. The sum of money the guy was paying to bring in not only food but an outside chef was astronomical and seemed like a waste to Drake, but he was learning, from hearing about some of Mackenzie's diva clients, that he knew very little about acting like a spoiled, entitled, self-important pain in the ass. His words, not Mackenzie's.

He had been working on Ellie's gym equipment list, scouring the internet for good deals on the pieces he wanted, and coming up frustrated. The weekly dinner date with his family had come at the right time, because he'd needed a break.

When they got to the front door, Drake opened it for Mackenzie and let her enter before him. The normal racket of the North family met their ears, and when she turned her brown eyes up to him, he guided her through the entry hall toward the open living-dining-kitchen area, where the scene was chaos as usual.

"The end is near," Gabe, the second oldest and usually the family peacemaker, called out good-naturedly as Drake and Mackenzie turned the corner past the central stairs and the group came into view. Gabe was in the kitchen with their mom and made a point to pivot around and look at the clock on the microwave. "For the first time in history, you're not late."

"We're early," Drake said smugly, sharing a look with Mackenzie, who had *convinced* him, they'd call it, to put his work away and get into the shower—alone, sadly—so that they wouldn't be late for her first time meeting his family.

"A whole two minutes," Mason, the oldest North brother, clarified from his position at the breakfast bar, where he was serving adult beverages and steeping their mom's tea.

"Two minutes is two minutes." Drake put his hand at Mackenzie's waist as they approached the dining table. "Everyone, this is Ezra's little sister, Mackenzie," Drake said. He gestured toward his mom, who fluttered, a little more slowly than her pre-heart-attack version, between the refrigerator and the counter and the sink. "That's our mom, Faye. Gabe is the smart aleck at the meat plate, Mason's the bartender, this is Cole and his fiancée, Sierra Lowell. Next to Sierra is Gabe's best friend, Lexie, who's practically earned sister status us with us."

Mackenzie nodded, pushing a thick lock of her hair off her

cheek as she skimmed her gaze over each person and said a blanket, "It's nice to meet you all."

His mom came over to them, her hands extended in welcome. "Hello, Mackenzie. We've heard all about you over the years. It's so nice to finally have you in our home." She pulled Mackenzie into a hug, and he noticed Mackenzie closing her eyes, as if she cherished the gesture.

"Thanks, Mrs. North," Mackenzie said as they pulled apart.

"Call me Faye," his mom corrected. "Come on in. Tell us all about you. Drake said you're just moving back to town?"

Drake pulled out the kitchen chair across the table from Sierra as his mom went back around the counter to continue with dinner prep. He watched his mom, as they all did now, to make sure she wasn't overdoing it and to discern whether she was hiding fatigue or anything worse. Since her heart attack a few months ago, she claimed her boys hovered over her, and that was probably accurate.

"I've been back from LA for less than a week," Mackenzie said without sitting. "And thank you for agreeing to store my belongings in your garage."

"Think nothing of it," Faye said with a wave. "I'm more than happy to share the space. I normally just ramble around in this big place until it echoes."

"What can I do to help?" Mackenzie went toward the kitchen, and again, Faye waved her off. "Not a thing."

"We've got it under control," Gabe said. "We're grilling tonight, and the rest we picked up from the deli to keep it easy. I've got the meat about ready to cook, and Mom is dishing up the sides before she sits and rests."

"I'm fine, Gabriel," she said. "Dishing up pasta salad is not particularly taxing."

"But wandering all over the yard with Lexie all day, planning your landscaping is." Gabe brushed more barbecue sauce over the raw chicken pieces.

"Lexie made me rest," their mom said. "A lot."

"Guilty," Lexie said with an affectionate smile. She gestured around the room at Drake's brothers. "These guys made me promise, and I don't know if you've noticed, but they're bigger than me."

"Everybody's bigger than you," Mason said, and since Lexie was about five feet nothing if she stood up really straight, no one could argue.

"Your boys, overgrown thugs that they are, just love you, Mrs. N. We don't want anything to happen to you again," Lexie said.

"That's the truth." Mason turned his attention to Mackenzie. "What can I get you to drink, Mackenzie?"

She glanced at the options on the counter. "White wine, please."

"The usual?" Mason asked Drake, and Drake nodded in reply as Mackenzie came back to him and sat in the spot he'd initially indicated.

"So what brings you back to Nashville?" Sierra asked Mackenzie.

"My job," Mackenzie said. "I work for a company that plans exotic honeymoons, and we're opening a Nashville office, in a manner of speaking. I'll be working from home to start with."

"Exotic honeymoons," Sierra said animatedly as she raised her brows at Cole. "Tell us about that."

Mason and Gabe heckled Cole about weddings and honey-moons from behind while Drake shook his head with a grin. In truth, Drake had never in his life seen Cole looking so...beyond content. As he sat there, entwined with the woman who'd captured his heart, he seemed happy on a soul-deep level.

"We get a lot of Hollywood clients, as well as tech industry," Mackenzie said. "We're hoping to tap into the country music world with the Nashville branch."

"Think high-dollar, over-the-top stuff," Drake said, taking the chair next to Mackenzie. "Diva celebrities and socially inept billionaires and what have you."

"And the occasional genuinely nice, down-to-earth person who has a very specific idea of what they want for a honey-moon and a large budget to pay for it," Mackenzie said cheer-fully. "I've worked with all types. So what about you two?" She aimed the question at Sierra and Lexie since she already knew the brothers worked for the family business. Drake had given her a rundown on the way over—Mason was the CEO, Gabe the VP of Human Resources, and Cole was a special projects manager who dealt with new properties for the company, overseeing remodels and construction. Zane, Drake's twin, was in the Navy, currently deployed. She accepted a glass of wine from Mason, who then delivered Drake's microbrew and took a seat.

Sierra's brown eyes sparkled with friendliness—and the same unmistakable contentment as Cole—as she replied, "I own a remodeling company that specializes in historical renovations. Anything from houses to commercial buildings."

Mackenzie's brows rose and she broke out into a smile. "Girl power. I love it."

"What she fails to mention is that she's also a television personality," Faye piped up proudly from the counter.

"What?" Mackenzie leaned forward, her eyes widening with interest. "You're on TV?"

"On a cable network," Sierra said modestly. "My company won a competition to remodel William Eldridge's mansion that was built in the early 1900s. Part of the prize is that the project is featured on a show on one of Eldridge's networks."

"For an entire season," Cole said, beaming. "And then, once the mansion is done, they'll follow her company's projects for the next TV season as well. My girl is a TV icon."

Sierra laughed and shook her head at Cole.

"That's impressive," Mackenzie said.

"These two just got engaged during the recording of the show," Drake explained to her. "The night you flew in."

"On the show? As in, live video?"

"Video, yes, but not live," Cole said. "I'm not sure I would've been brave enough if it'd been live."

"You would've done it anyway," Mason said confidently.

"Has it been shown on TV yet?" Mackenzie asked.

"No. They haven't told us the air date yet," Sierra said. "I've never been so shocked in my life. This guy, this afraid-of-being-on-camera guy, burst into the middle of the fireplace episode and went down on one knee."

"That's so romantic," Mackenzie said with a wistful look in her eyes.

"Cole's set a precedent," Faye said as she came over to the table and set out a plate of veggies and dip. "His brothers have a lot to live up to."

"Oh, Mom, how do I break this to you?" Gabe called out from the kitchen sink as he washed his hands.

"Not gonna happen," Mason said.

"The grandchild burden's one hundred percent on Cole," Drake added.

"Fools. Every one of you." Cole leaned over and kissed Sierra, obviously trying to make a point.

Their mom sighed. "A mother can always hope."

"So what constitutes an exotic honeymoon?" Mason asked Mackenzie.

"From what I've gathered, a six-figure budget," was Drake's answer.

"Not technically," Mackenzie said, "but the majority of the trips do end up with a high price tag. A lot of the people who use our company are those who are used to demanding whatever their heart desires and getting it, at whatever price. But it's the best job ever."

"It sounds like it," Lexie said. "Tell us about some of the trips you've coordinated."

"Let's see. All seven continents—"

"Antarctica?" Sierra said with a glance at Cole, who said, "We're not going to Antarctica."

"Penguin watching and sea kayaking are in higher demand than you'd think," Mackenzie said. "There's the riads—kind of like a private palace—in Morocco and exploring the markets and the medieval buildings, or a private diving and snorkeling sail on a schooner through Indonesia's Raja Ampat archipelago, or you could stay in a luxury tent on a safari in Botswana."

"Just for starters," Drake said. He'd traveled plenty in his life, but the trips Mackenzie had described in the past couple of days blew his mind and made him realize he hadn't seen nearly enough of the world.

"I'd choose something with a private beach," Sierra said. "A safari would be cool, but I don't see myself in a tent among the wildlife in Africa."

"I'd want to see the gorillas in Uganda," Gabe said.

"They have one at the zoo," Drake told him.

"I'm afraid to ask how you know that." Gabe carried the platter of raw meat into the dining area, heading for the door to the deck and the grill.

"The zoo is a great place to take a date," Drake told him. "You know, in case you ever get one."

"You might want to remember I'm cooking your dinner," Gabe said cheerfully as he opened the door and went outside.

"Lexie's getting married too," Mason said. "What are you and Raleigh planning for your honeymoon?"

"We're going to Europe," Lexie said. "My vote was for something shorter and closer to home, like Colorado, so I could take more time off work the week before the wedding, but I'm sure Europe will be amazing."

Drake couldn't help but wonder what kind of a schmuck dictated a honeymoon location instead of trying to please his wife-to-be.

"What kind of work do you do?" Mackenzie asked.

"I'm a landscape architect," Lexie said.

"She's going to redo Mom's backyard as a weekend project," Drake said. "It's been the same since we moved into the house. It's tired."

"Mature," Lexie corrected kindly.

"It needs some new life," Faye said. "Lexie's going to work her magic."

"So houses and landscaping," Mackenzie said to Sierra and Lexie. "Do you two ever work together?"

"Lexie's company is giant," Sierra explained, "and I'm just a small fish, so no. But maybe someday…"

"It's intriguing to think about," Lexie said.

"Definitely," Sierra said. "In the meantime, we three girls

should go out sometime. Soon. Mostly for fun, but if we go to Clayborne's, I might be able to introduce you to some country music types, Mackenzie. Sloan McGuire is the entertainment manager there, and she's very connected. Her boyfriend is Micah Sullivan, who's the drummer for Steele Hearts."

"I love Steele Hearts." Mackenzie was leaning forward, her elbows on the table, nodding frequently and enthusiastically.

"Then you're in for a treat," Sierra said. "I'm also friends with Gin Verdinelli, who's engaged to Tucker Steele, the lead singer. There's a recording studio on Hale Street, where I live. It's kind of a small world."

"I'd love to go out with you two, with or without the business potential. It's been years since I lived here, and I don't really know anyone in town anymore," Mackenzie said.

"I'm in," Lexie said. "My fiancé is out of town this week, so I wouldn't even need to coordinate with anyone."

"I'll check my production schedule and you two see what evenings could work for you," Sierra said. "Clayborne's is at the corner of Peach Boulevard and Hale Street, near downtown."

Mackenzie's face lit up like a kid on Christmas morning. "My schedule is open. It sounds fantastic."

"You girls will have a great time," Faye said as she brought a multicolored stack of plates around to the table.

"Someone needs to warn the surrounding businesses these three are on the loose," Cole said, sliding the plates toward himself and standing up to set the table. "Have a seat, Mom."

Gabe walked back in from the grill, set the empty meat plate on the breakfast bar, and sat next to Mason.

"So Mackenzie, can you tell us any of the famous people you've worked with?" their mom asked as she lowered herself to the head of the table. "Anyone we've heard of?"

"Wait till you hear who she's currently planning a trip for," Drake said. He met Mackenzie's gaze. "Is it okay if I say her name?"

"Ellie's? Of course. As long as we keep the details to ourselves."

His mom made an excited humming sound. "Ellie? Do you mean Ellie Grant?"

"I do. You must be a fan," Mackenzie said.

"No way," Sierra said, leaning back into Cole's side as he put his arm around her.

"I adore her," their mom said. "She seems like a wonderful person, at least in the media."

Mackenzie pointed her index finger, as if to say she'd hit the truth. "She is in person too. Drake's helping her out on a project himself, so he can tell you."

"My youngest son apparently doesn't tell me anything," his mom said, leaning onto the table expectantly.

"It just happened in the last two days," Drake said, "and it's not really a big deal. I'm helping Ellie outfit a brand-new home gym."

"You'd be good at that," Faye said.

"She wants him to be her personal trainer too," Mackenzie said, and Drake frowned at her.

"All she has to do is join my gym," he said lightly. "I can train her to her heart's content."

"So you're helping her with a home gym?" Cole asked. "Like, construction?"

"Not at this point, though if she wanted that, I'd know who to call. I'm just helping her decide on equipment and then ordering it for her. Which reminds me"—he addressed Mason—"why in the hell don't we have a home fitness line at North Brothers?"

"We do," Mason said. "We sell all kinds of home fitness equipment."

"I'm not talking about mini trampolines and yoga mats. I mean cardio equipment. Weight machines. The big-ticket items." Drake scooted his chair back and crossed a leg. "I've spent the weekend looking for a single supplier who has the brands I want all in one place. Someone local who offers competitive pricing. Money might not be an issue for Ellie Grant, but why should she pay more than she has to?"

"We've avoided getting into it because it's a big undertaking, and frankly, it's a little different market."

"Different, maybe, but it's a giant market, and only growing," Drake said. "And so is personal training. You could offer it all under one division. Maybe even home gym construction. A one-stop shop, so to speak."

Mason narrowed his eyes at Drake, the way he did when he was in business mode. "Intriguing idea. Why don't you put together some thoughts on it for me. Send me some bullet points."

Oh, Drake had lots of thoughts. They'd been brewing all weekend as his frustration at not finding what he was looking for mounted. "Sure thing. I'll see what I can come up with this week."

"You do that. By Friday?" Mason said.

Drake shrugged. "Friday's fine. But only ideas. I'm not getting involved beyond that."

Mason sized him up, then shared a look with Gabe, who was Mason's family cohort in all things upper management. Drake ignored it, because it wasn't his problem. He was certain enough that North Brothers Sports needed to get involved in exercise equipment that he would give Mason the info he'd requested, and that was that.

CHAPTER SEVEN

*I*t wasn't uncommon for Drake to go home for a dinner break from one of his jobs, as he was tonight. Grabbing some fast food would be easier, but he avoided putting crap food in his body whenever possible and preferred to throw something together in his kitchen. Apparently Mackenzie wasn't yet familiar with his tendencies, though, because if she had been, he never would've found himself in this situation.

As he came down the hall that angled from his front door toward the kitchen, he was happily surprised to discover she was there in the apartment, as her open bedroom door treated his senses to a steamy cloud of fragrant bath products from a recent shower and he could hear racket coming from the kitchen. Another handful of steps to the kitchen had him halting abruptly. His greeting got caught in his throat.

Mackenzie stood at the refrigerator with her head sticking inside of it, in profile to him, wearing nothing but a dark blue bath towel tucked under her arms and barely reaching to the tops of her thighs. Her slender thighs that would wrap around a guy just so. The towel gaped slightly at the bottom on the side facing him, gifting him with a view of silky-looking skin near her hip bone that made his mouth go dry and his blood pound southward.

Some distant part of his brain knew he should do something

besides stand there and take in the glorious sight of her, but he couldn't make himself either back out of the kitchen or say something to alert her to his presence.

As she reached up to the top shelf, her wet hair swung down the back of her neck, hitting just below her shoulders. Her delicate bare arm garnered his attention, and then he couldn't help but notice the way the towel was tucked in at this side of her breast, the swell of it barely visible. Just one little corner of material held it all together…

Drake swallowed hard, imagining how little it would take to undo it and let the towel fall to the floor, revealing every last inch of her.

She straightened with a bottle of Chardonnay in her hand, pulling her head out and affording him a glimpse of her collarbone. When she turned enough to notice him, she let out a short screech of surprise. She set the bottle down hard on the counter as she whipped earbuds he hadn't previously noticed—sue him for looking everywhere else first—out and let them dangle around her neck.

"You startled me," she said.

"Didn't mean to," he managed, noticing her phone on the counter, connected to the earbuds.

"I was just getting a glass of wine to sip while I get ready," she said unnecessarily, and Drake nodded. "Sierra and Lexie and I are going to Clayborne's." She took in a deep breath—which, he couldn't help noticing, made her chest rise and fall enticingly—and straightened, as if bolstering her confidence. In his opinion, she should have every ounce of confidence in the world. He didn't remember ever having a woman literally steal his breath, either clothed or unclothed, but that's exactly what this mahogany-haired beauty did. "I didn't expect you to come home so early." She turned to the cabinet to take down a wineglass, as if she wasn't three-quarters naked in his kitchen, and then set the earbuds on the counter by her phone.

"I gathered. I'm here for some food. Dinner break." He cleared his throat and attempted to follow her lead and act normal. Water, he decided. A big glass of water, because shit, his throat was parched. He went to the cabinet, took out a glass, and filled it at the spigot in the fridge, which put him right next to Mackenzie as she poured her wine.

"Shoot!" She hopped back from the counter as the bottle knocked into the glass and tipped it over, spilling some. The bottle wobbled, and Drake reached out to right it but instead sent it toppling onto the counter. Mackenzie shot her hand out, trying to prevent the glass from rolling off the edge but failing.

At the same time, the corner of her towel came untucked, and the whole thing started to slide down her chest, inch by inch, as if in slow motion as Drake's eyes locked onto it. She threw her arm to her chest at the last second, but not before he caught sight of the rosy outer edge of one tantalizing nipple.

"Good reflexes," he said stupidly, hoping to cover his disappointment and then silently scolding himself for being disappointed.

"I've had lots of practice at trying to stop mishaps as they happen," Mackenzie said, grinning self-deprecatingly, the slightest hint of a blush spreading over her cheeks. It was the same rosy color as her—

Dammit. Quit it.

"This is why I always drink white," she said. "It doesn't always stay in the glass."

Drake belatedly registered that the wineglass had shattered at her feet, and he looked down to verify it and saw that her feet were bare. "Don't move."

"Yeah," she said, glancing around her, as if judging where she could step that was safe.

"Nope," he said, and without thinking—because, damn, if he'd been thinking, he would have done something different, anything different—he swept her into his arms, one arm under her knees and one supporting her shoulders, eliciting another surprised shriek from her.

"Drake!" she said, laughing and, sadly, holding her towel tightly to her body.

Scratch that. *Not* sadly. Wisely.

Fuck, his brain was scrambled right now, as he inhaled the

scent of her and felt her smooth, bare leg beneath his fingertips. He fought to keep his gaze from roving to the bottom of the towel to see how far it traveled up, or to the top of it to see if it crept downward again, because he was trying to do the right thing and not act like a desperate, turned-the-hell-on man.

He swallowed, gathered his self-control, and carried her to the other side of the kitchen island, then set her down carefully, making sure not to let his hand trail any farther up her thighs in the process.

"My hero," she said, her grin wide as she gazed up at him, continuing to hold the towel with one hand and brushing the knuckle of her other one over his cheek. His cock responded by swelling even more. What he wouldn't give to really be her hero for a night.

Drake forced himself to grasp her hand lightly, briefly, a friendly gesture, he hoped, and then he stepped away. "I'll clean this up and bring you another glass."

Instead of heading back to her bedroom to get ready, as he'd assumed she would, Mackenzie slid onto a stool at the counter. In nothing but a towel. Not wearing any underwear.

He sucked in a quiet but deep breath, then tried to remember what he was doing. Cleaning up glass shards. Right.

He took out the dust pan and whisk broom and busied himself sweeping up the entire area between the cabinets and the island. He dumped it all in the trash can and took another glass down. The Chardonnay was close to empty, but it was the only bottle chilled, since he wasn't used to having a wine drinker as a roommate, so he poured the rest into the glass and handed it to her.

"Thank you," she said. "How are you doing on the bullet points for Mason? You had some great ideas on the way home the other night."

He turned back around and took out some roast beef and whole wheat bread. Keeping his back to her, he stuck the bread in the toaster and the meat in the microwave. "I sent them over today. We'll see what he says, but they'd be crazy not to pursue it."

"They'd be crazy not to convince you to be in charge of it."

He let the comment go unanswered. Maybe she would take her wine to her room and let him stick his head in the freezer to see if that would cool his blood.

"Okay, we can skip that topic," she said cheerfully. "How late do you work tonight?"

"Ten o'clock." His toast popped up, microwave dinged, and he heaped the meat on the bread, added a slice of cheese, put the top bread on, and turned around, mainly because it would be blatantly rude to eat with his back to her as he stood at the counter.

Mackenzie leaned her elbows on the island, her glass in front of her, as she absently wound a lock of her hair around a finger. The towel appeared to be secured tightly, but that didn't prevent him from getting an eyeful of her curvy, sumptuous cleavage. Did she have the slightest damn clue how alluring she was?

"Have you—" He stopped when his voice came out hoarse, cleared his throat, and tried again. "Have you heard anything more about your apartment?"

Her gaze jumped to his. "Have I overstayed my welcome?"

"No," he said quickly as he thought, *as long as you're fully dressed.*

She narrowed her eyes at him as if gauging his sincerity.

"Really," he said, and most of the time he meant it. The times when they stayed up late watching a movie or when they hit Carlotta's together before going their separate ways for the day, for example. Last night, they'd cooked dinner together, which had been an amusing give-and-take between his healthy preferences and her junk-food ones. They'd compromised with salmon filets with a side of mass-produced mac and cheese. He'd drawn the line at the orange stuff, insisting on no artificial colors, and he had to admit the whole dinner had tasted damn good.

"I talked to Nadine today. If all goes as planned, I can move in on Sunday. So you'll be rid of me soon."

Instead of letting slip how much that thought bothered him, he made a joke of it. "And then I'll never see you again?"

"You wish. I've been thinking of joining your gym."

An image of her in a sports bra and little workout shorts taunted his brain.

Once she moved out and the slumber party ban was over, he needed to get laid. Hell, who was he kidding? Though he would honor their agreement to not have a female guest while she was there, there was absolutely nothing stopping him from going home with a woman. Nothing except himself...or maybe the pretty girl who left little piles of Mackenzie shrapnel all over the apartment—her laptop and planner and a sweatshirt on the island, a pair of shoes by the couch, hairband and rings on the end table. He oddly didn't mind the signs of someone else in his space and admitted to himself that was probably because it was short-term.

"You should," he said. "I know a guy who could show you around, maybe give you some tips."

"I bet you do." She stood, grasping her towel, and said, "I might hold you to that. I need to finish getting ready or I'll be late. Enjoy your dinner." When she gestured to his sandwich, he realized he hadn't yet taken a single bite.

As he watched her walk toward her room, admiring those legs, he acknowledged he was starving, but not for a sandwich.

CHAPTER EIGHT

ackenzie thought she'd be relieved to ride off in an Uber toward the bar on Hale Street where she was meeting Sierra and Lexie. *Relief* hardly described her situation, though, as she thanked her driver and climbed out onto the brick sidewalk near the wooden Clayborne's on the Corner sign that jutted out from the building. *Relief* would mean that, by leaving his apartment, she could forget about Drake and what he made her body crave.

That was a big no.

Her body hadn't forgotten one iota of need.

When she'd seen Drake standing in the entrance to the kitchen, watching her, her first instinct was to hide. Though he was oh so desirable, she'd had no plan for him to find her in a towel, and on autopilot, she'd nearly jetted back to her room. But then she'd seen something in his eyes, interest, she was pretty sure, and he'd seemed a little flustered. She'd reminded herself that, generally speaking, guys liked to see girls in towels. And she'd acknowledged that she liked the way he was gazing at her. She'd thought, *This is Drake. See where it goes.*

Though she was a fan of sex and not a stranger to short-term flings, she wouldn't classify herself as sexually aggressive. Standing there, exposed, being checked out by a guy who looked like he did and who undoubtedly was used to gorgeous women, had required a micro-pep talk, and her nerves had caused her to spill the wine. But when he'd carried her to the other side of the room and set her down, she'd felt hard proof—rock hard—that he wasn't indifferent to her in a towel.

Though her brain could argue that that didn't mean anything except that he was a living, breathing male reacting to the sight of a female's skin, her body didn't care. Her body wanted to show him more skin and to peel his clothes off of him and run her hands over all of *his* skin.

It seemed her adolescent crush was alive and well and had escalated to a full-on *I want to make babies with him*. Except without the babies.

She blew out a big breath, trying to get herself in check before she entered the bar, peering down the one-block-long Hale Street. She wasn't familiar with this area of town, likely because it had only been redeveloped in the past couple of years, according to Sierra, who lived in an apartment above one of the businesses. It was easy to see it was a thriving, trendy block now, with shops on both sides, old-fashioned lampposts, and lots of people coming and going at the dinner hour. She'd have to make time to explore the stores and definitely that bakery across the street.

A group of people came out the main door of the bar, so Mackenzie grabbed the handle and went inside, glancing around for Sierra's chestnut hair or Lexie's espresso-colored locks. There was a small stage to the left of the door, lining the windows on the Peach Boulevard side, and high-top tables scattered throughout. A long wooden bar with loads of character and red-upholstered stools stretched along the left-hand wall, and there was a lofted second story at the back of the building, where it appeared there were more places to sit. Mackenzie wended through the tables, heading toward the stairs, thinking maybe her dinner dates were on the second level, but then she spotted Sierra at a high-top table for four along the wall that butted up to the stairs.

"Hey, you," Sierra said as she reached the table.

Mackenzie leaned in to give her a half hug, breathing in the citrusy scent of her. She noted the glass of red wine in front of Sierra was nearly full. "You weren't waiting long, were you?"

"Not at all. I met my sister here to go over some business stuff, and we just got done five minutes ago."

"Your sister works with you?" Mackenzie slid onto the stool with a back across from Sierra and settled in, loving the atmosphere and feeling like it was a place she could easily spend hours at. Most of the tables were full, as were the stools at the bar, and the din was warm, pleasant, that of people having a good time.

Sierra shook her head as she swallowed a sip of wine. "Kennedy's a marketing consultant. She's also part owner of Sugar Babies, the bakery across the street, which you have to try. If she's still here, I'll introduce you. Her husband is Hunter Clayborne, who owns this place."

"I'd love to meet her, and her husband too."

"Hi, ladies." Lexie appeared at their table with a shy smile.

"Hey, Lexie." Sierra pulled out the stool next to her. "So happy you could come."

"Your jacket is adorable," Mackenzie said of Lexie's fern-green suede jacket as she removed it and hung it on the back of her stool.

"Thank you." Lexie flashed another grin and hoisted her short body onto her seat. "Sorry I'm late."

"I just got here too," Mackenzie said.

A blond waitress came up to the table then and greeted them.

"Girls, this is Asia, my future sister-in-law," Sierra said. "This is Mackenzie Shaw. She just moved back to town, and she's staying with Cole's brother Drake for a while. Lexie Gallagher is best friends with Cole's brother Gabe." She gestured to each of them as she introduced them.

"Welcome. It sounds like you, my friend, are fully entrenched in your fiancé's family already," Asia said to Sierra, then turned her attention to Lexie and Mackenzie. "It's very nice to meet you two."

"You too," Mackenzie said. "I'm assuming you'll be a sister-in-law from the other side, since Sierra's the only one who's felled a North brother."

"Asia's engaged to my brother, Jackson. Did you two decide on where you're going for a honeymoon yet?" Sierra asked Asia.

"Not even close. We haven't had a lot of time and there's so many choices."

"You need a honeymoon planner like this girl here," Sierra said brightly, nodding to Mackenzie, making her laugh.

"I've never heard of one," Asia said, stepping closer. "So, like, a travel agent kind of thing?"

"Sort of, sort of more." Mackenzie slid into an abbreviated explanation of To the Stars, avoiding a sales pitch because she wasn't sure of the couple's means and didn't want to mislead them that she was the right person to help if they were looking for a modest trip.

Once Asia had lit up at the examples Mackenzie had cited, taken their drink and food orders, and hurried off to fill them, Sierra leaned in slightly.

"They need you," she said. "And trust me, my brother can afford it. He's a CEO and would give Asia anything."

"I wasn't sure if I should give her a business card," Mackenzie admitted.

"Give her a card. It's fate. Asia hardly ever waits tables anymore. She's an assistant manager here and usually has other duties, and she doesn't work many shifts at all because her photography business is taking off. Anyway, I'll put a bug in Jackson's ear too."

"Thank you," Mackenzie said. "I'd love to help them." She jotted a note with their names and wedding date on her phone, then took a business card out of her clutch wallet to hand to Asia later. "So you have Jackson and Kennedy and any other siblings?"

"Just the three of us. Jackson's the oldest and I'm the youngest. He's definitely the stereotypical overachieving first-born, but Kennedy doesn't have much of a peacemaker in her and I'm definitely not spoiled," Sierra joked.

"I have an older brother too," Mackenzie said. "Ezra. We're close, but I don't get to see him enough. What about you, Lexie?"

"I'm an only child, also not spoiled," Lexie said, making them laugh. "Ezra is friends with Drake, right?"

"And Zane," Mackenzie clarified. "They've been friends since, like, middle school. The three of them used to be inseparable. When Zane went into the military and Drake and Ezra went to college together, I stopped hearing Ez mention Zane as much."

Sierra set her wineglass down after taking a sip. "I met Zane when he was home for Christmas. I liked him, but we were only together twice for family dinners. He and Drake seemed kind of opposite, with Zane so serious and Drake…not. It must be weird for twins to be so far away from each other."

"Especially when they can't communicate as easily because of Zane's job." Mackenzie texted or talked with Ezra at least weekly, even though he was traveling the majority of the time. With their dad not really in the picture, they only had each other.

"Zane's a good guy," Lexie said, "but harder to get to know than Drake."

"You've known the Norths for a long time, huh?" Mackenzie said.

"Gabe and I've been friends since the first day of kindergarten. The twins weren't even born yet. Which makes me sound old," Lexie said with a laugh. "I'm thirty-six."

That made her eleven years older than Mackenzie, but it didn't feel that way. Maybe because Lexie looked about a decade younger or maybe because they had something in common—a history with the North family, though clearly Lexie was a lot closer with all of them than she was.

The North family, though it undoubtedly had its drama and ups and downs within it, seemed rock solid and so stable. Their mom had lived in the same house since before Drake and Zane were born, which meant somewhere in the three-decade range. No divorces, no new school districts, no upheaval. Mackenzie acknowledged that Mr. North's death must have been an unbelievable trauma for the whole family, but besides that, she envied the family's stability and deep roots. She'd vowed to build that for herself, for her future family, for her someday kids.

Both these women, who she instinctively liked upon meeting,

were a piece of the North family stability—Lexie from the past and Sierra into the future as she married and created her own family with Cole. While Mackenzie had no illusions of becoming that intertwined with the Norths, she was already beginning to feel a hard-to-explain kinship with these two such that their different ages didn't matter.

"You must have so much insight into the brothers," Sierra said to Lexie.

"They're family to me. More than my own is." Lexie's tone flickered with sadness, but then she seemed to deliberately brighten. "If you suspect Mrs. N is a saint, you're right. Those five have kept her on her toes for as long as I've known them."

"I want to hear all the stories," Sierra said, "especially about Cole. Oh! There's Sloan." She straightened and gestured to a raven-haired woman across the room.

By the time Asia delivered their food fifteen minutes later, not only had Mackenzie met Sloan, who seemed to be the queen of connections in the music industry and had sworn she was going to throw a party to introduce Mackenzie around, but Tucker Steele and his fiancée, Gin, had stopped by the table as well. Sierra had talked up To the Stars to them, and before Mackenzie could offer them the business card on the table, Tucker had jumped in, said Mackenzie was exactly the person they needed, and set an appointment to meet with her next week.

"Do you need a job?" Mackenzie jokingly asked Sierra as soon as Tucker and Gin walked off to get closer to the stage, where a couple of people were setting up for Wednesday Night Trivia, which Sierra promised was cutthroat and as fun to watch as a football game. "Because I'm ready to hire you as my PR girl. My mind is swimming with all the prospects."

"No kidding," Lexie said. "Is there anyone you don't know?"

Sierra said, "I always knew how music-centric this neighborhood is, in part thanks to the recording studio down the street, but what I didn't realize was how many people I know who are engaged. If you're looking for love, drink the water."

Mackenzie made a point of pushing her water glass away, eliciting a laugh from the others.

"Okay, so I have to ask," Sierra said as she dipped a fry into cheese sauce, "because Cole and I were debating… Are you and Drake…?"

Lexie let out an exhale. "Us too! Gabe and I went back and forth. Are you two together?"

Just the question made Mackenzie's temperature go up as the kitchen scene earlier this evening flashed through her mind. "No. I'm just staying with him for a few more days. Strictly platonic."

Sierra's enthusiasm faded slightly as her shoulders sank. "I could've sworn there was a connection there Sunday evening."

"There's chemistry," Lexie said, tilting her head at Mackenzie. "You can't deny that."

"Maybe the North brothers just radiate that vibe," Mackenzie said, her eyes on Lexie, "because when Mason first said you're engaged, I thought it was to Gabe for some reason."

"I got the same impression the first night I met Lexie," Sierra said. "Remember when the family celebrated Cole's job with North Brothers Sports?" she asked Lexie.

"How could I forget? Gabe is still so happy he's finally working for the family business," Lexie said and then took a bite of her sandwich.

"I asked Cole more than once if you and Gabe were a couple that night," Sierra said.

"You two seem…in tune," Mackenzie said as Lexie shook her head and finished chewing her food.

"Exactly," Sierra said. "And Gabe makes sure you have whatever you need."

"He's just a genuinely good guy," Lexie said with a shrug. "The type who's in tune with everyone, you know? Wants to make sure everyone has what they need."

"I can see that," Sierra said thoughtfully. "But you're engaged to someone else, so I guess that says it all. But this one here…" She pointed to Mackenzie with a wicked gleam in her eyes. "That was a nice dodge from you to Lex, but I want to get back to you. You're not engaged and there was chemistry that was nearly tangible between you and Drake."

Mackenzie shoved her glass to her lips and took a good swig

of her Moscow mule as she thought about that. Chemistry, yes. She blew out a breath as she set the glass down and felt flushed.

"Cole swore there was nothing going on because of your brother and some nonsense about a man code," Sierra said, "but I agree with Lex. There's no hiding that attraction."

Mackenzie glanced around, as if someone might be able to overhear. No one was paying any attention to them. And probably no one would care, but it wasn't her usual way to admit something so personal to someone so soon after meeting them. She was better at getting people to open up to her than she was at baring all herself. It was part of doing her job well, and she'd been heavily focused on doing exactly that for the past few years, in addition to navigating a variety of roommates she didn't know and didn't have a lot in common with. It'd been a long time since she'd allowed herself to consider building friendships that went deeper than the surface. These two, though… It felt right and she instinctively trusted them and, bottom line, she was dying to tell someone about Drake and get their input.

"It's…hard to deny," she said, grinning shyly. "We're not together—"

"But you want to be?" Sierra said.

"I knew it," Lexie let out with quiet exuberance when Mackenzie nodded.

"I'm pretty sure Cole was right that Drake doesn't want anything to happen between us," Mackenzie said, "because of Ezra." She knew her big brother, knew how protective he was. Nobody messed with his sister, even one of his best friends. Probably especially this one, because Drake was such a player. He had been in high school, she'd bet big money he was in college, and it was obvious he still was today, judging by his social media and the frequent texts that came in from numerous female names— and yes, she'd peeked a few times.

"But you're interested," Lexie said. "Your cheeks are pink."

Mackenzie let out a guilty laugh. "Have you seen him?"

"He's got that North allure for sure." Sierra's brows went up and she used her hand to fan herself, grinning.

"There's something about Drake though," Mackenzie said as

she scooped up a glob of cheese sauce on a pretzel bite. "I've always had a thing for him. He's the guy who talked to me whenever my brother had friends over. He's the one who made time to say hi, who teased me good-naturedly, who had a nickname for me."

"What was it?" Sierra asked.

Mackenzie shook her head and rolled her eyes. "It's stupid now, but when I was thirteen…"

"You can tell us," Lexie said.

"Shawlet. Because Ezra was Shaw, and I was the little Shaw."

"The stuff that raging teenage crushes are made of," Sierra said, her eyes sparkling. "Am I right?"

"Oh, completely," Mackenzie admitted.

"Nothing ever happened between you two though?" Lexie asked.

"I was four years younger. Still a kid, really, though I didn't think so at the time. And then it was crush interrupted when they went off to college. I didn't see him again until last week."

"I'd say he's interested now. Do you think?" Sierra asked.

Mackenzie glanced around again and then circled her finger around the rim of her copper cup as she recounted what had happened at Drake's earlier this evening. All the details. Because it sort of seemed to Mackenzie like he might be interested, and she wanted to see if she was, in fact, crazy.

"I mean," Sierra said when she'd finished the story, "you're pretty. And you've got these long, to-die-for legs—"

"You've never seen my legs," Mackenzie said, laughing.

Sierra waved a hand. "Maybe not in a towel, but I don't need to. They're long and gorgeous and most men would kill to have legs like yours all to themselves. And there's an obvious affection between you two. I'm betting he was hurting by the time you walked out the door tonight."

"For sure," Lexie said.

Mackenzie wanted to believe it. She wanted to believe it badly. "So what do I do?"

"What do you want to do?" Sierra asked.

"Tackle him. Have my way with him," she said as matter-of-factly as she could manage, but she couldn't help laughing again. Her drink was nearly gone and might have been making her feel giggly, but it was more likely the topic, the idea of tackling Drake North, who was twice her size and four times as strong. Maybe eight.

"Is that all you want? Sex?" Sierra asked.

"Definitely," Mackenzie said. "My whole existence is in upheaval right now. In my experience, relationships are just more chaos and instability. That's the last thing I want."

"That sounds right up Drake's alley," Lexie said before taking a drink of her lemon drop martini.

"Perfect match," Sierra said.

"So if it only happened once, would you be okay with it?" Lexie asked.

"I think you have the question wrong," Mackenzie said, grinning conspiratorially. "Maybe the question is, would I be okay with it if I *don't* have a one-night fling with Drake? Could I pass up that opportunity?"

"Smart girl," Sierra said, laughing. "And your answer?"

Mackenzie sat back on her stool, exhilarated and flushed from the topic, the alcohol, the atmosphere. She didn't have to think long at all. "It'd be the culmination of a teenage crush. How can I not try?"

Laughing, Sierra said, "I think you have your answer."

"Next question," Mackenzie said, sobering up. "I've had flings before, but I've never been the aggressor. So...how do I make it happen?"

CHAPTER NINE

Mackenzie wasn't drunk, but she wasn't sober either as she let herself into Drake's apartment. If she was going to do what she planned to do, she needed to be not quite sober, and she'd managed to achieve that by nursing two mules over the course of the last three hours with Sierra and Lexie as they watched the trivia battle, which turned out as fun as Sierra had promised. Maybe, the more she thought about it, she could really use a couple of double vodka shots right about now. Maybe but no.

The apartment was mostly dark, with just the light over the kitchen sink on a dim setting. Drake's bedroom door was open, which meant he wasn't in bed, and her first thought was that he'd gone out. But then she heard the TV in the living room, and as she went farther down the hall, she could see the flickering light of it.

Her nerves gripped her and she stopped in the hall before she could see the living room—or Drake.

Crap, this was crazy. Her shoulders started shaking with laughter at herself, first because she planned to be so bold and second because she was being a total chicken.

Since Drake apparently hadn't heard her yet, she took several steps back down the hall to her bedroom to collect herself or, really, re-talk herself into this.

"Do you want this?" she said to herself as she tossed her clutch wallet to the floor and kicked off her shoes just inside the bedroom door. She ran her fingers through her hair, wondering how bad it looked. "Of course you want this. Who wouldn't want this? But especially you. You want this so much that you'd be crazy not to—"

"What exactly do you want?"

She whipped around at Drake's voice *right freaking behind her*, lowering her arm from her hair as she did, and the next thing she knew, her elbow was knocking into his...jaw? He caught her opposite arm to steady her, probably a good thing, and she found herself chest to chest with him as he rubbed the side of his face.

"Crap. I'm so sorry," she said, and she reached up and brushed her fingers along his jaw as he lowered his hand.

"Hurricane Mackenzie."

"More like a wrecking ball, honestly," she said, frowning. "Are you okay?"

"I'm fine. What do you want so much?"

Oh. Yikes. He'd heard everything. What exactly had she said?

She peered up to find him staring down at her, and when their gazes met, she couldn't pull hers away. He was holding both of her arms now, and there was barely room for a breeze to go between them. Mackenzie's breath stuttered out of her, and a little voice in her head pointed out that exactly what she wanted was right there. He smelled deliciously masculine, as if he'd showered recently with some kind of manly smelling soap that mixed with plain old super-sexy man.

Mackenzie leaned in, stretched up on her toes, that same little voice saying *what the hell* as she dared to press her lips to Drake's. Their mouths sort of bounced together for a second, and she met his gaze again, expecting him to refuse her, set her away from him, burst out with a hell no, but all he did was peer down at her with heavy-lidded eyes.

"This," she said, barely above a whisper. "This is what I want." She went back in for more, her arms winding around his torso to ensure she didn't lose him now that she had him.

Their lips flirted with each other for several seconds, tapping, touching, testing, and then his hands slid from her upper arms to the back of her head, and he held her to him as he turned it into a real kiss, one that she'd been dying for for nearly half her life. Their tongues met and all tentativeness vanished.

Her insides melted as he swirled his tongue with hers and tilted his head for a better angle, still grasping the back of her head with one hand as the other trailed down her back and his fingers dug into her waist as he pulled her closer. His hardness jabbed at her abdomen, leaving no doubt he was as into this as she was.

She dipped both hands under the hem of his T-shirt in front, skimmed them upward, and marveled at solid, sculpted abs, so defined she could feel the ridges. As the kiss deepened, her hands continued upward, over an awe-inspiring set of pectoral muscles. When she grazed both hands over his nipples, Drake groaned, deep and slow, and then the next thing she knew, he ended the kiss.

It was a toss-up what she needed more—oxygen or his lips back on hers. She decided on him, but he pressed his forehead into hers, keeping his lips just out of reach.

"This is a bad idea," he said in a gravelly voice that made her knees go weak—until she registered his words.

"I don't think so."

"We aren't supposed to let this happen."

"You've thought about it," she said brazenly. "You wanted that kiss as much as I did. You can't tell me otherwise."

"It's not about want."

"It is." She lowered one hand to his erection and grabbed it through his athletic pants, which left little to the imagination. "Drake, I'm not asking for anything besides right now."

He groaned again as she rubbed her hand up and down a couple of times. He pushed his body into her. "Your brother would kill me."

"He won't know. It's one night. And even if he did, he has no say."

Before he could come up with more excuses, Mackenzie reached up to the tie of her shirt—a halter style with off-the-shoulder sleeves—at her nape and undid it, then tugged it up her torso and over her head. Drake's eyes were glued to her as she reached behind her and unhooked her peach strapless bra and let it drop to the floor, baring her from the waist up.

———

DRAKE CONSIDERED himself a fairly strong person, but faced with Mackenzie's wisp of peach silk lingerie and then her glorious naked tits, he was a fucking goner. There was no way he could stand there without touching them, palming them, kneading them, tasting them. He managed to hold himself in check just barely.

"You don't play fair," he said, and his words came out shaky, with so much need he couldn't think straight.

"I know what I want."

Her hands went to the waist of her jeans next, undid the button, rasped the zipper downward, and Drake swallowed, afraid to breathe, dying for her to keep going and knowing on some level he should stop her.

She stuck her fingers into her jeans at the sides and slid them down her hips, pushed them to her ankles, stepped out of them. Her skimpy panties barely covered anything, just a small triangle where her gorgeous thighs met, and then she pushed them down her legs and tossed them to the side. She stepped to her purse, which was sitting askew on the floor near the door, bent down, unzipped it, and grabbed something. Setting aside the oversized wallet, she held up a square packet so he could see it was a condom and then stood, facing him.

His cock was throbbing for her painfully, insistently as he feasted his eyes on every inch of her naked, luscious body.

"Say yes, Drake," she whispered, looking up at him expectantly, and there was a flash of insecurity in those beautiful brown eyes. That would've done him in if he wasn't already done the hell in.

"Fuck yes. Get over here, Mackenzie."

She was in his arms in a heartbeat. He plucked the condom

from her fingers and tossed it to the bed until he was ready for it. While his lips ravished her mouth, his hands were all over her, from her hips, over her rounded ass, up her slender torso, to her lush, silky breasts. He broke the kiss to taste her nipple and run his tongue around the hardened nub, swirling, teasing, loving the gasp he pulled from her. His free hand trailed lower again, to the wet heat between her thighs, and he dipped a finger inside of her, nearly losing his mind at the slick, soft, womanly feel of her.

He moved his mouth to her other breast, laving it, sucking, toying with it, his fingers doing the same to her core, and before he could even think about stopping for long enough to take his shirt off, she was panting, grinding her hips in circles on his fingers, clinging to his biceps as she came apart and her insides contracted around his fingers.

"God," she said, breathing hard, leaning her weight on him as her legs seemed to wilt.

Pressing his lips to her temple as he held her up, he said, "That was the most beautiful sight I've ever seen."

Her lips found his, a tender, caring, just-had-the-orgasm-of-the-decade kind of kiss, while his blood pounded through him with an urgency he'd never experienced before. He picked her up with his hands at the backs of her thighs. Mackenzie wound her arms around his neck, and when his fingers trailed back to her center, she moaned and then gasped.

"Drake."

He could listen to her say his name all damn night, preferably with him buried deep inside of her. As he carried her over to the bed, he nibbled at her ear and whispered, "You're so damn hot, Mackenzie. Making me lose my fucking mind."

When he felt the mattress at his knees, he carefully set her down on the middle of it, then stood and whipped his clothes off in record time. He grasped for the condom, opened it, and wasted no time sheathing himself. Then he crawled over Mackenzie, supporting his weight on his arms, and directed himself to her opening. He sucked in an uneven breath, trying to slow down, reminding himself to make it good for her, but then

Mackenzie grasped his ass in both hands and impaled herself as her legs came around his waist.

He bit his lip in order to not lose it, mentally reeled himself in for a few seconds, and then Mackenzie squirmed beneath him, urging him to move. So he did. He pulled out almost all of the way, slowly, telling himself he had control, but then he felt a nip of her teeth on his shoulder. With her fingers on his jaw, she angled his lips toward hers and pulled him into a tantalizing mating dance of tongues that matched what their bodies were doing, and he was lost. He gave himself over to the rhythm his body demanded, understanding that she was right there with him. Perfectly there with him, as if their bodies were made to be joined like this and everything before Mackenzie had just been passing time.

As her fingers played over his body, every touch pushing him higher, he burrowed his face in her hair, engulfing himself in the scent of her, all of his senses overwhelmed by her, and every thought slipped out of his head. His body climbed toward release as he registered the sexy, needful sounds coming from Mackenzie. He managed to pull himself back enough to ensure she went over the edge before he did. Barely.

As Mackenzie shattered around him and called out his name, he drove into her a final few times and climaxed so hard he saw stars. He was still coming back to himself, letting the world fall back into order around him, when the sound of the apartment door opening reached his ears.

What the—

He pushed himself up somehow, his muscles still feeling liquid and useless, and got his fingers on his pants as the front door shut. It wasn't loud—he wouldn't have heard it if they'd closed the bedroom door, but they hadn't. Why would they?

With his heart thundering, he somehow got his legs into the pants and yanked them up just before sticking his head out the bedroom door to the hallway—where he ran head on into Mackenzie's brother.

CHAPTER TEN

The absolute worst person who could walk through Drake's door right now?

Ezra.

Without a question.

Worse, even, than Drake's mom.

"Hey," Drake said, trying like hell to sound pleasantly surprised to see his friend instead of guilty like a thief in a church service. He eased the guest bedroom door closed behind him to protect Mackenzie as he stepped fully into the hall, wishing he'd had time to grab his shirt. "What are you doing here?"

Why in the name of all things holy had he ever thought it was a good idea to give Ez a key so he could let himself in whenever he was in town?

"I just got in from Australia," Ezra said. He wore a suit, minus the tie. He rolled a compact suitcase behind him and had a leather messenger bag on his shoulder. "I thought I'd crash on your couch and surprise my sister in the morning." His eyes narrowed. "Wait. Where is my sister?"

"How about a drink? I bet you're exhausted." Instead of leading Ez to the kitchen, Drake stood firmly in front of Mackenzie's door.

"Drake, I said where's Mackenzie?" Ezra's voice was low and threatening. Drake sized him up in the dim hallway, searching for a sign of weakness even though he knew he wouldn't find one. Ezra had a rep for choosing hotels all over the world for their twenty-four-hour fitness centers so that he could work out in the middle of the night when he couldn't sleep, which was always.

"Come on," Drake said. "Let's go to the kitchen. Are you hungry?" It was damn hard to do, but Drake moved in that direction, leaving Mackenzie's door vulnerable. If he continued to stand guard, though, it just made them look guilty.

As if there was any question what had been happening five minutes ago. *Five damn minutes.*

Drake stopped when Ezra didn't follow him.

"What the hell is going on?" Ezra demanded.

The bedroom door opened, and Mackenzie stood there, fully dressed in the jeans she'd been wearing earlier and a wrinkled gray T-shirt. Her hair was a mess, as if she'd been thoroughly… yeah. Five damn minutes ago. "Ezra!" She threw her arms around her brother. "What a happy surprise." Her joy was real, Drake could tell, even if she was pouring it on a little thick.

Ezra accepted her hug stiffly. "What…the…fuck, Drake?" Rage came through in each evenly measured word. Loud and clear. "Tell me you didn't do what it looks like you did."

Mackenzie ended the hug. "It's not your business, Ez. I'm an adult. I make my own decisions."

Ezra set her aside, closed the space between him and Drake, and punched him, all in a single move, and even though Drake was expecting it, the blow to his jaw hurt like a son of a bitch. He stepped back, holding his cheek, but he didn't retaliate. He would do the same if he had a sister.

"Ezra!" Mackenzie yelled. "What are you doing?"

"What are *you* doing?" Ezra yelled back, sparing her a confused look and then returning a death glare to Drake. He advanced another step, and Mackenzie jumped between Ez and Drake, as if Drake needed—or deserved—a protector.

"Ezra, cut it out!" She pushed her hands into his chest, futilely trying to stop him, and lucky for Ezra, he stopped himself. "I am a grown woman," she said. "This doesn't involve you."

"The hell it doesn't." Ezra's voice was low and measured. "You slept with my sister," he said to Drake. "When you said you'd take care of her, I didn't know that's what you had in mind."

"Dammit!" Mackenzie said, slapping her brother's arm ineffectively. "Butt out."

Drake couldn't stand the way his friend looked at him in that moment, particularly because he had every right to. "I didn't have anything in mind, man. I made a mistake."

At the word *mistake*, Mackenzie whipped her head toward Drake, her mouth open and hurt radiating from her eyes, and he instantly realized how that must sound to her. *Shit.* But he also knew, now that they were both dressed and not touching each other, he'd been weak. He'd made the wrong decision. What his body wanted hadn't mattered.

He hastily told her, "That's not about you, Mackenzie—"

"Go to hell," she said, the look in her eyes, of so much hurt and disappointment, gutting Drake. Hurting her was the last thing he ever wanted to do. "Both of you. Beat the crap out of each other. I don't care." She swung an angry look back at her brother, then turned on her heel and stomped back into the guest room.

"Way to go, jackass," Ezra said. "That's exactly why you were never supposed to touch her. How dare you fucking hurt her like that." He pivoted and followed Mackenzie into the bedroom, and Drake heard him ask her if she was okay.

Mackenzie's vulgar response was short and not at all sweet and impossible to misunderstand, for Drake as well as the rest of the people who lived in his high-rise building.

With his stomach knotted, Drake turned and went into the kitchen for that drink he now needed like he had never needed a drink before. As Ezra tried to reason with her in the other room, Drake took down a cocktail glass and the whiskey and poured it till the glass was three-quarters full. He swigged a mouthful of it and closed his eyes as the liquor burned all the way down his throat and into his belly.

He couldn't have fucked up things any worse if he'd tried.

"Get out of here!" Mackenzie yelled at her brother.

"I'm not the bad guy here, Mackenzie—"

"Go!" she yelled.

Drake took another gulp and closed his eyes, wishing the whiskey would burn up the regret that was drowning him.

Ezra came storming out of the bedroom, gunning for him, and Drake put a hand out to stop him.

"You got your hit in," Drake said, still holding the glass in his other hand. "You try it again and I won't just stand here." He set the drink down hard on the island and straightened, just in case. He almost hoped Ezra would take another swing, because it would feel damn good to punch back.

Ezra turned away and grasped the counter on the island with both hands, as if trying to get control of his anger. He shook his head, jaw locked tight, visibly working to calm himself down. Drake had rarely seen him this out-of-control pissed off. Ez didn't often explode in anger.

Drake leaned against the opposite counter, his gaze zeroed in on the floor. The only sounds were coming from the guest room, where Mackenzie was… He wasn't sure what she was doing, but it wasn't quiet and it wasn't calm. He needed to apologize to her, but not while Ezra was here.

Without facing him, Ezra asked, in a deceivingly calm voice, "What were you thinking?"

Drake let out a scoff at himself. "I wasn't thinking," he said quietly. An image of Mackenzie flashed in his mind, that moment she'd stood on her tiptoes and kissed him, softly, awkwardly, and his body had lit on fire. Thinking was the last thing he'd been doing; in fact, she'd looked so irresistible in that instant, so vulnerable and sexy at once, that he was pretty sure his brain had short-circuited and he'd been operating on sheer physical instinct, the kind that ensured the species was carried on.

He shut down the memory, swearing up a blue streak to himself.

"You never think," Ezra said, louder now, less calm, facing him and pointing a finger at him. "It's all about the moment for you and you never consider the aftermath."

"I said I messed up," Drake said, his volume rising to meet Ezra's.

"Fuck yes you did," Ezra said. "How are you going to unfuck this, Drake? Answer: you're not. This time your charm and good looks aren't going to help a damn thing. You. Hurt. My. Sister."

"That was never my intention," Drake bit out. He picked up his glass and swigged down half of what remained.

"Mackenzie deserves someone who cares about her, who treats her like a queen, who doesn't take advantage of her just because she's across the hall and convenient, and who doesn't tell her she's a damn mistake."

"She does deserve the best," Drake agreed, "and we both know that's not me, but I did *not* take advantage of her, nor did I see her as 'convenient.'"

"Bullshit."

Drake wasn't about to point out that Mackenzie had initiated sex or that she'd said she didn't want a commitment. None of that was Ezra's business. But… "The mistake comment… I regret that. But that's between her and me." He slammed the nearly empty whiskey glass down hard. He lowered his voice a few decibels, fighting to keep his cool. "The only thing that concerns you is that I broke your trust, and for that, I apologize."

Before Ezra could respond, the apartment door slammed, and Drake realized it must be Mackenzie.

"What's she doing?" he said, taking a step toward the hall.

Ezra intercepted his path. "Leaving. She was throwing all her shit in her suitcases as she ranted at me."

"Where the hell is she going?"

"How would I know? She wasn't in a sharing mood, thanks to you and your dumb-ass move."

"Shit," Drake muttered, not trying to get around his friend even though he didn't want Mackenzie to leave. They had things they needed to discuss—fully clothed and preferably with a table in between them. On some level, he recognized that she might need to calm down before they could have that discussion.

"You need to leave now," Drake said. "I've apologized. I'll do my best to make things right with Mackenzie—"

"Stay the hell away from her," Ezra roared. "For the love of God, leave my sister alone." He stared Drake down, breathing hard with anger, then stormed back down the hall, grabbed his luggage, and went out the way he'd come in, slamming the door behind him just like his sister had.

"Later, dude," Drake said to the empty room as he lifted his glass in mock salute. It was a good thing Ezra hadn't waited for him to agree to leaving her alone, because like it or not, he and Mackenzie had unfinished business.

CHAPTER ELEVEN

The next morning, Mackenzie exited the Wentworth Hotel and pulled her jacket tighter around herself to fend off the brisk late-March wind. The hotel was perched at the opposite end of Hale Street from Clayborne's, and she took in the lively neighborhood from this new perspective as she walked down the curved driveway.

She wasn't completely calmed down after the dramatic shit storm that had been last night, but a few hours of deep sleep on a lush bed in a quiet, upscale hotel room and the bright morning sunshine were helping. Carbs and coffee were the next steps in clearing her mind and gearing up to have a productive day. She scoped out the nearby breakfast options.

The concierge had recommended Frank's Diner for a hot meal or Sugar Babies for pastries and muffins, after getting a pitch in for the hotel's own restaurant. There was really no decision—anything with *sugar* in the name drew her in like a homing pigeon to its nest. The bakery was at the far end, on the left side. As Mackenzie headed that way, she took her time, window-shopping the dresses in the Pincushions window, the home furnishings at Henry Interiors, and the mosaic artwork at World in Pieces. The stores weren't open yet, but she'd make a point of exploring them later, maybe over lunch, after she checked out of the over-her-budget Wentworth.

She pushed open the door to Sugar Babies and inhaled the sweet scent of fresh-baked vanilla and cinnamon. The place was adorable and bustling even though it wasn't quite seven thirty a.m., with several people sitting at the small cafe tables scattered in the front and three in line at the shell-pink old-fashioned display case. The case was stuffed full of exquisite colorful desserts and pastries, and on top were antique-looking display platters overflowing with cinnamon rolls and muffins in a variety of flavors. Whereas Carlotta's, in Drake's building, was a coffeeshop that offered a few treats, this place was all about the sweets, and Mackenzie wondered if she could make it her permanent address.

A few minutes later, after saying hello to Sierra's sister, Kennedy, and being introduced to Violet, who was another of the owners and was working the counter, Mackenzie took her oversized triple berry muffin—and a coffee from the connected bookstore—to a place near the window. As she settled in and held her coffee cup below her nose, breathing in the invigorating aroma and waiting for it to cool enough to sip, Sierra herself walked through the door, with Cole at her side.

Mackenzie waved, and Sierra's face lit up as she said something to Cole, then made her way toward her through the maze of tables. Cole joined the line, sending Mackenzie a nod.

"Hey, you," Sierra said as Mackenzie stood and they hugged. "What are you doing here?" She lowered her volume when she said, "You're supposed to be curled up in bed with a certain North brother."

Mackenzie blew a breath out and forced a smile. "Yeah. That. Do you have a minute to sit?"

In response, Sierra lowered herself to a chair and leaned in, her eyes wide. "What happened? Did the mission fail?"

Mackenzie sat again and pulled off a chunk of muffin. "No," she said, glancing around to ensure no one was paying them any attention. "The girl got the guy in the strictest sense possible, but then it all blew up, literally within minutes." She explained in partial detail her brother's entrance, the fight, and what Drake had said to defend himself. *I made a mistake.*

"A mistake?" Sierra repeated, enunciating the word as if in disbelief.

"Direct quote," Mackenzie said. "I can't decide who I'm more pissed at—him or my brother."

Sierra leaned back in her chair, seeming to ponder the tale, and her eyes narrowed. "Drake doesn't usually do that—say the wrong thing. In fact, he always seems to say the right thing, the most charming thing possible."

"I guess things change once he gets the girl into his bed. Or the girl gets him into his guest bed. Whatever."

"I want to hit him."

"Be sure to get video, because I want to watch," Mackenzie said, biting down on another piece of muffin and then calming herself slightly by savoring the perfect blend of fluffy muffin and sugar-sweet bits of berry.

"So he said that, and then what happened? Did he apologize? Kick your brother out?"

"I don't know. I packed my stuff and left while they were yelling at each other." She'd had to leave a suitcase there in order to get out in a single emphatic trip, but she'd stuffed the most important things in the two she'd taken.

"Brothers can be so annoying, thinking they have any say in our lives."

"Particularly our sex lives," Mackenzie said. "The idiot. I'm the one who came on to Drake."

"So where did you go when you left?"

"I found a last-minute deal for the Wentworth on a travel app. It was more than the chain hotels, but not by much, so I figured I deserved some historical Nashville luxury to lick my wounds. Just for one night. I'll find something more reasonable to move to later today."

"You should've texted me," Sierra said. "My couch is super comfy and you're welcome to it."

"It looks like you were probably busy." Mackenzie shot a raised-brow smirk in Cole's direction, who was almost to the front of the line now. "If I'd known he was waiting for you last night, I wouldn't have kept you out so long."

Sierra waved the comment off. "It was no big deal." She leaned closer, grinning widely. "We decided to move in together. We're going to start looking for a house this weekend."

"That's exciting," Mackenzie said, a little piece of her green with envy at the prospect of a home.

"We've been staying at my place a lot because we love the neighborhood, but he has a cat we need to take care of, so it was either unsettle the grouchy cat twice with two moves or just buy a house."

"That makes sense. I'm in love with this street though."

"I do love my apartment," Sierra said. "The only thing that could get me to move is Cole. Maybe you should check it out. I know there's an available unit a few doors down from here. And mine is coming soon."

"My place is supposed to be ready on Sunday." She'd told Sierra the crazy story about the Buick last night at the bar. "Hale Street is tempting, but I just need to make it a few months in an apartment while I organize and house hunt."

"Short-term sacrifice," Sierra said. "And maybe you can do it even sooner than you plan. Everything can change so fast. A few months ago, Cole was just my employee. If you'd told me I'd be engaged to him and buying a house, I would've laughed in your face."

"Have you set a date yet?"

"We're working on it."

"Working on what?" Cole asked as he set a steaming cup of coffee in front of his fiancée. In his other hand was a turquoise box that likely held a dozen or more treats and a smaller one on top that was the size of a single muffin.

"My hero," Sierra said, picking up the cup and scooting her chair back as if preparing to stand. "A wedding date."

Cole's lips eased into a smile. "By *we*, she means her and Kennedy and Hayden. Three-woman wedding-planning typhoon."

"It's a lot of logistics planning around the show," Sierra rationalized.

As Sierra stood, Mackenzie asked, "Off to work?"

Sierra nodded and pointed to the large box. "Fuel for my crew and the production people."

Mackenzie rose, came around the tiny table, and hugged her new friend again. "I'm so glad we ran into each other."

"Same," Sierra said into her hair. As the hug ended, she added, "If you need a place to stay, let me know. You could even stay in my apartment and Cole and I can go to his place."

"I thought you were staying with Drake," Cole said.

"I didn't want to wear out my welcome," Mackenzie said offhandedly. She felt her phone vibrate in her pocket but ignored it. "Thanks for the offer, but I'd feel awful kicking you guys out. And I really need a place to office as well, so a hotel will be good for the last couple of days until my apartment is ready."

"If you change your mind…"

Mackenzie nodded and smiled, grateful to realize she was well on her way to building her Nashville life with people she really liked. "Thanks, Sierra."

"Let us know if you need help moving in," Sierra said. "I can bring the muscle." She shot a loving look up to Cole.

"Anytime," he said. "We both have trucks."

"I might take you guys up on that. Either way, we need to do dinner or drinks again soon."

They said goodbye as Mackenzie's phone buzzed a second notification, and she took it out as she sat back down. It was a text message from her blockheaded brother.

Where are you?

Mackenzie locked her jaw down and debated whether she wanted to answer. Her coffee was finally cool enough to drink, so she took a sip, let the smooth flavors of both bitterness and sweetness roll over her tongue. It was the one thing in her life she didn't add sugar to, preferring the sharpness of straight-up black coffee, and this brew from the bookstore next door was exceptional.

Come on, Mackenzie. I know you're awake. Answer me. I'm worried about you.

Damn him. That last line got her. Ez had always been the one to worry about her, even when their mom was alive, and though she wanted to head-butt him into next week, she couldn't keep ignoring him.

She typed, *I'm awake. Still pissed.*

I know. We need to talk. In person. I fly home to Houston tomorrow and I don't want to fight with you.

Her anger ebbed a little, because their time was limited. Always so limited. They saw each other every three or four months, usually when her brother could schedule a flight through LA in the midst of his business travel, and she didn't know how easy that would be anymore since she'd be living in Nashville instead.

Fine, she typed. *I'm in a bakery on Hale Street called Sugar Babies. Can you find that?*

I think I can manage that. Do they have blueberry muffins?

Yep.

Grab me one and I'll be there in fifteen.

After buying his breakfast and setting it across from her, she replied to several business emails on her phone—one to Cora, her boss, and two to resort people for Ellie Grant's honeymoon, one of which had mentioned the possibility of flying Mackenzie there for a tour. She'd love to go—it was something she did whenever possible so she could develop closer relationships with resort staff and assure herself the high-dollar honeymoons she coordinated went as flawlessly as possible—but it depended on whether she could make it work, time wise, as she got business rolling in Nashville.

She happened to glance up as her brother walked by the bakery window, heading for the entrance, and she forced her mind from work to take in a deep breath and fight down the lingering irritation with him.

Ezra searched her out with his gaze as soon as he was in the door and then headed toward her. Despite her annoyance, she looked him over as he approached, since she hadn't really had the chance last night and hadn't seen him for four months before that.

He was dressed casually, in jeans and a camel-colored sweater. His dark hair was the same as always, a little longer on top but well groomed, with facial hair that was more than a scruff but not quite a full beard. His tall, wiry body didn't hold an ounce of fat and it was obvious he still worked out, probably too much if she knew him. As he neared the table, she took in the fatigue in his eyes, not just from fighting with his best friend last night but more of an ongoing weariness. It wasn't surprising considering the nonstop traveling, all in the name of work, that he did, but it concerned her and softened her even more toward him.

"Ez," she said, standing and stepping into his embrace. He might be overbearing at times, but she loved him fiercely.

He kissed her forehead as they ended the hug. "Hey, you. It's good to see you." He held her back and looked her up and down quickly. "The move to Nashville is agreeing with you?"

"So far so good," she said as they sat, he in the chair across from hers. "The city's changed a lot—like this street, for example —but it still feels like home in a way LA never can."

"First time I've been here." He gestured to the street. "It looks lively. Thanks for the muffin, Kenz," he said as he turned his attention to it and split it in half.

"You're welcome. Ezra—" she said, reaching her limit on small talk when she was still annoyed beneath the surface.

"Look, I'm sorry our reunion last night was ruined. I flew in just to see you and wanted to surprise you—"

"Oh, you did," she said, eyeing him unapologetically. "You need to understand a few things."

"What I understand is that Drake is not the right kind of guy for you, Kenz."

Just like that, her irritation was back up, nearing a ten. She bit down on it momentarily, to avoid making a scene, and instead, after sucking in a breath, she said in a mostly calm tone, "I know what kind of guy he is. He's not a relationship guy."

"Yes."

"Women are like a hobby for him."

"Yes."

"He's too charming for his own good, and funny and fun."

"Yes."

"Sort of irresistible," she said, catching herself slipping into a smile as she remembered the flirtatious look on his face several times in the past week when they'd bantered, over movies, books, food, and any number of other topics.

"That much was clear," Ezra said in a hard voice. "Mackenzie, what are you doing with him? You know you can't change him, right?"

She scowled at him. "I'm not trying to change him. How stupid do you think I am?"

"I don't think you're stupid, but messing around with him... You know he's my best friend, but he is not the right guy for you."

"Not the right guy for what?" she said, her volume rising, generating a couple of looks of interest from the people around them, which was enough to make her reel it in again. She leaned forward and lowered her voice. "Ezra, reality check. I'm twenty-five, not fifteen. I've had boyfriends and I've had one-night stands." She said it for the shock value, her anger propelling her beyond the discomfort of talking about her sex life with her brother. "That's what Drake was, and I knew it and he knew it and we were fine with it, and then you came butting in and messing everything up because you think...what? I need to be saved?" She glanced around again, assuring herself the onlookers were no longer paying attention to them. "Here's the truth: I'm the one who started it. Not him. As he pointed out, he gave in, but he was not the pursuer. So you can quit being mad at him."

Ezra took a large bite of his muffin as he let what she'd said sink in. After he swallowed, he swigged some coffee, then set his cup down. "Really?" he finally said.

"Really. Why would I make that up?"

"I'm sorry," he said after another hesitation. "I forget you're a capable adult sometimes. I'll always want to protect you from the bad stuff, and Drake would be bad for a girl who's looking for any sort of relationship."

"I'm not that girl. I don't want a relationship. I'd think you would understand more than most that what I want is some stability, and that's why I moved back to Nashville. I want to settle down, by myself, because from what I've seen, having a guy in my life does not lead to any kind of stability."

Ezra nodded, and she could see in his eyes he did understand. To them, after growing up with their family life, a dad who'd left before Mackenzie was four and a mom who'd been about as stable as the fluff of a cottony dandelion, standing on their own two feet was the only way to guard against upheaval.

"Where are you staying now?" he asked once his dainty porcelain plate was empty.

"The Wentworth for another three hours or so. What about you?"

"I got a room downtown, in case you or Drake or both wanted to hit Broadway tonight."

"I would, unless he goes," she muttered.

"I won't be asking him."

"Better idea," she said, remembering a tabletop sign at Clayborne's last night. "Steele Hearts is playing tonight, across the street at Clayborne's. I met some people last night and I could see if I can get us in."

"Steele Hearts? Aren't they a little big for playing bars?"

"From what I gather, Sloan, the Clayborne's entertainment manager, is tight with Tucker Steele and his fiancée, so they sometimes play there."

"I'd love to see them. Maybe I'll switch to the Wentworth."

"And I'll switch to not the Wentworth. In fact," she said, pulling her phone out and checking the time, "I need to get going. I have a lot of work to finish before checkout."

"Don't stay with Drake again, Kenz."

"Ezra!" She threw her head back in exasperation. "What part don't you get? I'm not about to." She stood and picked up her trash and plate, grabbed her bag, then spun on her heel toward the trash station near the counter. Ezra was following her but she didn't care. She headed for the door, then burst out onto the sidewalk and turned toward the hotel.

It only took a few seconds for her brother to catch up.

"I'm sorry, Mackenzie," he said, falling into step beside her. "I get it. That popped out before my brain engaged." When she kept walking, he reached out and grabbed her arm, stopping her, and she allowed him to, facing him as they stood in front of the recording studio next to the diner. Ezra nodded as if he was silently running the facts through his head. "I won't bring it up again. Come on." He nodded toward the Wentworth. "You have work to do today. I have some calls to make. Let's go to the hotel and I'm going to get a room for me and pay for yours until your apartment's ready. Tonight we'll go see Steele Hearts if you can get us in."

"Is paying for my room your penance?" she asked, her lips playing with a sorta smile.

He studied her for a few seconds, and then, as if he knew that was the only way to get her to agree, he said, "Absolutely."

"You realize how much you're going to pay, right?" He could afford it just fine, a hundred times over, which was the only reason she'd allow him to do it.

Ezra pulled her into a side hug and started them walking down the sidewalk again. "You're worth it, brat. Whether we can get in to see Steele Hearts or not, we'll have a good time."

Mackenzie soaked in the contentment of having her brother beside her, taking care of her in a sense, and solving her dilemma of where to stay for the next few nights. Her day was stacked, and not having to find a different hotel and move would let her get more of her to-do list done so she could play tonight.

As they crossed the street toward the main doors of the hotel, she allowed herself to hope that some quality brother time would help her keep her mind off everything else. Every*one* else. Because Drake "I made a mistake" North did not deserve her time or her energy or even her thoughts.

CHAPTER TWELVE

s Drake drove his Jeep down Hale Street Friday morning, keeping an eye out for a parking spot, he didn't have a plan. Just a goal.

He'd only found out where Mackenzie was staying a couple of hours ago, thanks to Cole showing up at the gym for their early-morning workout and giving him crap about "running Mackenzie off." Apparently Mackenzie and Sierra had been in frequent contact since Wednesday night, and Cole had heard enough to give Drake intel, even if Cole didn't realize that was what he was doing.

Mackenzie was giving Drake the big blow off, but he'd learned she was staying at the Wentworth. She and Ez seemed to have made peace and had gone to see Steele Hearts at Clayborne's last night. For Mackenzie's sake, Drake was glad to hear they'd worked things out, even if he himself still wanted to punch Ezra.

As he neared the end of the lively block-long street, the flower shop on the corner caught his attention. Flowers. Yes.

He ended up parking in the public garage behind the Wentworth, and a few minutes later, Drake hurried through the drizzle to Buds 'N Blooms. He paused as his eyes and senses adjusted to the wood-floored flower market. It was a kaleidoscope of colors and greenery, and the air was filled with the sweet scent of flowers and plants.

"Good morning." The voice was female but had a lower timbre and a roughness, as if she was a smoker or just not awake yet.

"Hello," Drake said as he spotted her in all the colorful chaos. It was no mystery why it'd taken him a second—the clerk behind the counter had a head full of bubblegum-pink hair, which went right along with the bundles of colorful flowers throughout.

"What can I help you with today?" the girl said as she stuck a stem of greenery into a vase among a spray of vivid orange and yellow blooms.

He pivoted, taking in the dozens of options—from buckets of single-stem flowers to floor-to-ceiling coolers of elaborate arrangements to racks of gift items and cards. "I don't know." He was no stranger to buying flowers. A bundle of tulips for his mom, roses to impress a date, a vase of spring blooms to butter up Vera, the office manager at the gym. But there were so many choices here, and they needed to be just right. "I'm at your mercy," he said, giving her his winningest smile, "in dire need of your expertise."

"Well," the girl, who was early twenties or so, average height, and wearing a delicate pink sweater that matched her hair, plus black skinny jeans and black combat boots, said as she came out from behind the counter, "who are you buying for?"

"A friend," he said easily.

"A female friend?" She eased up next to him, warmth emanating from her eyes, and he read the name on her name tag —Jadyn.

"Yes."

"So red roses and chrysanthemums are out," Jadyn said to herself as she looked around at all the options. "Unless...is it strictly platonic?"

Damn good question. "Not strictly," Drake said after half a second's thought. To hide his uncharacteristic unease, he flashed her a self-deprecating grin. "It's complicated."

"Which is why you're here," she said knowingly. "Because

flowers can cut to the chase and say things that you can't even get straight in your head."

Drake's brows rose and he nodded. "That's exactly what I need."

"So a friend but not strictly platonic. Caring but not in love?" She went to a bucket of pink tulips and plucked out three perfect blooms.

"Yes," Drake said easily.

"Attraction though?"

Drake held back a scoff at the word *attraction*. It wasn't strong enough for what he'd suffered through for the week Mackenzie had been sleeping under his roof. But… "Sure. There's an attraction," he managed to say without giving away more. He wouldn't admit out loud that he'd gone home alone last night in spite of plenty of female attention at the bar and his burning desire to get Mackenzie out of his head.

Jadyn picked out some small yellow and white flowers that looked like miniature tightly petaled roses. "These are supposed to say *I'm dazzled by you.*"

Drake narrowed his eyes, took in the small flowers again, and shrugged. "I don't know if I've ever used the word *dazzled,* but okay."

"You want to sleep with her, right?" Jadyn said, pausing in her flower selection to gaze at him.

"Well…" Drake laughed at himself. What the hell. If a bouquet of flowers could fix things with Mackenzie, he might as well give Jadyn more to go on. "She's my best friend's younger sister." Possibly *former* best friend.

"Oooh," Jadyn said, switching course from a bucket of stems that had multiple coral-colored blooms on them and taking a step back. "So she's off-limits."

"She was." Right now, he didn't give a shit what Ezra thought. All he cared about was getting Mackenzie to listen to him, to let him apologize. He'd texted her multiple times yesterday, but each time, she'd ignored him or told him she couldn't talk. She'd shut him down completely, and he wasn't okay with that. "Look, I screwed up some stuff, so if you could sprinkle some *I'm sorry* into that along with all the other magic ingredients…"

Jadyn cracked a half grin and shook her head slowly at him, muttering something about how guys like him were the key to their business success, then turned toward the inventory and busied herself, putting some flowers back, selecting others, pausing every once in a while to eye the varied bunch that was growing in her hand.

"The purple ones are I'm sorry?" Drake asked, unsure if he bought into this whole language-of-flowers thing, but if it could help get Mackenzie to forgive him, he'd go with it.

"That's right."

"Maybe add some more?"

With a laugh, she said, "Aesthetics are important. A little dark purple goes a long way." The pink-haired flower fairy carried all the blooms to a worktable behind the counter. "Do you want these in a vase or wrapped?"

"Vase, please. She's staying at the Wentworth."

"Fancy."

"I don't suppose you know an insider over there who would slip me her room number?" It didn't hurt to ask.

Jadyn laughed at him, her hands moving quickly, arranging the bunch in the vase. "You're so screwed." After a few more adjustments and a final trim of a sprig of leaves, she set the vase on the counter next to the register. The finished bouquet was a tasteful splash of pink and yellow and purple and white amid lush green accents.

As he handed over his card, he asked, "What are the big white ones?"

"Gardenias," she said as she swiped his card and handed it back. "Traditionally a symbol of…secret love." Her blond eyebrows rose and her eyes lit up.

"I'm not looking for anything that starts with *L*."

She shrugged. "Well, they look good anyway, right?"

"Are you telling me your flowers *don't* have magical powers after all?"

"I personally have no proof either way, but honestly, female point of view here, if you tell her you're genuinely sorry and that you care about her and then flash her just the right smile—and don't tell me you don't know how to work those to your benefit —I think you'll end up just fine."

Drake studied her for a couple of seconds and finally said, "You're very wise, pink-haired flower mage. I'll do my best."

With an engaging smile and a nod at her, he turned and headed out the door, toward the hotel, knowing full well, flower power or not, he had his work cut out for him.

CHAPTER THIRTEEN

Clayborne's was rapidly becoming one of Mackenzie's favorite places on the planet. Besides having really good bar food and hosting some excellent bands, it was also turning out to be her best source for potential new clients.

In addition to Jackson Lowell and Tucker Steele, both of whom Mackenzie now had appointments with next week, she'd met an agent friend of Sloan's between sets last night. Dorian Bradley was in the market for a "magical, one-of-a-kind honeymoon" as a surprise for his fiancé, Eric, and couldn't wait to meet with her to start the planning.

Mackenzie was going to owe Sloan and Sierra a half-dozen really nice dinners of thanks at this rate, and she would treat them with pleasure.

The Steele Hearts show had been unforgettable. The band was working on a new album and had played a couple of brand-new, never-heard-before songs as well as their biggest hits. For them to play in such a small, intimate venue made it all the more memorable. Going with Ez had been the cherry on the four-scoop sundae.

After his apology at the bakery yesterday, he'd checked into the Wentworth and paid to extend her stay through the weekend. Nadine had confirmed her apartment would be ready Sunday, so Mackenzie was soaking up the luxury while she could.

She'd spent a few hours working, and then she and her brother had gone car shopping. It'd taken no small miracle to get him to shut up and let her negotiate with the salesman at the Acura dealership, but when they'd walked out several hours later, the keys to a shiny cherry-red ILX in her hand, he'd admitted she'd attained a ballsy deal. She attributed it to a combination of just the right amount of flirting with Cliff, the salesman, and lots of practice getting what her clients wanted from resorts and other worldwide travel companies. Ezra swore he was going to fly her to Houston when he bought his next wheels.

Now she was ensconced on the thick-cushioned, sumptuous love seat in the sitting area of her hotel room, files and notebooks spread around her, laptop on her legs as she dove into finding the perfect tropical spot in the South Pacific for Ellie Grant and Thomas Maywood. The couple had narrowed it down to some-place warm, tropical, and exotic and given Mackenzie some parameters.

To the Stars sent a lot of clients to that area of the world because there were thousands of islands, with everything from populous cities to private paradises. Ellie wanted a small, inti-mate, luxurious resort, with waterfront casitas. Something with lots of privacy and all the amenities. Mackenzie knew of several and was researching a few others, including Bellamore, the one that had mentioned comping a trip for Mackenzie to check it out. Mackenzie was drooling over its website when her cell phone signaled a text message. She dragged herself away from the photos of turquoise water and sleek private beach casitas and picked up the phone from the cushion beside her.

Hey was all the message said, but it jump-started her heart anyway because of the sender.

She pressed her head into the cushion behind her, gazing at the ceiling, running her options through her head. To reply or ignore.

She'd managed to blow Drake off all day yesterday, and it had been mostly justifiable because she'd been busy with Ezra, buying a car and going to a concert, in addition to working. But if she pulled the same thing today, he might conclude she was upset about what had happened. She was—who wanted to hear, mere minutes after being naked with a guy, that they were nothing but a mistake to him?—but he didn't need to know that. It might make it seem like she cared more than she did.

Oh, hell, who was she kidding? She cared, and there was a part of her that was overjoyed to hear from him. An ill-advised, stupid part.

With a long, loud exhale, she tamped down that part and tapped in a noncommittal *Hi*.

Dots appeared to show he was typing, and then, *I'm in the lobby. Can I come up?*

"What?" Mackenzie slid her laptop to the coffee table and leapt up off the love seat. "He's bluffing. He doesn't know where I am." But it struck her that his brother Cole knew where she was, and the chance of Drake somehow getting that info did exist.

A single glance in the full-length mirror outside of the bathroom confirmed that she was *not* presentable *if* he was indeed here at her hotel. She still wore what she'd slept in—striped silky boxer shorts and an old, thin long-sleeved tee—and she hadn't brushed her hair or teeth yet.

What lobby? she typed as she ran a brush through her tangled hair.

The Wentworth.

If her adrenaline hadn't been flowing previously, it was now pumping hard. Before she could figure out how to reply, he sent more.

I need to talk to you and have something for you.

Something for her? She momentarily forgot her panic and wondered if it was food. She'd meant to get room service for breakfast but had yet to call it in, two hours after she'd sat down to work.

What flavor of something for me? she replied, stalling for time, fishing for details as she raced around the room, searching for her black leggings and a bra. Because she knew she had to let him in, get this over with, whatever *it* was exactly, so she could go on with her life and stop thinking about her dreadfully timed tryst with her brother's best friend.

What flavor do you want?

On the floor in front of the window, on the bottom of a pile of clothes, she found her leggings, grabbed some clean underwear from the suitcase, whipped her boxers off, and yanked both layers on. Then she typed, *You know what I like.*

Right after she hit send, the double meaning hit her and she grimaced. Food, she meant. Breakfast. Though she'd only stayed with him for a week, he did know her preferences, as they'd hit Carlotta's almost every single day. She was partial to fruit flavors in her sweets and nothing but beans and caffeine in her coffee.

What if it's not food? he texted.

Tell me what it is, she replied, pulling a sweatshirt over her head and hurrying toward the bathroom.

If you want what I've got, tell me your room number. Otherwise I can go door to door looking for you, and if that doesn't work, I'll stake out the lobby until you have to come out for something.

She doubted he would, as he didn't do well with sitting still or being idle, but she had to get this discussion over with anyway. Besides…she was hungry and maybe it was food. Plus, something in her needed to lay eyes on Drake again. Call it closure for a night that had started out spectacular and ended up a disaster.

With her toothbrush hanging out of her mouth, she typed in 322, tossed her phone down, spit out her toothpaste, and hastily arranged her hair in a messy bun. She'd just come out of the bathroom and was about to gather all her clothes off the floor and throw them in the closet when a knock startled her even though she was expecting him. She shrugged at the mess—in addition to the clothes and toiletries everywhere, her work stuff remained spread out and her laptop was still on the Bellamore website.

Turning toward the door, she closed her eyes and took a moment. *Not going to let him affect me. Not going to…*

He knocked again and she let out a quiet curse at his lack of patience.

When she opened the door and saw him standing there, wearing nothing special, just athletic pants and a Jim's Gym T-shirt—which happened to reveal some fabulous biceps—she couldn't help thinking about how those specific biceps had held his body over hers and how that facial stubble had felt against her skin.

She was so *damn* affected.

When he offered a stunning vase of flowers, which he'd been holding out of her sight, her mouth opened, but she couldn't find words. She managed to take it from him and couldn't help leaning forward to breathe in the sweet scent of the blooms.

"Hey, Shawlet," he said in that low, lazy drawl of his that could turn a girl inside out.

But not this girl. She straightened and moved away from the door, into the room, to show him—and herself—that it was no big deal to be in a hotel room with Drake and a king-sized bed looming across the way.

"Drake," she said, businesslike. It would take more than the nickname and some pretty flowers to get her to forget about being a *mistake*. "Thank you. These are gorgeous."

"But probably not as edible as you were hoping for, so I picked this up from the cart in the lobby."

He handed her a small paper bag. She peeked inside to see a blueberry scone. "Thank you," she said, trying not to show how much his thoughtfulness got to her. He was obviously working all the angles and clearly wasn't a novice at it.

Drake took the vase from her and set it on the coffee table, then took the pastry bag in one hand and Mackenzie's hand in the other and gently tugged her to the love seat. "Sit," he commanded. Because he was taking the scone out, she did as he said, biting down on her tongue and trying not to think about the warm strength of his hand. "You eat while I talk," he said as he handed the pastry to her, along with a napkin.

Instead, she set the scone and napkin on the coffee table next to the flowers while he stacked the folders, placed them next to her, and lowered himself to the table, planting his still-perfect ballplayer butt by her laptop, pushing the table farther away from the love seat in order to fit his long legs in front of it. Glancing at the screen, he said, "Bellamore. That place looks amazing."

"I'm researching it for Ellie," she said. "It's on a tiny island called Jiva."

"It sounds like what she said she wants."

He leaned his elbows on his knees, which brought him closer. Mackenzie shifted away to the corner of the cushion and pulled her legs up next to her, knees to the side. She put more space between them because she could smell him, clean and masculine and uniquely Drake, and she needed to not.

"I owe you a multifaceted apology," he said, his eyes averted.

"Okay." She narrowed her eyes at him. "Did Ezra put you up to this?"

Drake glared, not at her, more at her brother, it seemed. "Hell no. I haven't talked to him. This is all me."

"Okay," she said again, believing him but holding tight to a big dose of caution.

"I'm sorry for calling what happened a mistake, Mackenzie." He brushed his knuckles back and forth along her lower leg, and she tried to tell herself it was affectionate and not seductive. It wasn't really working. *Seductive* was his middle name, no matter what his intentions were.

She forced her attention from his long, talented fingers to his face, and he met her gaze, nearly made her breath catch with those intense blue eyes.

"*Mistake* insinuates that something was wrong, and believe me, there was not a thing wrong between you and me."

She couldn't look away, and she couldn't breathe. And she couldn't wait to get this sweatshirt off because it was suddenly broiling in the room. But she fought the urge to shed it, because no matter what Drake's words did to her insides, she needed to keep an even keel on the outside.

"I know and you know that I didn't take advantage of you, but Ez doesn't want to see that. All he sees is his baby sister hooking up with a guy who doesn't do relationships."

"I don't want a relationship," she said adamantly. "And I told him that."

"You and I agree on that, and that's all that matters between us. Whatever happens between Ezra and me is separate. I don't want us"—he gestured between them—"affected by Ezra."

"Fair enough," she said. "You're forgiven for the mistake comment. I don't know that you have anything else to say you're sorry for."

"I'm sorry as hell our night was ended abruptly and early," he said, taking one of her hands in his, "because in the short time we had, you blew my mind."

She fought hard not to melt, but she felt the same way. Cheated. Regretful that she didn't get the chance to spend one full night with him. But in some part of her brain, she acknowledged that it was for the best. Because, objectively speaking, if her goal was to *not* fall for this man, then blowing each other's minds even more was a bad idea.

"Things work out the way they do for a reason," she said, trying to sound indifferent as she spouted philosophy she was only about fifty percent sold on. "Let's just say it was fun while it lasted and now it's over."

Still holding her hand, he studied her, as if looking for a hint that she was bullshitting him or saying what he wanted to hear. Mackenzie raised her brows to emphasize she meant it and gently pulled her hand away, smiling to show she was A-okay, fine, un-damn-affected.

She would be un-damn-affected as soon as he wasn't close enough to touch, smell, see the faint beginnings of smile lines at the corners of his sky-blue eyes.

She hopped up off the love seat and put several feet between them. "I really need to get back to work." *And get you out of here.*

Slowly, Drake stood, still eyeing her. "We're okay then? Friends?"

"We're okay," she said easily. "I hope you and Ez can work things out. You've been friends forever."

"We'll see," he said noncommittally.

"Thanks for the scone and the flowers. They're beautiful."

"The flowers are from the shop across the street. Supposed to have magical powers." He was making his gradual way toward the door, and he halted when he was even with her. Peered down at her, seeming to devour her with his eyes, and there was a vibe in the air between them that had her wondering if he was going to lean down and kiss her on the lips in a more-than-friends way.

Instead, he brushed her cheek with his fingers, pressed a friendly kiss to the top of her head, and said, "I'll see you Sunday."

"Sunday?"

"Moving day. At my mom's house. I'll be there to help."

Right. At his mom's. With others around. Totally safe. "That sounds good." She opened the door for him. "I'll see you then." She gave a stupid little wave before he turned and went on his way, and then she shut the door, leaned against it.

She'd have her defenses back up by Sunday and be prepared to see him as only a friend and a pair of strong arms to help her move. Because if she didn't, she had a feeling she could so easily plummet in the other direction and screw up all the things that were most important to her.

CHAPTER FOURTEEN

he office of the CEO of North Brothers Sports was nothing special. It was the not-too-big, not-too-fancy corner office on the second floor of an unimpressive, nondescript building, the same place it'd been from day one of the corporate office.

Since the creation of the company in the 1970s, there had been exactly three CEOs—Harrison North, who was Drake's dad, then Hamilton North, Drake's uncle, who'd stepped up when Harry died, and then Mason, who was the oldest of all the children of the two original North brothers. Mason was also the most driven, the biggest workaholic, and in the running for most serious, though Drake's twin, Zane, would give him a run for the money on that.

Drake hadn't been in this office for ages. Prior to this Monday morning meeting, he'd had no reason to be. He could count on one hand the number of times he'd visited it in the few years since Mason had taken the helm. And still, the room was familiar enough to cut to the bone.

It was his dad's desk that Mason sat behind. His dad's wood coatrack in the corner, where there was a trench coat hanging but no suit jacket, as, true to form, Mason was fully suited up at the moment. Drake was more than a little stunned at the emotional punch of being here, meeting with his brother and the marketing

VP, in the place where he had countless memories of seeing his dad.

He'd been devastated just like the rest of the family when Harry had been killed in a car wreck. Drake and Zane had been fourteen, and it still caused a deep ache to think about his old man now, which was why he made a point of not thinking about him too much. But sitting here, it was impossible not to recall all the times he'd come to work with his dad as a kid.

Drake and Zane and his mom used to deliver dinner to Harry on evenings when he worked late. Some of Drake's favorite memories were of playing spy with Zane in the sparsely populated after-hours building while their parents sat in this very room and discussed business or family or whatever they needed to catch up on that particular day. He and his brother would split up and stealthily creep from hiding place to hiding place and see what intel they could overhear, the goal being to avoid detection. Drake's crowning success was when he'd hidden under this very desk and eavesdropped on his parents' discussion of Cole's three-day suspension from seventh grade after a fistfight in the middle school library.

Now Drake tuned in to what Melody Schafer, from marketing, was saying about the potential market for a home fitness equipment division. They'd been discussing it for the past forty-five minutes, and it was clear there was a big opportunity for North Brothers Sports here, one that business bulldog Mason would never let pass.

"So Drake, you can go first at the board meeting," Melody said, "and give the fitness expert's perspective—benefits of a one-stop shop for the best brands of home equipment and a place where the customer can test them out, as well as how it would work to offer personal training in the home, from liability insurance to marketing our services to finding qualified trainers. I'll give an overview of the SWOT analysis afterwards. It should be a no-brainer, though Bill will probably have a thousand objections."

Bill Santini was the VP of Finance. He was in his late fifties and did what finance guys did…tried to rein in spending at every turn. Mason was a big believer in spending money to make money, so while the two frequently went head-to-head, they balanced each other out in the end, or so Drake picked up from family gatherings.

"I'll handle Bill," Mason said. "The meeting's Wednesday at nine a.m. You need to be here on time." The last part was directed toward Drake, and while Drake was fully aware that timeliness was not his strongest attribute, he didn't need Mason riding his ass about it. His brother should be thankful Drake had agreed to help them sell the idea to the board.

"I'll be here," Drake said curtly.

"Send me your talking points by tomorrow night?" his control-freak brother carried on. "Your bullet points from last week are good. Just expand on them."

"I got it, Mason. I may not work in the stuffy offices, but that doesn't mean I'm stupid."

"Not stupid at all," Melody said, her green eyes alight and her voice full of enthusiasm. "This is such a good idea. So much potential." She tapped her tablet, where she had all her notes, closed the cover on it, and stood. Drake rose as well, to shake her offered hand and let her past him. "It's been a pleasure to see you again. See you on Wednesday."

"You too," he said. He'd only met Melody, a brunette in her early to mid-forties, a couple of times before, at the annual company picnic, or maybe it was the holiday party, but he liked her.

Once she was gone, he sat back down, fully aware Mason would have more to say. He always had more to say. Before the CEO could start, though, Gabe wandered in.

"How'd it go?" Gabe asked. "Melody looked happy."

"It went well. We're presenting it at the board meeting," Mason said, entering something on his computer—notes on the meeting, Drake would bet. "Drake's put together a lot of good info, and Melody's findings were even better than we expected."

Instead of taking the second guest chair in front of the desk, Gabe wandered to the side table along the wall and leaned against it, crossing his suit-clad legs at the ankles, arms over his chest. "I wanted to catch you two together. I had an idea."

"You sure I need to be in on it?" Drake asked, glancing at the time on his phone. He had a shift at NBS in less than an hour.

His two oldest brothers were infamous for their frequent business discussions. Didn't matter if it was work hours or not, in the office or outside of it. Mason handled a hell of a lot, and he generally kept Gabe, who was VP of Human Resources, in the loop. Of all the brothers and cousins, they'd been with the company the longest, along with their cousin Cooper. Mason had already been in the corporate office when their dad died. The ten-year difference in age between Mason and Drake was more than evident when it came to their roles in the company. Mason acted like an old man, and Drake...didn't.

Drake appreciated the hell out of the two oldest North brothers' devotion to the business because it took the pressure off him. Keeping this company, their dad and uncle's company, going strong was paramount. It was their legacy and would hopefully be in the family for generations to come. Drake valued it just as much as the others did, but he'd always known Mason would lead it. He himself would always have a part in it—that's why he worked the retail end of it instead of putting in full-time hours at the gym—but he savored his freedom and his lower stress level.

"This isn't business related," Gabe said. "I was thinking about Cole and Sierra, now that they've set a date. What do you think about the three of us, and maybe Zane too, going in on a dream honeymoon as their wedding gift? Something Mackenzie could coordinate? Something Cole probably wouldn't think to spring for."

With a half grin, Mason said, "Cole definitely wouldn't think of it, and Sierra would never ask for it. I like it. What about you?" He aimed the question at Drake.

"Easy. I think it's a great idea."

"Maybe Mom would want in on it too," Gabe said.

"I bet she would." Mason leaned back in his chair now that he was done on his computer.

They were spot on about Cole. He was a black sheep in a lot

of ways and had signed away his share of the business when he was eighteen years old, then spent years working his ass off in construction, when literally millions could have been his. It was only recently that he'd joined North Brothers Sports, and he'd reluctantly accepted his vastly multiplied company share back as part of the deal. The guy was brilliant about a lot of things but hardheaded as hell. Cole was not a big spender and wasn't used to being well-off and then some.

Sierra deserved a trip to the moon if she so desired it, for putting up with the surliest North brother and figuring out how to make him happy.

Beyond that, Drake was a fan of giving Mackenzie some business. She didn't need charity, was more than competent, from what he'd seen, but he knew she wanted to make a big impression on the company owners fast, to show them the decision to move her to Nashville was a wise one. The more business she could drum up quickly, the better.

"Any idea where you want to send them?" Drake asked as he started to filter through some of the places he'd seen her working on when she was staying with him.

"Sierra said she wanted something with a beach at dinner that night when Mackenzie was there," Gabe said.

"You think Cole would like that?" Drake asked.

"Cole will like whatever makes Sierra happy," Mason said. "That sucker has it bad."

All three of them shook their heads, mocking their weak-ass brother.

"How are you thinking we'd work it?" Drake asked. "Tell them up-front what we plan to do and let them choose all the details? Or plan it all ourselves and surprise them?"

"As busy as those two are, I'd like to take the planning off their hands," Gabe said. "But we need to prevent them from planning a honeymoon themselves somehow. I'm not sure how best to handle it."

"I'll talk to Mackenzie. I'm sure she'll have some insight." Drake jumped on the opportunity to be the point man for two reasons. One, he didn't want either of these clowns spending time with Mackenzie, and two, it was just the excuse he needed to see her again.

"See what she suggests, what she needs from us," Mason said. "Once we have more information, we can decide how to proceed."

"I'm on it," Drake said, standing to leave, taking out his phone to send Mackenzie a message.

She hadn't been unfriendly yesterday when he—and Cole and Sierra—had helped her move her belongings out of his mom's garage into her apartment, but there'd been a coolness in her demeanor, a distance between them that wasn't his doing. A definite message of *things are different now* with a healthy dose of *that night was a fluke, so don't get any ideas.*

Not that he was.

Not too much.

Okay, ideas, yes. He couldn't get that night—before Ezra had blown it to hell—out of his mind. But actual intention of a repeat, no. He had no expectations of sleeping with Mackenzie again, but he missed her, had grown used to daily interaction with her. Besides that, he never liked to have someone upset with him, either outwardly or subtly. He was determined to get back in her good graces, and this would be the perfect opportunity.

CHAPTER FIFTEEN

*M*ackenzie loved her job even without the perks, but the perks... They made working for To the Stars over-the-top and unbeatable and something she would be hard-pressed to ever walk away from.

It was Tuesday afternoon, just after five o'clock. She'd been in her apartment for two days and had unpacked the necessities and made it comfortable for now—story of her life, though at least this time there was an end to the cycle of packing and unpacking almost in sight.

She'd ordered two barstools online and they'd arrived just before lunch today. Assembly had been quick and painless as she stuffed a sandwich down so she could get back to work. Now she sat on one of the stools, her laptop on the counter in front of her, on a video call. After several emails back and forth with Giovanni Rossi, the owner of Bellamore, the new resort on the island of Jiva, they'd finally found a time to connect. He was most insistent that the resort would fly Mackenzie to the other side of the world for a five-night stay so she could experience firsthand the exquisite luxury and impeccable service that her clients could be enveloped in.

She couldn't turn him down. Not even considering how chaotic her life was right now. Going would be good business— the more relationships she could build around the world with people at key resorts, the easier her job became. But beyond that, how crazy would she have to be to say no to soaking up sun and luxury on the other side of the world—at no cost to her? Yes, she had loads of work to do, but she could do a lot of it poolside with an umbrella drink at her side. She'd gone on numerous other business trips like this, to all parts of the globe—the Maldives, Thailand, Peru, Turks and Caicos, Austria, and probably a dozen others. Sometimes they ended up being overpacked with sales-pitchy activities, but Giovanni had assured her multiple times she could spend her time as she wanted to. These were the perks she lived for.

Giovanni had momentarily muted the call and stepped away while he checked available dates for her trip. The twelve-villa resort had opened three months ago, and he was working hard to get its name out there.

While Giovanni was away from the call, she glanced at the clock on her computer, noting it was twelve minutes after five. Not surprisingly, Drake was late for the appointment he'd set with her to discuss some kind of mysterious business he'd refused to elaborate on. If it was anyone else, she'd be less skeptical, but what business could he possibly want to discuss?

She couldn't help suspecting he was using "business" as an excuse to come over, though why, she couldn't figure out. They'd made their peace last week. They'd gotten along fine on Sunday, when he, Cole, and Sierra had helped her move in. Once Sierra and Cole had left, Drake had hung around, offering to assemble this or unpack that, but Mackenzie refused his help at every turn and finally told him he had to leave so she could take a nap. At last, he'd given up and gone, but the look on his face as he walked out was one of reluctance.

She'd had no intention of napping but had needed him out. Away. Because she was still struggling hard to cut off her attraction to him, still fighting the urge to replay every moment they'd been in bed together.

Today, she wasn't feeling at all optimistic it would be any easier, but if he showed up, she'd find out what he wanted and then get him out the door again. She hoped one day she'd be able to spend time with him without obsessing or remembering, but today was not that day.

Giovanni, who had dark, collar-length hair and sparkling brown eyes and looked to be in his early thirties, surprisingly young for a resort owner, appeared on the screen again. He paused before unmuting and gave his attention to someone off-screen, holding up his index finger to Mackenzie, then mouthed an apology and stepped off camera again. It made her slightly antsy that he was taking so long, but how could she hold it against him when he was arranging a trip to paradise for her?

She pulled her planner in front of her to check out her schedule for tomorrow, but before she could get it open, a knock sounded on the door, causing her heart to hammer. As reluctant as she was to see Drake, a part of her danced in anticipation.

After a quick glance to verify that Giovanni was still away, she hurried to the apartment door, rammed her foot into the empty barstool box that she'd set aside to take out later, swore to herself and righted the box, then twisted the knob, pulled the door open, and…

God. He made her breath catch every time.

She tamped that reaction right the hell down and wrapped a cloak of indifference around her. "I'm on a video call with a resort," she said, her voice hushed even though the call was still muted. "Come on in, but pretend you're not here when Giovanni comes back on."

"Giovanni?" he said, amusement lacing his tone.

"Shh," she said as she heard noise from the call that sounded as if Giovanni was back. She rushed to her stool just as the handsome resort man appeared and flashed her a winning smile.

"Hello again, sweet Mackenzie," Giovanni said. She could appreciate his dark-haired good looks, but they were altogether ineffective on her, especially now that six plus feet of testosterone was settling in next to her, just out of view of the camera. Six plus feet that let out an almost inaudible grunt of amusement. "Thank you for your patience. I've reserved the Sea Sanctuary casita for you, one of our very best, for a five-night stay beginning on this coming Sunday. I've tentatively booked a six-fifteen a.m. flight out of Nashville, Tennessee, on Saturday morning. You'll arrive in Fiji, where you will be met by someone from my resort. I cannot wait to meet you in person and show you all the pampering and amenities of Bellamore."

"That sounds amazing," she said, triple-checking her planner for those days, knowing even if there was something scheduled, she would cancel it or postpone it. "The dates and times are fine. Let's go ahead and do it, Giovanni."

"As you wish, pretty lady," he said, typing away on his keyboard.

"Pretty lady," Drake said, again under his breath, and Mackenzie smacked his thigh with the back of her hand off camera, keeping her eyes on Giovanni to make sure he couldn't hear any of it. She risked a quick glare at Drake, telling him with her eyes, if he made one more comment, she would do true physical harm to him. Drake put both his hands up in surrender.

Mackenzie finished up the call quickly, with Giovanni promising to forward all her travel info via email, and when she disconnected, she breathed out in momentary relief that Drake hadn't said anything further.

"How old are you?" she asked.

"That guy," he said, shaking his head. "Subtlety isn't one of his strengths."

The guy was flirty, but she could ignore the random *pretty lady* as long as that was all it was. "He's harmless," she said as she marked the days of her trip on her planner.

"How do you know?"

With a shrug, Mackenzie said, "He's a flatterer and a flirt. Not a big deal. I can handle a guy like him."

"You're really going to go meet him in person?"

"I'm going to take advantage of the trip his resort has booked for me, check out the property for my clients—including Ellie Grant—and take in a little turquoise water while I'm at it. This isn't an unusual thing in the industry." She hopped up and went into hostess/business mode. "Can I get you something to drink?"

"I'm good," he said, leaning his elbows on the counter and gluing his gaze to her.

She busied herself getting a glass of ice water, feeling his eyes on her back with every movement. When she'd gotten dressed this morning, with their meeting at the top of her mind, she'd felt dumb putting on the jeans that Cora said made her butt look good but had done it anyway, and now…thank God. Taking one more cube out of the ice tray, she bolstered herself as she plunked it into the glass. Instead of facing him, she poured water into the empty sections of the ice tray.

"So…you said you have a business proposition," she said as she put the tray back into the freezer.

"My brothers and I would like to hire you to plan a honeymoon that will blow Cole and Sierra's mind."

Closing the freezer door, she spun around. "Wow. Really?" she said stupidly.

In theory, she knew all the Norths were well-off, verging on filthy rich. Living with Drake for a week, she'd discerned that he didn't spare any expense for the things he wanted, and seeing the vehicles each of his brothers drove the night they'd gone to his mom's for dinner, there was no question—they were *not* worried about money. But they were all fairly down-to-earth and came across as everyday guys in a lot of ways, so it was easy to forget they were in the same league as her actors and entrepreneurs and other clients.

"Really," Drake said, his lips twitching up into an amused half grin.

"And let me guess…you're the point person."

"In the flesh."

"Do you think it would be better for me to work with one of your other brothers instead?"

"Not even a little bit," he said. "They don't have time anyway."

"This isn't just a ploy to work your way into a repeat of what happened between us?" She said it with her own halfhearted grin.

The smile that appeared on Drake's face now was full-throttle, one-hundred-percent flirtatious, and there was not a doubt in her mind he'd used that exact look to get what he wanted a thousand times. In the last month. "Is there a chance of having a repeat?" he asked, raising his brows hopefully.

"Not even a little bit," she mimicked.

"Can't blame a guy for asking. But no, not a ploy for anything. Gabe came up with the idea yesterday. He, Mason, my mom, and I are all in, and maybe Zane, too, once we get ahold of him."

"Do you know what you want? Where you want to send them?"

"Sierra mentioned the beach."

She set her water glass on the counter, quickly forgetting about it, her mind revving up with possibilities. "It's hard to go wrong with a beach trip. Anything more specific?"

Drake shook his head. "We're open."

"Do you have a budget in mind?"

"Whatever it takes to give them a spectacularly memorable trip. Cole has a history of thinking he's an outsider in the family. It's never been true except to the extent he's distanced himself from us. This is our way of showing him he's one of us. And Sierra… She's the one who helped Cole turn his life around. How do you pay someone back for giving your brother the kind of happiness she's brought to Cole?"

"The honeymoon of a lifetime is a really good start," Mackenzie said.

"They both deserve it."

In that moment, Drake's love for his brother and his soon-to-be sister-in-law were so clearly etched on his face that she couldn't help but see a deeper dimension of him, beyond the all-around charming, friendly guy. He was a man who cared deeply, who didn't always make it easy to see how deep he went.

And didn't that just draw her in another three or four levels. Maybe five.

"Okay then. Let's do this. Let's figure out a 'spectacularly memorable' trip for Sierra and Cole," she said.

Without hesitation, Mackenzie went back around the counter, sat down next to him, and drew her notebook near. Drake pulled his stool closer to her, as if to better see everything she wrote down and any websites she might pull up, and she wavered. Because she could smell him, that same scent she'd been lost in the other night when she was engulfed in his arms. She felt the heat of his thigh up against hers, even through the denim and polyester.

Scratch all that. She sat up straighter, put a whisper of space between their legs, and reminded herself that she could do this, she could do business with Drake and keep it strictly business. She was as hardheaded as she was determined, and he was not going to get to her.

CHAPTER SIXTEEN

For three days, Drake had managed to keep himself ass-crazy busy, busy enough to avoid thinking about Mackenzie's pending trip. He'd organized a rock-climbing day trip with a couple of guys he knew, gone out each night to the bars, played a double-header volleyball game for the North Brothers Sports intramural team, cleaned out his mom's garage, met with Cole and others regarding Cole's new baseball training foundation, and worked a couple of shifts—one at the gym and one at the store.

But now, at 3:47 a.m. on Friday night, or technically Saturday morning, none of that did a damn bit of good, and he'd do just about anything to pass out cold and get some god-forsaken sleep so he could stop thinking about Mackenzie's imminent departure. Six fifteen in the morning, to be exact.

He bolted upright in his overlarge, over-empty bed, cussing up a storm, then threw his legs over the side. He grabbed his sweatpants from the floor and tugged them on. A few long strides took him to the balcony door, and he unlocked it and threw it open, stepped out into the brisk early-April night. Which did exactly zero bit of good.

The street below was deserted. Windows in the building across the street were mostly dark. The only noises were the distant din of a car starting, a dog barking. Most of the world was asleep, like he should be, but instead, he stood there breathing in the crisp air as if it could clear his head or calm his soul.

It didn't.

For a minute, he considered a motorcycle ride, but even that idea didn't appeal.

Mackenzie could take care of herself, just like he himself had told Ezra back when he'd picked her up at the airport barely two weeks ago. She'd traveled all over the world before. And if he was honest with himself, it wasn't that kind of worry that had him tied up in knots. It was the thought of that flirtatious motherfucker meeting her on the other end of her day-and-a-half-long, around-the-world journey.

He pushed himself off the iron railing, spun on his heel, and strode back inside, slamming the door shut behind him. Though the lights were out, he could make out the stack of three books on his nightstand, and none of them, not the new-release thriller, not the rock star memoir, not the Ted Williams biography that he'd finally gotten around to picking up, not one of them roused his interest right now.

The covers on the bed were twisted and pulled out from under the mattress, visible proof of his two hours of attempted sleep so far tonight, and though he'd always been a big fan of his ultra-comfortable top-of-the-line memory foam mattress, the thought of even sitting on the edge of it right now made him want to punch the wall.

He stormed out into the hall, made his way to the kitchen, fighting to blank his mind. Without a thought as to whether he was legitimately hungry or not, he opened the fridge and took out the remains of a chicken and veggie bowl and tossed it into the microwave. For the two minutes of cook time, he emptied the top level of the dishwasher, and when the ding sounded, he removed the bowl and sat on the edge of one of the stools, then started shoving steaming food into his mouth without tasting it.

Mackenzie might think the resort douchebag was just being friendly, but Drake knew that the chances of that were slim. She could catch the interest of any single guy, and she'd definitely caught the resort owner's. Drake couldn't help but wonder whether the attraction might go both ways—he could see with his own eyes the guy was sculpted like a Greek god. He let out a growl.

Drake shoved the half-eaten bowl away and catapulted off the stool, unable to lie to himself anymore that he was fine to sit back and passively wonder whether Mackenzie would hook up with Adonis for the next week. He went over to the living room and pulled his laptop off the lower shelf of the coffee table, where he'd left it.

He was on the reservations page of the Bellamore resort within a minute, typing in Sunday's date, hitting the search button impatiently as he muttered out loud, "Come on. Show me what you've got."

His plea was answered quickly, as the site came back with two different beach casitas still available, including the one called Honeymoon Haven, which gave him an idea. Maybe that would be suitable for Cole and Sierra. Maybe he could check that out in person.

He clicked on the other available place, Reefside Retreat, and skimmed over the details—king bed, spa tub, two stairs to the sand, and another twenty steps to the water at high tide. The nightly price was sky-high, but he didn't blink when he hit the reserve button.

Before filling out the reservation form, he opened another tab and did a search for flights. He didn't know her exact itinerary beyond her six-fifteen-a.m. departure, but it didn't matter. The earliest flight that came up didn't leave until ten a.m. It wouldn't get him to Fiji until the morning after Mackenzie arrived, but that was okay. He changed to Monday on the resort site, then switched back to the airline ticket and clicked on it.

Only one seat left, it said in red letters of the ten-o'clock flight, and that's how he decided this was the right thing to do. Mackenzie might not agree, but he'd deal with that problem when he had to.

With that, he completed the reservations on both sites, shoved up off the couch to go pack a bag, and felt more at peace than he had for the past three days.

———

TWO FLIGHTS down and two to go. Six hours invested so far, and he wasn't even halfway there. Not even a third of the way.

Drake had kept his mind continually occupied by starting the Ted Williams book on the flight to Dallas and by bingeing a few episodes of *The Office* on his tablet between Dallas and San Francisco, but now, as he headed from the airport pub where he'd grabbed a quick dinner to his gate, certain thoughts were hard to keep burying.

Specifically, what the ever-loving hell was he doing?

His pace was leisurely, thanks to a two-hour-plus layover. He barely noticed the throngs rushing past him in all directions as he paused in front of the departure board to check the status of his flight. Still on time, just like his app had told him.

As he turned onto one of the international flight wings, his messenger bag on his shoulder and duffel in his hand, he glanced at the overhead signs and spotted the gate he was looking for halfway down the terminal. He slowed the closer he got, and once he arrived in the general area, he found a spot on the wall of the main walkway to lean against instead of wandering into the maze of seats near the door to the jetway.

He double-checked the flight board—Suva, Fiji—and leaned his head back against the wall, eyes closed, thinking.

He could still double-back the way he'd come, find the next flight east, and return to Tennessee. Because once he got on that overnight flight to Fiji, there was no turning back. He'd be full-on committed then.

It was impossible to ignore the glaring truth any longer that, if he boarded that plane, he was chasing a girl literally around the world.

Drake didn't chase girls.

He'd never even chased a girl to the other side of Nashville.

He'd never had to and never wanted to. If a girl needed to be chased, he backed off, because chasing could give the impression that he wanted a relationship, and he didn't want a relationship.

Except…he couldn't deny that he still wanted *something* from Mackenzie. The R word was taking it a little far, but he was aching to see her, spend time with her. He wanted to have a full night with her, where he could worship her body with his, take his time pleasuring her, learn the best ways to make her come apart. And it went beyond sex too. He wanted to pick apart movies with her, watch her face as they parasailed or zip-lined or island hopped via Jet-Ski, lie next to her on the warm sand as they watched the sun set.

The admission caused a kernel of hot fear to blossom in his gut. He pulled out his bottled water and poured the cool liquid down his throat to extinguish it.

He could still turn back.

But the island of Jiva would be one hell of an adventure. And he'd already cleared his schedule, found replacements for every single shift for both jobs, told his mom he'd be out of the country for the next week.

He wasn't one to shy away from adventures. Ever. And no matter how much it made his gut tumble just thinking about it, he couldn't shy away from his original harebrained plan to chase Mackenzie. Because he wanted more with her. He wanted adventures with her. He wanted to hear her laugh and see her smile and smell her fresh, flowery scent. For the first time in his life, he wanted…more.

Straightening away from the wall and hoisting his duffel back up, Drake took in the chaotic travel scene in front of him and, with no more hesitation, walked toward the boarding area and got in line to board.

CHAPTER SEVENTEEN

hirty-plus hours of travel might give some people pause, but the availability of Wi-Fi on the longest leg allowed Mackenzie to get a lot of work done in between a couple of lengthy naps. Plus, there was that whole hard-to-find-fault-with-a-free-trip thing. By the time she landed at the airport in Fiji, she was ready for food, tropical air, and a good night's sleep, but at the same time, she was invigorated on both a business and personal level.

The tropical air part of her wish was fulfilled as soon as she stepped off the plane. It was dark—local time was just after nine p.m.—and the warmth and humidity rolled over her as the faint smell of the sea filtered through her nose. She focused all of her attention on descending the flight of stairs to the tarmac, because the last thing she needed to do was stumble down them and break a leg in a foreign country.

Once she was on solid ground, she stepped to the side, out of the way of the other passengers, and got her bearings. Before she could take in much, she noticed her name on a placard less than twenty feet away, with Giovanni himself holding it up. She had to admit it was sort of nice to see a familiar face this far from home.

"Pretty Mackenzie," he said in his flirtatious baritone that had somehow seemed less aggressive over video chat. "It's so good to see your beautiful face in person." He lowered the sign and held it in one hand, offered his other to her. When she shook it, he grasped it for an extra moment, which put her on alert. This trip could get uncomfortable fast if he thought they would be anything more than business associates.

She pulled back as nonchalantly as she could, ready to give him the benefit of the doubt, and said, formally, "It's nice to meet you, Giovanni."

"Welcome to Fiji. Have you been here before?"

"I haven't, but I've been to American Samoa and New Zealand and the Marshall Islands. It's such a breathtaking part of the world. I can't imagine living here."

"It is a special area, for certain," Giovanni said. "One of the most romantic places in the world."

"That's exactly why I can't wait to see firsthand what your resort offers honeymooners."

"Honeymoons are our specialty. We aim to give lovers the most romantic setting for memories of a lifetime. Do you have bags that we need to pick up?"

"Just this one," she said, motioning to her rolling carry-on. If Drake were here, he wouldn't be able to say she'd packed like a girl, she thought with a little pang in her chest, because that had happened before things got screwed up between them. She hadn't improved at packing, but all the clothing she'd brought consisted of smaller bits of material, like shorts and thin tops and bikinis and coverups.

"Allow me," Giovanni said as he reached for the handle.

"Oh, thank you, but I've got it."

He tried once again, with a wordless gesture at the suitcase, which she answered with a short shake of her head and a bigger smile to reassure.

"Very well," he finally relented. "Our ride is this way."

After a short trip in a taxi, during which Giovanni sat in the front seat next to the driver, they arrived at a small marina. He led her to a boat with the Bellamore Resort logo on it, a vessel that had both enclosed and open-air seating and could probably hold twenty people.

"We can ride on the top if you don't mind getting a little windblown," he said as he waved at the uniformed man who she guessed was the captain. "We'll have a fantastic view of the stars tonight."

She couldn't pass up the opportunity, and he showed her to the stairs. When he followed her up, she was a little thrown to realize he really did mean *we*.

"Do you meet all your business associates at the airport?" she asked as she chose a seat. Naturally, Giovanni took the one right next to her.

"I wanted to give you a warm personal welcome. I hope to form a strong alliance with your company that will last many years into the future."

She relaxed a degree at his businesslike reply. Maybe she had her guard up a little high after such a long trip.

Without delay, the boat departed from its slip, and they were on their slow way, just the two of them plus the captain, and when they reached open water, they picked up speed.

Being out on the ocean, open-air, in the dark, was magical and exhilarating. The wind whipped her hair across her face, but after so much stale airline air, she relished the freshness. Giovanni pointed out several tiny nearby islands, most of which appeared as only a mass of darker black in the distance and a handful of which had a few lights.

"A couple of our competing island resorts," he explained, leaning close to her ear so she could hear him over the noise of the wind and water, "though we have a good relationship and refer customers back and forth depending on who has vacancies on desired dates. But of course, our goal is to be better than them." He had a lighthearted gleam in his eyes.

"How long is the ride to Jiva?"

"Forty minutes total." Giovanni looked at his watch. "We have approximately twenty-three minutes left. In that general direction is Kanakana Island. We offer many activities and excursions in cooperation. Zip lining, scuba diving, snorkeling, helicopter and balloon tours, cultural cuisine adventures, just about anything you can imagine doing. I would be happy to book you on your choice of any of these."

"That sounds amazing. As long as I can balance it with some work, I'll take you up on it."

He ran down some of the options in more detail as the boat made its way across the vast water.

Soon, he gestured to the scene in front of them.

"Welcome to Bellamore," he said with a flourish of his hand. "We're passing in front of one row of luxury casitas, some of which you can see lights in. As you can tell by the darkness in between, they are ensconced within clusters of trees, which gives each casita the feeling of being isolated and private. We're approaching the main pier."

She stood to see better and could make out a narrow dock with low lighting evenly spaced along what must be a hundred or so feet of walkway from the water end to the land end. Most of the casitas were tough to make out, but one was lit like a Christmas tree, the lights showing that almost the entire seafront side was glass.

Beyond the row of casitas, she could make out a few lights that she assumed were the main resort complex. Between Giovanni and the website, she knew there was a lounge with a wine cellar, a spa, a kitchen, a recreation room, a pool, and a workout room—everything her clients could possibly need.

The captain directed the boat to the dock, and a girl in her late teens assisted from the dock. Once again, when Giovanni offered to carry Mackenzie's suitcase, she declined, but she did grasp his offered hand as she disembarked, purely for the sake of not tripping and ending up in the water. She retracted it before he could hold it for an extra moment again, and then they made their way to the reception "hut," which was a gorgeous wooden building with a peaked roof and open-air sides.

He led her to the main counter, where there was one employee working. "Good evening, Alima," he said. "Mackenzie is here to check in, please."

The dark-haired woman wearing a white Bellamore polo shirt and khaki pants returned his greeting and said, warmly, "Hello,

Giovanni. Welcome to Bellamore, Mackenzie." She asked for her last name, then typed away on her keyboard.

Alima made several *mm-hmm* sounds and then filled Mackenzie in. "It looks like you've been scheduled for a spa session in the morning."

"I didn't—" Mackenzie started.

"I took the liberty of scheduling one for you," Giovanni said. "A massage is the best thing for travel fatigue, but feel free to cancel or reschedule it."

"I'd be stupid to turn it down," she said, thinking that Giovanni was a considerate host, whether he sometimes seemed too forward or not.

"Very well. You can look over the services here"—Alima handed her a brochure—"and just show up at the spa area at nine." She pulled out another glossy piece, this one a map of the resort, and pointed out the spa as well as the Sea Sanctuary casita, where she'd be staying.

After filling her in on all the amenities, she programmed Mackenzie's key card and then handed it to her.

Giovanni said, "I'll show you to your casita and make sure everything is to your liking."

"I think everything is going to be to my liking," Mackenzie said with a laugh.

Three minutes later, she and Giovanni exited the golf cart that had made short work of the twisting stone paths that connected everything on the island. He led her to the door.

The casita consisted of a large bedroom that faced the sea and looked out on a partially covered, dimly illuminated deck that was at least as large, with a dining table, a sumptuous-looking round-cushioned lounge chair that could fit two, a pair of single loungers, a wet bar and kitchenette, a modest-sized plunge pool, and, as promised, two wooden steps down to the sand. Nestled behind the bedroom was a spa-quality bathroom with a soaking tub, granite vanity, indoor and outdoor showers, and enough space to hold a yoga class.

"I'm sure you're ready to crawl into bed after your long

voyage," Giovanni said from his spot near the door, where he'd waited while she gave each space a once-over.

"More than," she admitted, nearly drooling at the thought of crawling into the luxurious, heavenly king-sized bed.

"I'll wish you a wonderful night's sleep. Please dial the front desk if we can get you anything at all."

She offered her hand, but instead of a businesslike shake, he raised it and pressed his lips to it briefly. He released her before she could tug away, and when she looked at him questioningly, he merely winked and let himself out, leaving little doubt that he was attracted to her.

After locking the door, she wandered out onto the deck and took a long, slow inhalation of humid, salty air. So far, Giovanni had been subtle, but if he became more forward, she would have to be frank with him. Not the most comfortable situation in light of their plans to nurture a business relationship, but she would handle it.

After a handful of breaths, it was easier to shift her thoughts from the resort owner to a more comfortable subject—business. That was the reason for the trip, after all.

What she'd seen of the resort so far was spectacular, the luxury unparalleled and the location idyllic. Tomorrow, she would take pictures for Ellie and Thomas, because she suspected this was exactly what they were looking for. Cora had briefed her on one of her clients who might be interested in Bellamore as well, and based on the client's wish list that Cora had shared, this resort could be perfect.

And maybe Sierra and Cole, Mackenzie thought, but that immediately brought Drake to mind, and she was back to feeling uneasy. Because instead of focusing on her business meeting with him a few days ago, her mind insisted on replaying the sex with him—the good parts, before Ezra had ruined it. The good parts had been off-the-charts amazing and apparently impossible to forget, even thousands of miles away.

"You're an idiot," she said out loud to herself as the breeze rustled her hair. "You're on a dream vacation to a dream part of the world, and Drake North is anything but your dream man."

Except maybe in bed, she silently acknowledged, then shook her head at herself. "He's as unsettled as a guy can be."

Turning from the expanse of sand and open water that dimly sparkled from the moon above, she promised herself to put Drake out of her mind and focus on two things only for the next five days—building her business and soaking up every ounce of pampering and extravagance that was Bellamore.

CHAPTER EIGHTEEN

*M*ackenzie didn't see how her morning could get any better.

She'd taken the advice of Levani, her brilliant massage therapist, changed into her emerald-green bikini after the massage, and returned to the main pool deck to enjoy her midmorning breakfast—a fresh fruit medley of melon, pineapple, and bananas with whipped cream on top and a pitcher of refreshing, rejuvenating cucumber water.

Though she had every intention of getting some work done today, she hadn't yet been able to pull herself from the relaxed stupor caused by the massage and the warm rays of the sun.

When the heat became too much, she immersed herself into the picture-perfect swimming pool. There were actually two resort pools in one—an irregular-shaped lagoon-like one and a long, narrow rectangular one for laps, which lined one side of the lagoon pool, overlooking it and spilling water down into it. Cushioned teak loungers were scattered around the area, along with round tables with thatched umbrellas and chairs.

A man and a woman had been in the pool when she first arrived, but they'd disappeared in a hurry, obviously honeymooners. Otherwise Mackenzie had the area mostly to herself, with an employee or guest walking through periodically.

She pushed into a lazy back float and gazed up at the cloudless, perfectly sky-blue sky. Keeping her mind on low speed, she allowed herself to start a mental list of work goals for the day—taking and emailing photos to Ellie and Cora, researching accommodations and tourist sites in Eastern Europe and South America for Tucker Steele and Jackson Lowell, respectively, and corresponding with a handful of resorts on behalf of Dorian Bradley.

The longer the glorious sun beat down on her face, the more she realized she probably should either hit the shade or apply some sunscreen. She wanted to get some color on her skin, but lobster red had never been her hue. Eventually she rolled to her front and dove underwater, then swam slowly toward the steps at the end of the pool. When she surfaced, she tilted her head back to get her hair out of her face and wiped both hands over her eyes. She rose to her full height in the waist-deep water and strolled the rest of the way to the stairs.

As she took the last step out, with water washing down her body, she spotted Giovanni off in the distance, exiting the reception hut. He waved as his gaze roved over her, and even from here, she could see appreciation in his eyes as he smiled widely. She merely nodded in acknowledgment and hurried toward her lounger to retrieve her towel, relieved she'd worn her modest, plain bikini instead of the black crisscross string one that showed even more skin.

Just before she reached her chair, the sound of her name behind her had her halting abruptly. The familiar voice resonated deep within her body even before her brain could make the connection, and she whipped around in surprise.

"Hi," Drake said, standing there all nonchalant, as if they were running into each other at a gas station in East Nashville, not on the other side of the damn world.

"H-hi," she managed, her mouth seeming to be stuck open in shock.

Before she could attempt to make sense of the fact that he was standing there at an exclusive beach resort in Jiva, her brain cells registered how delectable he looked. He was dressed for comfort in gray athletic pants and a shoe-logo T-shirt that couldn't hide his gym-honed pecs. His hair was slightly mussed, and there was a little more scruff on his chin than usual. His eyes were locked on her, burning over her skin, making her wish she'd chosen the black string bikini.

Snapping out of her stunned admiration, she said, "What are you *doing* here?"

Drake's lips eased into a slow, gorgeous grin as he closed the distance between them. "What a coincidence," he drawled.

It clicked that he was obviously there to check up on her or follow her or do something relating to her. Tempt her, maybe.

Crap, he was so damn tempting.

"You followed me?" she said, stunned, determined not to betray any eagerness at his appearance. "I... What... It takes a day and a half to get here."

"I wanted to check out Jiva for Cole and Sierra," he said, not putting much effort at all into making her believe his line of BS.

"Liar."

"What? This looks perfect for them." He swept a hand in a gesture encompassing the whole resort, and Mackenzie strove to summon some annoyance at his ridiculous claim.

"It is, and that's why you hired me. So I could research their options, either online or in person. This is *my* job. So again, why are you here?"

He stared into her eyes for a good long time, as if deciding on his answer. "I don't trust the smarmy guy."

"What?"

"Adonis."

"You mean Giovanni?" Her chin dipped down as she let that sink in. "You can't be serious." She suspected, from his expression, that he might be though, and she processed the implications of that. Did he think she couldn't handle herself? What if she wanted to get to know Giovanni better? She didn't, of course, but what if she did? Was Drake back to older-brother mode or was he...jealous? "You can't... That's not... You know that's crazy, right?" she sputtered.

"Pretty Mackenzie, is everything okay?" Giovanni spoke from behind and to the right of her. His overprotective tone was all it took for inspiration to strike.

She threw her arms around Drake in a tight, welcoming hug. In his ear, she whispered, "Play along with me, please?"

She didn't know if it was agreement or not, but Drake pulled her into him and made the embrace believable. At least it wasn't a stretch for Mackenzie as she breathed in the scent of him and felt the roughness of his jaw at her temple and savored the familiarity, the safety, the pure irresistible maleness of him. Then she felt Drake's palm slide over her upper thigh to rest possessively on her not-quite-covered butt, and it was as if her turned-on switch had been flipped from warming up to full power.

When Giovanni made a sound in his throat behind them, she was jerked back to the ruse.

"Drake," she said, her voice sounding a little shaky to her, so she cleared her throat. "This is Giovanni Rossi. He's the owner of Bellamore. Giovanni, this is Drake North." Looking into Drake's eyes, she added, "A close friend of mine."

It took Giovanni several seconds to reply. "You seemed a little upset when I approached."

With a laugh, Mackenzie said, "Shocked is a better word. He came all the way from Tennessee to see me. In the US. It's… crazy." She looked back at Drake as she said the last, piercing him with her gaze, trying to discern his true reasons for traveling so far, because the idea that he'd traveled for more than a day because of Giovanni was preposterous.

He held the eye contact, and it was all she could do not to get lost in it.

"Sometimes a little crazy is called for," Drake said to her. It didn't escape her notice that he had yet to directly acknowledge Giovanni. "Want to help me find my room?" he asked her.

"Casita," Giovanni corrected.

"I'd love to," Mackenzie said, dying to grill him in private. Drake pulled her to his side possessively, as if he was just so happy to see her, or maybe just so happy to flaunt it in Giovanni's face.

For the first time, she noticed a duffel and a messenger bag on the chaise behind Drake and asked, "Have you checked in?"

He retrieved his key card from his front pants pocket and

held it up. "I'm in the Reefside Retreat, which I gather is that way." He pointed.

"It is," Giovanni said, slipping back into his gracious host persona. "Right next to Sea Sanctuary, as a matter of fact."

"Ah," Mackenzie said, "I know exactly where it is then. Thank you, Giovanni. We'll see you later."

He gave her a single nod, his expression blank except for a professional smile. "Very well. Enjoy your morning."

She thought to pick up her white mesh cover-up but didn't take the time to put it on. She interlocked her elbow with Drake's, and they headed down the stone path toward his casita. Once the walkway took them past the lounge, around a curve, and out of sight, Mackenzie pulled away and put several inches between them, fighting internally to get her equilibrium and her right mind back.

CHAPTER NINETEEN

Drake hadn't seen any of that coming at all.

He hadn't known what kind of reception Mackenzie would give him, but he definitely hadn't anticipated her throwing herself into his arms. He'd also not expected to find her, first thing, looking like five feet and ten inches of sin personified in a simple, plain bikini that said she wasn't even trying to make men lose their minds over her.

He sure as shit was not complaining about either.

Even if she had pulled away as soon as they were out of the sleaze-ball resort guy's sight.

After a five-minute walk, he spotted a sign that said Reefside Retreat with an arrow that pointed down a short, narrow path. Both sides of it were lined by lush, jungle-like bushes with bright blooms in oranges and pinks and yellows and reds.

He led her to the door and opened it with his key card, then allowed her to enter first. With a cursory, distracted glance around the room, he registered that the accommodations were top-notch as he tossed his bags on the king-sized bed that was front and center, but he was more focused on the woman before him. The woman who silently padded over in her bare feet to one of the glass sliders that opened onto a deck, powder-fine white sand, and a killer view of the calm, crystal-blue sea.

She stood on this side of the glass with her back to him, her cover-up in one hand, looking out, which gave him a moment to take in the gorgeous picture she made in her bikini. Her legs were long and slender, her ass two delectable globes that made his palms itch with the desire to touch them, knead them. The sample feel by the pool had had him going hard in an instant, and his erection throbbed painfully again now. Her top was held up by two ties. He wanted to untie them both, watch the material fall to the tile floor, and then stand there in total enthrallment as she slowly turned to face him, offering her perfect breasts to him.

"Don't think for a second I bought your excuses for being here," she said, crashing his fantasy to an end.

"They're true," he said, knowing full well they weren't the only reason. He needed to tell her the main reason now, but he was chartering yet more new-to-him territory, and it took some thought as to how to say it.

Mackenzie whipped around. He tried not to let her chest catch his attention as it bounced slightly with the movement. "Are you here to piss Ezra off? Is this an amusing way for you to pass your time?"

He flinched inwardly. "Is that really what you think of me?" He was a lot of things, but spiteful, vengeful, and cruel weren't traits he generally embodied.

"I don't know what to think," she said, tossing the cover-up to the chair in the corner and crossing her arms over her chest.

"I'm not here to piss Ezra off. He doesn't know I'm here. I haven't talked to him since…that night." He'd stopped giving a shit what Ezra thought. "There's nothing funny about me being here." Swallowing, he searched for courage. "I'm here because I wanted to see you."

She narrowed her eyes the slightest bit, almost indiscernibly, but he caught it because he was scrutinizing her for any signs of anything.

"Really," he said, because he could tell she couldn't decide whether to believe him. Drake closed some of the space between them and acknowledged, "When I first got the idea, I tried to tell myself it was because I didn't trust Mr. Smooth out there." He gestured in the general direction of Adonis.

"I can take—"

"I know you can take care of yourself," he preempted. "I was...jealous."

There. He'd said it.

Mackenzie's features softened by several degrees and she tilted her head. "There's nothing to be jealous about between me and Giovanni."

"I've never felt jealousy about a woman before," he said, "but that jealousy made jumping on the plane in Nashville seem like a perfectly justified thing to do."

"Maybe a little extreme," she said, her tone lighter, not hiding her amusement.

"Maybe. When I boarded in San Francisco, though, I had to stop lying to myself. I had to admit that the driving reason for jetting around the globe after you is because I want to spend time with you, Mackenzie."

As she stared up into his eyes, she inhaled audibly, then pressed her lips together, as if preparing to say something. Instead, she let out the breath and turned away to face the glass door again. "The problem with that is that you didn't take into consideration for one second what I might want."

He stared at the back of her head, her copper-brown hair still wet and hanging down messily to the tops of her feminine shoulders. "That might be a fair assessment," he said. He took two long strides so that he stood next to her, leaned his upper body against the window, facing her profile. "And if so, I apologize. My decision was impulsive, but even so, I stand behind it now. I'm telling you I want to spend time with you. And now I'm asking you if that's what you want too."

Her long-lashed eyes remained fixed on the view straight in front of her, so Drake waited her out, staring, sweating, dreading what her answer would be the longer she remained quiet.

"It's not that easy, Drake."

"It could be that easy." He couldn't resist touching her and trailed his finger from her shoulder down the silky skin of her upper arm.

Instead of softening, she stiffened, straightened, and a

wrinkle popped up between her brows. "I made a promise to myself when I decided to move to Nashville. I promised myself no drama, no entanglements, no anything right now except building up the new office of To the Stars and finding my forever home. No roommates, no boyfriends, no extra chaos."

"And I'm chaos?" He flashed her one of his most charming grins.

"That's a fair assessment," she mimicked, her lips hinting at a smile.

"Did somebody hurt you recently?"

"Nothing like that. It's…" She shook her head. "It wouldn't make sense to you."

"Now you're calling me stupid?" he said, grinning. "I'm more than just a dumb jock."

Finally, she met his gaze, measuring him with those deep brown eyes, and he realized in that second how badly he wanted to measure up, be whatever she needed him to be.

Her hesitation stretched out and her eyes shifted back to the water view. Just when he'd decided she was going to blow him off, she spoke. "Well, first there was my mom and all the times she moved us. I think that had more of an effect on me than I ever realized."

"I can understand how that could happen."

It had always seemed like that's what the Shaw family did—they moved. Ezra hadn't talked about it much. Only later, once he and Ezra had finished college, did he realize how much that way of life had affected Ezra. Mackenzie's brother seemed to thrive on bouncing from hotel room to hotel room, rarely spending more than a couple of nights in any one city, including his home base of Houston.

"Didn't she take a job in the Bahamas before you were done with high school?" He remembered Ezra talking about it, trying to figure out how to help his sister. There'd even been a brief discussion about Ezra taking a break from his senior year in college to move back to Nashville with Mackenzie so she could finish her last year of high school. She'd ended up living with a friend's family.

"Yep. That one was a man-and-job combo she couldn't pass up, and I like to think it was where she finally found some contentment. I know a lot of kids have it a lot worse than I did. I had a decent place to live and a loving family. I didn't realize until later how much moving all the time affected me. Not until I was on my own in LA."

"Where you moved a bunch more times." She'd mentioned it the night she'd moved back. "But that couldn't be because of your mom anymore."

She held up her hand, counting on her fingers. "There was freshman year, moving into the dorm. Summer after freshman year, subleasing an apartment. Sophomore year, my same roommate and I got a campus apartment together, which we shared until I dropped out junior year and had to move because I was no longer a student." She held up three fingers, added a fourth. "The roommate I found when I quit school turned out to be crazy, so after ten months with her, I moved in with a guy—"

"What guy?" Drake couldn't help asking. She'd lived with a guy? "Was he a friend or…?"

"A mistake. I dated the brother of one of my clients. I stupidly thought I was in love and I unstupidly needed to get the hell away from the crazy roommate."

"He didn't work out, huh?"

"He couldn't make it six months without cheating. Even though he was the one who asked me to move in."

Drake narrowed his eyes and felt a strong urge to make a stopover in LA on the way back to pound the guy's face in for hurting Mackenzie.

"After that, more roommates, more apartments. I've been saving to buy a house since I quit school. I have a decent bit saved up. Just not enough for LA real estate. I can afford a house in Nashville, and once I find it, that will be the last time I move."

"Ever?"

"For a long time, at least. I'm dying to have my own place. Buying a house may sound not that big of a deal to someone like you who could buy six houses if you wanted to, but I crave stability the way a homeless person craves a cheeseburger."

"Fair enough. You've moved a dozen and a half times in twenty-some years."

"I need *my* place," she said. "I need steady and predictable and certain, and people are none of those and—no offense—but especially you. And this all sounds incredibly stupid because all you want to do is sleep with me."

He laughed quietly, even though her words made him uncomfortable, because though he wasn't sure what, exactly, he wanted, he was pretty sure it wasn't *just* sex, and that had been fucking with his mind since San Francisco. "You make it sound so crass."

She exhaled, and it was noticeably shaky. "I'm attracted to you, Drake. I think that's obvious. I thought, by seducing you that night, I would give in for one evening and move on, but here we both are on the island of Jiva all the way around the world two weeks later. The attraction is crazy hot between us, but you're the opposite of stable and settled and peaceful. You're the last guy I should have in my life *if* I were going to break my own rules and have a guy in my life."

As much as he wanted to focus on the *crazy hot attraction* part of her diatribe, he was more caught up on the last bit. He couldn't argue with a word of it.

He wasn't stable, life-wise. He'd never wanted to settle down. He didn't lead a peaceful, predictable life. He wasn't the man Mackenzie needed, not long-term.

But that didn't negate the fact that he wanted more time with her. He wasn't ready to let her go, didn't want to move on just yet. "I get it. But we're on this big adventure in paradise. We want each other. We like spending time together. So why not make this trip a time-out from reality and indulge ourselves, knowing full well there's an end date when we go back to the real world?"

Mackenzie crossed her arms and slowly rubbed her hands up and down her upper arms, gazing outside but, he suspected, lost in thought and not seeing what was in front of her. She was considering his proposition, thank God.

He needed her to say yes. He wanted to snorkel and deep-sea

fish and sunset watch with her, absolutely, but even more, he needed to touch every inch of that sun-kissed, baby-soft skin and run his tongue over her and in her to see if she tasted like the coconut tropical scent she gave off today and sink his body into her until his eyes crossed and he didn't remember what planet they were on. If she said no now…

"Just while we're here?" she asked in a lower, huskier voice.

"Just the next four days. As soon as we step off the plane at BNA, we go back to just friends. You go back to your promise to yourself and focusing on house and job, and I go back to my happy, commitment-free existence."

She turned from the view to face him fully, met his gaze head on, still looking thoughtful and so damn pretty. "This is supposed to be a working vacation for me."

"You can work." *In between orgasms.*

He'd never been one to not use every tool he had to get what he wanted, and now, at what felt like a crucial moment, would be a foolish time to start. He ran a finger up her arm, from her elbow to her shoulder, then over her sexy collarbone. Then lower. He traced the outer edge of her bikini top over the curve of her breast, then he dipped his thumb below the green fabric, lightly massaging in little circles, veering toward her nipple but never quite touching it, just enough to tease her.

Her eyes dilated and she stuttered out a shallow exhale. "Okay. Until Nashville." Her lids fluttered shut momentarily as she took hold of the biceps of his other arm. When he inched his thumb farther and finally rubbed it over the hard, distended tip of her nipple, she sucked in her breath.

With his other hand, he reached around to her back and untied her top, first the bottom tie, then the one at her nape. The green fabric fell to the floor, and the sight of his thumb on her silky pink nipple… Yeah. Thirty-four hours of travel was worth it for this.

He kissed and swirled his tongue over the exact spot his thumb had been as he drew the bottoms of her swimsuit down to her ankles and she stepped out of them. He reached around her and palmed both cheeks of her ass, then lifted her and carried her to the bed.

After lowering her to the middle of the thick mattress, he went to his messenger bag, dug deep for the condoms he'd packed, set them on the nightstand, and shucked all of his clothes off, his cock throbbing painfully. He climbed onto the bed and sat up, his back against the dozen pillows in front of the headboard, and lifted Mackenzie on top of him. With a lust-dazed look in her eyes and the heat of her center rubbing against him, she leaned in to kiss him deeply, sensually, thoroughly, and his eyes rolled back into his head. He pulled her to him, their hands all over each other, teasing and exploring and enflaming.

This woman was perfect. Perfect for him. Perfect for right now.

He couldn't allow himself to think beyond that as he matched up their bodies and pulled her down onto him and lost himself in an ocean of divine sensation.

CHAPTER TWENTY

Mackenzie had succumbed to the magic of the tropical island hours ago, maybe the second she entered Drake's casita, and she refused to worry about it.

This, with Drake, was temporary, and that fact made it just about perfect.

She was in Drake's arms, fully clothed now, in a casual black dress. The dance floor was an area on the patio cleared of tables and chairs, and they were the only ones on it right now. The Fijian musicians—two guitarists and one playing a ukulele—on the tiny stage of the outdoor lounge area were winding down a love song they'd played at Drake's request. Their style was island music all the way, with a bit of a reggae beat to it—upbeat, happy songs that would forever take her back to tonight in her mind.

"Those guys are incredible," she said, smiling up at him, "but I'm not sure what makes this a love song compared to the others. It's not like a sappy American ballad."

"It's the lyrics," Drake said matter-of-factly, which made her laugh because the words were in a different language, and though he'd gotten Felise, their server, to teach him *please* and *thank you* in Fijian, she was sure he didn't understand any of the song. He laughed with her, and then he lowered his lips and kissed her as the music ended, lingering over her mouth for just long enough to spike her pulse with the unspoken message that this was a prelude to more, later, when they were alone.

Someone started clapping, drawing their attention to the stage. The ukulele player grinned widely and aimed the applause at her and Drake. Hamming it up, Drake bowed, then gestured with a flourish to Mackenzie, who, playing along, attempted an awkward curtsy. They all laughed, Mackenzie included, and Drake nodded his appreciation to the musicians as he wove his fingers with hers and led her back to their table.

There were several other couples scattered around the lounge deck, most at tables and one of them heading out to the "dance floor." The atmosphere was laid-back yet romantic. How could it not be with the sound of the distant surf audible in between songs and the scent of the sea and tropical flowers hanging in the warm night air? There was a straw-roofed cabana along one side that served as the bar, with a bartender working the counter and Felise, the one and only server, handling table service.

Early that afternoon, Mackenzie and Drake had eventually passed out into a long, deep jet-lag nap after a couple of rounds of life-changing sex. She'd woken to an island breeze blowing over Drake's bed and an atmospheric twilight temporarily disorienting her until she remembered where and when—and with whom—she was.

The resort offered personal chef services and a choice of eating in the room, out here at the lounge tables, or anywhere else on the private island. They'd chosen the lounge, in part so Mackenzie could experience as much as possible for professional reasons. All thoughts of her job and To the Stars slipped away when she'd tasted the exquisite citrus coconut cream fish baked in banana leaves and the greens and the coconut bread on the side. Her mai tai had a mini yellow umbrella sticking out of it and no shortage of rum. All that, plus sitting across from Drake, with him as the main scenery, made for an unforgettable evening.

When they returned to their little table for two now, Felise had replaced their beverages with full ones, as they'd requested. They sat and each took a drink to quench their thirst after dancing to a half-dozen songs. As Mackenzie set her glass back down on the table, she spotted Giovanni heading their way and managed to bobble her glass enough to spill a little. She soaked up the spilled cocktail with her napkin.

"Good evening, Drake and Mackenzie," Giovanni said warmly as Drake reached to her side of the table and interlaced their fingers possessively.

"Hi, Giovanni," she said. "Want to pull up a seat?"

Drake's fingers stiffened a bit in hers, and she saw annoyance when she glanced at his face. She gave him a quick shake of her head and squeezed his hand.

"Only for a minute," Giovanni said.

When he went to the next table to grab an extra chair, Mackenzie whispered to Drake, "Be nice. I want to do business with him."

His eyes sparkled with a moment of mischief, and then he squeezed her hand, let go, and sat back in his chair, as if acquiescing.

"Drake, you're a lucky man," Giovanni continued, "and I'm pleased to meet you. Mackenzie, I'm sorry to put you in the position I did."

"What position is that?" Drake asked.

"Sometimes I may seem"—he searched for a word—"dense, but I observe many people, and I believe your embrace this morning, upon Drake's arrival, was for my benefit, to show me that you were not receptive to my...personal interest. Am I right?"

"Drake and I have known each other since we were kids," Mackenzie said. "I didn't expect him to show up here. The hug was real."

"Oh, I don't doubt your feelings for each other," Giovanni said, his mouth sliding into a grin. "The affection between you is undeniable. But I'm taking the tiniest bit of credit for pushing the two of you together because I believe your relationship has deepened since this morning."

"Giovanni—"

"I am wise about some things," he said knowingly, and Mackenzie figured it wasn't worth arguing about. "And I am hoping for the best for the two of you." He nodded slowly at Drake.

Drake eyed him, and Mackenzie waited to see how he would respond. "Thank you, Giovanni." His gaze shifted to Mackenzie, and the look in his eyes made her feel melty inside, nearly as much as his next words. "Mackenzie is a special woman. I can't fault you for noticing that."

"Keep Bellamore in mind for the honeymoon, yes?" Giovanni said with an even wider grin, and they all laughed, even if Mackenzie was a bit thrown by the idea. "If not Bellamore, then my family has numerous island resorts I can connect you with."

"Really?" Mackenzie said, sitting up straighter as she snapped into business mode. "Why haven't you told me of these before, Giovanni? Are you holding out on me?" She kept her tone light.

Giovanni leaned his forearms on the table and steepled his fingers, his gaze falling to his hands. "I suppose I will let you in on the secret. I have six brothers and I am the youngest."

"Your mother had seven boys?" Mackenzie said with a combination of awe and horror. "Any sisters?"

"No. My parents were blessed only with boys," Giovanni said with a little grin. "We grew up on Malta, in the Rossi Resort—"

"The Rossi?" Mackenzie said. "You're one of those Rossis?"

With a humble laugh, Giovanni said, "My parents are those Rossis, and I suppose we seven were too, as we lived and worked there. Have you stayed with my family before?"

"Not personally, but I've had clients stay there," she said. "It's a beautiful place, from what I've seen, and it has an impeccable reputation."

"Thank you. My parents have been very successful there. They have groomed each of my brothers and me to run our own resorts and have financed each property. But they did not want us to infringe on their Mediterranean Sea territory," he said with a laugh, "and so we're all here, in this part of the world."

"So you're all in competition," Drake said.

"For everything, not only customers. I will admit I wanted to keep a beautiful girl like Mackenzie away from them. They are much too old for you anyway," he said to her.

Mackenzie laughed. "Giovanni, you're going to hook me up with information on their properties, right?"

"Yes. I have conceded on a personal level, and I will also open up the field for business, even though the competition between my brothers and me is cutthroat. You are welcome," he said with humor.

"Thank you. Keep in mind I can send you all lots of business. No need to feel competitive about my company." Mackenzie couldn't wait to see which places were owned by his family. It could be six other strong business relationships for her. Seven if she included his parents. But she was getting ahead of herself.

"I will put together a list with all their contact information and websites," Giovanni said. He pushed his chair back and stood. "In the meantime, I have outstayed my welcome at your table. I'm going to check in with the other guests before I retire to my residence for the evening. I look forward to doing lots of business together, and I hope we are friends." He offered a hand to Drake.

Drake stood, all hints of jealousy now gone, and shook Giovanni's hand. "Friends," he said. "And I hope you and Mackenzie have a business relationship that benefits both of you."

They all said good evening, and the resort owner made his way to another couple.

"Thanks for being friendly," Mackenzie said once Drake sat back down and it was just the two of them.

Drake shrugged. "He's not so bad, as long as he knows where we all stand."

"It must be lonely to be him." She plucked the pink umbrella out of her drink and spun it between her thumb and fingers. "Most of the people who stay here are probably couples. He seems to work every day, so he doesn't have a lot of ways to meet women."

"But look at this place. The dude literally lives in paradise. I don't feel too sorry for him."

With a laugh, Mackenzie said, "Ha. It might be beautiful here, but you couldn't live without your twenty thousand women, paradise or not."

"Twenty thousand. I'm flattered." He took a drink of his bottled beer and set it back down. "That many women sounds like a lot of work," he said with a wink.

"Speaking of work…" Mackenzie glanced at the time on her phone, which she'd left on the table under her clutch. "This is a working vacation for me. I'd planned to work this afternoon instead of sleeping like the dead. I need to get a couple of things done yet tonight."

Drake frowned. "What is this working vacation you speak of?"

"Reality for those of us who don't have a trust fund or whatever it is you North brothers have."

"No trust funds here," he said, smiling, and that was a technicality because she knew he had millions. "I read up on things to do in this part of the world during my flight. Cave exploring, waterfall hikes, seaplane and helicopter tours, shark diving, kayaking, snorkeling… Are we going to get to do any of that together?"

"Shark diving is an easy no," she said.

"I'd keep you safe," he said, the low, intimate timbre of his voice resonating deep inside of her, taking her thoughts from business dedication to that big, comfortable bed in the center of his room. Or hers. She wasn't picky.

A faint alert sounded in her brain. She could have some fun, spend some time with Drake, but what she couldn't afford to do was blow off work altogether.

"I can split my time between work and play," she said, in a way compromising with herself. "But still no shark diving."

"Phobia?"

"Ez went through a *Jaws* phase when I was maybe four or five years old. Still traumatized."

"How about an hour of work tonight, and while you do that, I'll see what we could do tomorrow," Drake suggested.

"Deal." She took a sip of her sweet, rum-heavy drink. "So I've been thinking about how best to handle Cole and Sierra's honey-moon. Their engagement party is coming up, right?"

"In May sometime, I think."

"So why don't I put together three detailed options for them and you guys can present the choice to them at their party. They'll still have plenty of time to choose one. That way, they have some control but not the burden of planning."

"I like that. And I definitely think this place should be one of the three," Drake said. "They would love it."

"I agree. And I have ideas for the other two whenever you're ready."

"Let's wait till we're back home. My brothers will want to be in on that decision."

"Fair enough. Speaking of your brothers, what ever happened with the home fitness idea for North Brothers? Are you still helping Mason with that?"

Drake leaned his elbows on the table and groaned. "I am, sort of. He's trying to get me to come on board full-time."

"That would be a perfect fit."

His face didn't say *perfect fit*.

"I thought you were excited about the possibility of North Brothers doing this."

"Oh, I am," he said. "North Brothers should absolutely dive into it. They'd be stupid not to."

They. Not *we*, she noticed.

"You love your family's company, right?"

"I do." His voice was flat when he said it.

She watched him, but Drake diverted his attention to the dance floor, where another couple danced to another upbeat island song.

"It seems like that would be a really good opportunity for you," she tried.

He pegged her with piercing eye contact then. "I can be supportive of you doing some work while we're here, but for me personally, there will be no working on this vacation. Let's talk about something else. Anything else. Please."

"Okay," she said without flinching, because she got it. All too well.

That right there illuminated the difference between them and highlighted the precise reason that she couldn't have him in her life once they got back to the States. They were in different places in their lives. It remained to be seen whether Drake would ever be able to take responsibility and settle down. And that was the exact reminder she needed that, for them, temporary was the only way to do it.

She would enjoy every second of right-now Drake for the next three days, and then, as hard as it would be, she would move on. Just like she'd promised herself.

No regrets and no wavering.

CHAPTER TWENTY-ONE

$\mathcal{M}$ ackenzie suspected, the second her phone rang with Ezra's ringtone the next evening—Tuesday —she'd made a mistake.

"Crap."

She and Drake had been back in her casita for ten minutes at most after an incredible afternoon on a neighboring island, where they'd gone swimming in a picturesque crater after a scenic horseback ride to get there. Afterward, they'd had dinner at a beachside shack, for lack of a better word, where the seafood had been simply prepared and some of the best food she'd ever tasted.

That was also where she'd uploaded a dozen photos from the day to Instagram, including a selfie of her and Drake overlooking the crater pool.

"You going to answer that?" Drake asked from the deck, where he was peering out at the sea, waiting for her to change her clothes so they could head out to the lounge for a drink and maybe some dancing if the band started up.

She headed to the chair, where she'd flung her purse and phone when they came in the door, her instincts telling her she'd be much better off not answering, but then Ez would worry.

"Hi, Ez," she said into the phone after she pulled her casual short dress over her head and let it fall into place.

"What the hell is going on, Mackenzie?" her beloved brother bellowed into the phone, confirming her suspicion. She'd mistakenly thought he checked into social media close to never, and that's what had given her the courage to post the pic of her and Drake. She'd buried it within a group of photos, just to be safe.

"Well, I'm just getting ready to go to the lounge for a cocktail," she said, playing dumb.

"What is *he* doing there?" Ez said, his volume lower, his anger more intense.

Intense and unfounded and irritating her more by the second.

"He's vacationing, as one does in the South Pacific."

"Kenz, don't play stupid with me."

"I thought we already argued about this, Ezra. It wasn't your business then, and it's not your business now."

"It is if you lied to me."

"I didn't lie. We're still just having fun. Nothing for you to worry about."

"You said it was a one-time thing," Ezra said.

Drake had come inside, obviously hearing everything on her end through the open door. "Let me talk to him," Drake said, holding his hand out.

Maybe it was a stupid move, but she handed her phone over to him, because frankly, she didn't have more to say to her brother on the topic, nothing new anyway, and he'd obviously not listened to *it's none of your business* or *I can make my own decisions* the last time they'd had this argument.

"If you're pissed, take it out on me, not your sister," Drake said into the phone, and though Mackenzie didn't catch the exact words, she couldn't help but hear Ezra's roar over the line. "She didn't know I was coming. I showed up as a surprise, not that I need to explain myself to you."

Ezra ranted some more, and Mackenzie squeezed her eyes shut as she wandered out onto the deck. She could still hear the argument, but she tried to block it out.

She hated that those two were at each other's throats. It killed her that it was because of her. If they were girls having this disagreement, they'd fight it out and talk it out and then eventually make peace, but with these two hardheaded testosterone-laden males, she wasn't sure if they'd ever work it out. Two decades of friendship could be out the door like yesterday's trash, all because of Ezra's misplaced concern, otherwise known as butting in. And yet she couldn't fault him for wanting to "protect" her, even if she didn't need to be protected from Drake.

Well, in theory.

But Ezra couldn't pull off the kind of protection her heart might need after these few stolen days with Drake. Mackenzie had brought it on herself and she'd pull herself out of it when the time came. That just wasn't yet.

Drake came back out on the deck and handed her the phone, which had gone dark.

"The fucker hung up on me," he said.

"I'm sorry," she said quietly.

"What? You have nothing to be sorry about."

"I shouldn't have posted the picture of us. But Cora wanted to see one of us, and it's a really good picture and—"

"You can post whatever pictures you want," Drake said, his voice gentle and completely lacking the heat from when he'd talked to her brother. "We don't have anything to hide. We're not doing anything wrong. Come here."

He pulled her into his arms, and she burrowed into his chest, closing her eyes again as she took a deep breath.

"Don't let him ruin our time together," Drake said. "We don't have much of it as it is."

"I know." She wished she could let it slide off, but it wasn't that easy.

"Even if I flew home right now—which I'm not about to—he's still going to be pissed. So we might as well just go back to what we had planned and finish out a pretty fucking awesome day."

She nodded, knowing he was right. She didn't want him to leave. Yes, he'd had to work to convince her to spend these few days together, but once she'd made that decision, she was wholeheartedly in. She wanted every second she could get with Drake. It was just going to take a little while for her to shake off the call from Ezra. She held on to Drake for a good while, breathing in the security of him, the strength and the caring and the protection she felt in his arms.

"I'm not really in the mood to go to the lounge now," she said. The lighthearted mood they'd been in when they'd returned from their excursion had vanished. Being social and friendly and around others no longer appealed.

"Me neither," he admitted. "So how about a late-night swim instead?"

"We swam earlier."

"But we had swimsuits on then. Have you ever swum naked in the ocean?"

She glanced toward the calm sea, her body coming alive at the thought, and shook her head.

"Me neither. You up for it?"

As their bodies were still aligned, she could feel he was quite up for it. She was emotionally spent and physically tired, but she couldn't deny the lure of forgetting herself and her frustrating brother by losing herself in Drake. Their time together was ticking. She could deal with the backlash later.

She nodded with a flushed smile. "I'll get some towels."

CHAPTER TWENTY-TWO

*D*rake didn't do sitting still well—he never had. It gave a guy too much time to think, and he'd much rather *do*. But Mackenzie had been working half days, so he'd had lots of opportunities to do it, both the sitting and the thinking.

Drake was free to do what he wanted while she worked, but he'd chosen to stay on Jiva instead of going off island. It was tough to fit in travel time to and from another island and then some kind of activity before she was done working, and he didn't want to miss any free time with Mackenzie.

There was only so much you could do to entertain yourself on an island no bigger than a city block. The resort had a state-of-the-art workout center that he'd taken full advantage of, and he'd finished the two books he'd brought with him and started a third on his phone. He'd run on the beach twice a day, swum a few laps, joined a beachball volleyball game in the sand, and tracked down Giovanni to hammer out a surprise for Mackenzie. Still, he'd had plenty of time left over to sit and admire the view, and he'd endeavored to do that, appreciating the beauty of it and trying to embrace the peace of it. That's where the thinking came in, and he wasn't sure he liked some of the conclusions that were staring him in the face.

It was just after nine p.m. Wednesday, and once again, he was waiting for his brunette beauty. They'd spent the afternoon and evening on a guided six-mile hike on one of the nearby islands, complete with a picnic dinner at the base of a stunning waterfall. When they'd returned to Jiva, she'd had one business call to make that she couldn't take care of earlier due to the time zone difference, something about a Latvian castle that offered overnight stays. She'd said it would only take a few minutes, so he'd gone out to her deck and wandered down onto the sand to wait in one of the two teak lounge chairs.

It was dark and private out here, and the only sounds were the gentle surf, a breeze in the trees, and the occasional feminine laugh in the distance. His phone buzzed in his pocket with a notification of a message, and he pulled it out to see who it was.

Mason.

Shit.

Drake didn't need to read it to have a pretty good idea of what it was about, but he opened the app anyway.

What the hell are you doing, Drake? You were supposed to give me an answer on Monday. Then I found out today, from Mom, no less, that you're in the South Pacific? What is your hesitation? You're the best person for the job. You would rock the hell out of it. I'll pay you what you're worth, probably more than you're worth. All you have to do is accept.

Without responding, Drake clicked it closed and knocked his head into the wooden back of the lounger.

"Hey," Mackenzie said as she came down the steps into the sand, her voice melodic and cheerful and in contrast with the tempest that was gathering strength in his head. "That was worth the late-night call. It sounds like exactly what my client is looking for, so thanks for being patient."

Instead of taking the lounger next to him, she lowered herself to his and sat sideways on it next to his thigh, half facing him. Her smile disappeared as she got a closer look at his face. "You doing okay?"

"Let's go on a walk," he said, bolting up off the chair on the opposite side, not because he wanted away from her but because he couldn't handle sitting any longer.

"We walked all day…"

He was already halfway to the waterline, aiming for the outer reaches of the beach, where they could make a full circuit of the island. At least one.

Mackenzie caught up with him and grasped his forearm as he slowed his pace for her benefit. "What's going on, Drake?"

He glanced down at her bare feet, knowing she'd likely slipped her shoes off the second they got in the door, as she always did, regardless of where they were. "Want to put shoes on?"

"That depends. Are we doing some kind of a race or a leisurely moonlight stroll in the sand?"

"No race."

"I'm fine without shoes then."

She moved to the water side of him, where the very edge of the waves teased her feet. He was still wearing his hiking shoes and stayed just out of the water's reach.

He took her hand, thinking that if there was anything that could settle him a bit, it was her. They walked in silence for a few minutes, past his casita and the others on this side of the island. As they angled around to the next side, he felt her scrutinizing him from the side. Before she could question him again, he spoke up. "Did you get everything done that you needed to?"

"Most of it. I need to do some more research for Jackson Lowell, but I can do that tomorrow."

"What do you think about working on the plane the day after tomorrow instead?" he said. He'd booked the same flight as her so they could travel together. "I'll even help you if I can. I've set up a surprise for you tomorrow that will take most of the day. I was hoping you could afford to take our last day here off completely."

"Oh." He could practically see the gears working to change directions in her head, and he waited with bated breath to see how hard he was going to have to work to persuade her. Because he'd put a lot of effort into this idea, and he was determined to get her to agree. "I was going to finish up the Bradley proposal and then do research, but I guess I could do it all on the plane. We'll have plenty of time to kill then, huh?"

"And how often are you going to be on a private island in the South Pacific? You deserve one full day off." What he didn't want to tell her yet was that his surprise would help her with her job, even though he wouldn't consider what they'd be doing work at all.

"You're right," she said, and she reached up and pressed a quick kiss to his cheek. "Yes to the whole day off. You're sweet."

"You deserve something special. You work hard." They were halfway down the second side of the island, most of the casitas dark but not necessarily unoccupied, but the one they were passing now had the deck lights on low, and a man and a woman were in the plunge pool. Once they passed the trees between casitas, Drake said, "I admire your dedication to your job."

"Really? I was afraid you'd been privately cussing out my dedication with all the hanging around and waiting you've had to do." Her tone was light, verging on teasing, but there was a thread of concern there too.

He shook his head, unable to throw out a flippant response. "I suspect it's time for me to be more like you in that way. Past time. I'm not sure how though."

"How to work too much?" she said with a grin.

"I've heard when you love what you do, it doesn't feel like work."

She considered that for a second. "It's work, but you don't mind it." They reached the end of the row of casitas and curved left to the next side just as the island band at the lounge started up, adding an unobtrusive mellow accompaniment to the evening. "Is this about the job with North Brothers?"

He hated to get into it, didn't really want to talk about it, but he'd been pushing it aside for days now, and it wasn't going to go away. A part of him didn't want it to go away. "I must seem like a pretty big idiot to you. To everyone. The ideal position for me, handed to me on a silver platter, and what do I do? I skip out on giving my brother an answer."

"What is the position exactly?" she asked, and he noticed she didn't argue with his stupidity.

"I'd head the new home gym division, which will offer everything from designing home workout rooms to custom outfitting them to personal training. We'll eventually have a staff of personal trainers who become specialists in gym design, not so much the architecture and construction of it, but from the workout side of it. Just like what I'm doing for Ellie, essentially, but with the training element as well."

Mackenzie blew out an impressed breath. "That's exciting. It *is* ideal for you, Drake."

He silently counted the seconds until the next words came out of her mouth, knowing what they would be. It took less than three.

"So why are you so unsure?"

Boom.

It was his turn to let out a loud breath, but it wasn't one of being impressed but rather overwhelmed, confused, frustrated with himself. As they neared the end of this row of casitas, he realized he'd picked up speed at some point and was going too fast for a leisurely beach stroll. He made a point of slowing his steps, taking in the scene around him, which he'd mostly not noticed for the past ten minutes.

The pier came into view as well as the open beach, the "public" side, where the resort sometimes organized beach activities like volleyball and cookouts and bonfires. Tonight it was deserted and offered a refuge.

"Want to sit for a while?" he asked, gesturing to the dry sand.

She lowered herself to the ground, stretching her legs out in front of her, knees up so she could hug them, and Drake sat right next to her, nearly touching but not quite.

He gazed out at the endless water, the half-moon casting just enough light to make out the vast ocean as something more than a dark void. To the right, near the horizon, there was a light on a ship of some kind, and straight ahead was an island that looked uninhabited from here, just a dark blob in the night. The scene had a way of making him feel smaller, making the problem that had been plaguing him for a couple of weeks—or really, half his life if you wanted to get technical—seem less significant.

But it was still a problem.

"Drake?" Mackenzie broke into the silence. "Talk to me."

He craned his head back and registered the vastness of the sky above them, the infinite number of stars twinkling at them, and forced himself to start talking, even though he was still working things out in his mind.

"I'm turning thirty soon," he said.

"I know."

"I still act like I'm twenty."

She didn't say anything but he could almost hear another *I know* hanging in the air.

"My mantra has always been no settling down," he said when she didn't bail him out. "Complete opposite of you, right?"

"*Settling down* makes it sound like I want to get married, get a dog."

"Do you?"

"Not today," she said with a light laugh. "Someday, for sure. Do you?"

"I've always tried not to think about it."

"Because no settling down," she said. "What's so bad about settling down? Not the marriage kind, even, but what's preventing you from taking this job?"

He watched the light on the ship, trying to discern whether it was getting anywhere or just sitting still. "I don't trust feeling settled," he said after a while. "That stability kind of thing you're going for..." He shook his head. "Unlike you, I had a pretty stable childhood. Until *bam*! One day I didn't." Those words were hard to force out because, damn, did they make him feel vulnerable.

"When your dad died?" she asked quietly.

He swallowed around the lump that popped up in his throat. This was why he hated talking about this, why he avoided thinking about it. But after seeing closeup how Mackenzie lived her life, how much meaning her job had for her, how effective she was at it... She had purpose, and that was something he respected the hell out of. Purpose beyond having a good time. She was doing something with her life, and though he'd told himself for all these years he didn't want that, opportunity and age and his own cowardice were closing in around him.

"That was the big one," he said finally.

She put her hand on his leg and leaned her head on his shoulder. Drake pulled her to his side and squeezed his eyes shut. He couldn't remember ever needing another human as much as he needed to touch Mackenzie right now, to feel that she was there, with him and for him.

"It must've been awful," she said.

"We went from this mostly normal family with our Dad owning a growing company, our Mom working part-time so she was always around when we needed her, a nice house, baseball all the time, and then in a heartbeat, it was all stolen away."

She squeezed his leg and tucked her head in a little tighter against him.

"I didn't know how to handle it," he said, his voice thick with fifteen-year-old grief that was resurfacing with a vengeance.

"I don't think anyone would."

"Zane and I...we were there for each other, but he didn't know any better than I did how to handle something so big and terrible. We mostly just stuck together and stayed quiet. But I knew he was there, you know? Ez too."

Drake and Zane had had lots of other friends back then, but when their dad died, a lot of them backed off. He understood now they probably hadn't known how to handle his and Zane's loss, what to say. Ezra had been different.

Mackenzie nodded. "My brother's a good guy."

Shit, that part wasn't easy to talk about either—not since he'd broken Ez's trust.

"That wasn't the only time he stuck by me when bad shit happened," he said, his voice thick and low. He expelled another loud breath. "When we were seniors in high school, Ez, Zane, and I had everything planned out. We were all going to college together in Memphis. We had a suite together in the dorm, baseball scholarships for Zane and me, had it all lined up. We'd been talking about it for years. But a couple months before graduation, Zane informed me he'd changed his mind. Without me knowing it, he'd applied to multiple military academies and had even gone on interviews without telling me."

"Ouch," Mackenzie said. "And then just *guess what* one day?"

"Pretty much. I'd had no idea he was remotely interested in the military. He left me out of the whole process, like he didn't trust me with it. I like to think I would've been happy as hell for him if I'd had any idea. But he just…blindsided me. It felt almost like a betrayal. We've worked through stuff, but we're not as close anymore."

"I wondered. I thought maybe it was just because he's far away and has been for years."

"It's more than that," Drake said. He shook his head, unable to explain better. "Anyway, I've made a point of not getting too attached to anything since. Not jobs, not women, nothing, really. Quantity over depth. I'm not proud of it. I know it's stupid or immature or whatever you want to say, but it's my way of dealing with having the rug pulled out. If you never let the rug settle in the first place, it won't get yanked and fuck up your life or your head."

"I get it," Mackenzie said thoughtfully. "You lost your dad, and in a way, you lost your twin."

He inhaled a shaky breath and nodded, steamrolled by emotion he hadn't allowed himself to feel for ages.

"I'm sorry, Drake. That's rough."

They were quiet for a couple of minutes, with only the sound of the gentle waves on the shore breaking the silence. Then Mackenzie sat up a little straighter. "So that's why the twenty thousand women now," she said, her tone light, with a hint of smart-ass thrown in.

Drake gave a half laugh in spite of himself and shrugged.

"There's an upside of never feeling settled in your life, I guess," she said more seriously. "You're not worried about it getting yanked away. You can't lose what you never had."

"I must seem like an ass, complaining about losing something you've never felt like you had."

"Not at all. God, your dad died. Mine is barely in my life, but at least I know he's out there and I could talk to him if I needed to." The only thing Drake knew about her father was that he was a contractor for the military who worked overseas and that he only talked to his kids once or twice a year.

He caressed her shoulder, again glancing up at the sky, wondering how his life would be different if his dad had never gotten in his car that day. A pointless line of thoughts to go down, he supposed. "So now I need to commit to something. To this job. Just…stop worrying that if I go all in, something will ruin it or take it away."

"Take everything else out of the mix. Does the idea of building up this division of North Brothers appeal to you? Can you see yourself doing the work? Planning home gyms, working with vendors, overseeing trainers?"

His blood rushed with a thrill at the thought of it, in spite of his trepidation. "I can," he said.

Mackenzie straightened and pivoted on her butt in the sand to face him. "When I went to Ellie's with you, I could see it. You loved doing that. When we walked into her pool house, you lit up. And you're good at it. She's told me more than once how happy she is I hooked her up with you."

"It's what I know."

"It's more than that. It sparks you. If you ignore the fear—which is perfectly understandable, by the way—and just dive in, I have a feeling you'll be too busy to think about what could go wrong or how it could all fall apart."

"Maybe."

"And the best part is, you have the backing of a large, successful company. North Brothers Sports isn't going away any time soon, so it's almost like there's no risk."

Instantly, his brain locked up and he only felt his heart thundering, his body temperature shooting up into an inferno of panic. It took an inordinately long time for him to get a breath of air in, and his senses went blank to everything outside of him. He didn't hear the waves, didn't smell the sea air, didn't see the stars or the ship. He just…shut down. Then he felt Mackenzie take his hand, squeeze it with both of hers, dragging him out from that black void. After sucking in a deep breath, he forced out the words, "I could fail."

He lay back on the sand, as if the fear was too heavy, too much for him to stay upright. Mackenzie followed suit, stretching out on her side, propping her head up on her hand, peering at him. His eyes were closed, but he could feel her inspection.

"You could, but you won't," she said. "You're an expert in fitness equipment and workout programs. Mason will give you the tools to learn all the other aspects. He wants you to succeed as much as you want to succeed. And if, for some reason, something goes wrong, you'll be okay. You'll have this successful company and your family on your side, figuring things out with you."

Mason had said a lot of the same things last week after the board meeting. Drake did trust his CEO brother, hell, all of his brothers, to have his back. And Drake did know his stuff. He lived the subject every day, between his own fitness and his job as a trainer.

It occurred to him that he was just throwing up obstacles now, dragging his feet, being a damn pussy. Time to quit that shit. He sat up quickly, his heart racing, because he knew saying it out loud to Mackenzie was as good, as binding, as saying it to his brother. "I'm going to tell Mason yes. As soon as we get back."

Mackenzie popped up next to him.

"Just dive in," he said, noting the ship had definitely made progress and was farther to the right.

"Yessss," Mackenzie said, her smile audible.

Drake switched his gaze from the distant orange light to her beautiful face, his insides a jumble of emotions—exhilaration, fear, relief, and even a kernel of excitement. Before he could sort it all out, he felt Mackenzie's lips on his. Her soft, sweet, seductive lips…even when she wasn't trying to seduce.

What the hell was he doing wasting time with life decisions when he only had this woman for two more nights?

He pushed the job stuff and the life stuff far, far away and maneuvered Mackenzie onto his lap without losing contact with her mouth. Then he stood, with her in his arms, both of them laughing at the awkwardness and then quickly forgetting it as she threw her arms around him and kissed him again. Lips still locked with hers, Drake trudged off through the soft sand, heading for her place and another night of pure magic with the most beautiful girl in the world.

CHAPTER TWENTY-THREE

*I*n the wee hours of Thursday morning, Mackenzie awoke in the big, messed-up bed in her casita, alone, naked, and disoriented…and sore in places she hadn't known she could be sore in.

Her next cohesive thought was of Drake, and a dopey private smile crept across her lips. That man… the things he could do with his…

Wait. Where was Drake?

She forced her eyes open and registered two things. One, it was dark. Still the middle of the night. Two, Drake was…in the shower?

As she sat up, she heard the water shut off and the glass shower door open. Had he lost his mind? They'd showered together last night as soon as they'd come in from the beach, deciding to wash all the sand off instead of taking it to bed with them. It had turned into the most unforgettable shower of her life, and her body woke up at the memory. Her brain lagged behind.

Collapsing back on the mattress, she opted to wait for him to emerge and explain himself. No way was she crawling out of these high-thread-count sheets for anything. They'd stayed up so late that they shouldn't be conscious for another few hours at least.

Her eyes had drifted shut and she'd curled into the massive king-sized pillow when the bathroom door opened, letting light into the room. Drake walked out, fully dressed in athletic pants and a lightweight pullover hoodie.

"You're awake," he said, sounding fully, ridiculously alert.

"Why?" was all she could manage.

"Time to get up, sleeping beauty. We've got plans."

With her eyes closed again, she reached out for the nightstand, fumbled around, feeling for her phone. Once she laid her fingers on it, she grabbed it, pulled it close to her face, and squinted one eye at it. "Five oh nine in the morning? Did you get your time zones confused?"

He laughed, a sexy rumble in his chest that was much too far away for her liking. What was wrong with waking up gradually, with the sun shining in, and spending a leisurely morning in bed? It was their last day on the island. Shouldn't they be taking advantage to the fullest?

"I told you we have a full day of plans and that we'd start early," he said.

"There's early and then there's stupid."

Again, he laughed, apparently in a chipper, happy mood, and she briefly wondered if maybe she could send him on his chipper, happy way to do the plans himself. But then it hit her that it wasn't only their last day on the island. It was their last day together. Shoving aside the uneasiness that thought brought with it, she gathered her willpower and, in one sudden motion, threw her sheets off, popped up, and swung her legs over the side of the bed. Naturally, one foot got tangled, and the sheet came with it, so she had to work to free it.

"God, you're gorgeous, and I might be the dumbest fool alive to not just crawl back in bed with you and spend the day seeing how many different ways I can make you scream my name."

She felt an uncharacteristic heat in her cheeks, and she laughed quietly, because she had done plenty of screaming his name in the past several hours. With a burst of energy, she stood and flung her arms out to her sides, thinking to tempt him. "This could be yours. All day."

The heat in his eyes as he gazed at her naked body had every nerve ending in her girl parts tingling in anticipation and need and hope.

With a growl, Drake took three measured steps to her, peered down at her with heavy-lidded, lust-filled eyes, and seemed to consider her proposition.

"You were sent to me by the devil himself," he said with a mischievous grin, and then he wound his arms around her, palmed her butt with both of his large hands, and hoisted her up into his arms.

When she thought he would tumble onto the bed with her, he carried her into the brightly lit bathroom instead and set her on the cool granite countertop next to one of the sinks. The only reason she didn't complain was because he didn't step away. Instead, he kissed her as she locked her legs behind him. He ran his thumbs over both her nipples, sending a shock of urgency to her core.

"God, Drake," she breathed out.

With a sexy laugh, he said, "Not screaming, but we'll get there."

He kissed her lips while he continued to knead and tease her nipples, and she arched into him, aching for more. She'd learned this week that he was an incredible, unselfish lover, but his favorite thing to do was drag out her pleasure, tease her till she couldn't breathe before treating her to a cataclysmic orgasm or three. She attempted to rein herself in a degree now and revel in his thoroughness, because it seemed he was just getting started as his lips trailed slowly to her neck.

Lowering his mouth to one breast, he laved the nipple, suckled, teased, drawing everything inside of her taut and tight and needful. Mackenzie furrowed her fingers through his hair with one hand, supported herself with the other on the counter behind her, and threw her head back toward the mirror. He made her feel like a goddess as he worshipped her body with his mouth and hands. Every last cell was awake now, heedless of the way-too-early hour, buzzing with need, begging for his attention.

He rose back up so that his mouth teased her ear, giving her the best kind of shivers, and then he said, "Apologies in advance for rushing this. We've got a schedule to meet." At the same time, she felt his hands on her upper thighs, and then he gently spread her legs farther.

When his finger dipped inside of her, she arched involuntarily and gasped. Her eyes were closed, but she felt him staring at her. She opened them to confirm it, and his heated, adoring look was one she would never forget for all of her days. The corners of his lips tugged up into a smile, and then he dropped to his knees on the hard tile floor and his mouth joined his fingers at her center and her eyes rolled back in her head as she gave herself over to him and thanked the universe for his "rushing."

It turned out, when Drake was determined and on a schedule, he could make her scream his name in less than sixty seconds. It took her longer to recover and come back to herself as he made his way back up her body, peppering her with kisses and playful nibbles along the way. He veered to the side of her neck and her ear again, and when he lightly sucked the lobe between his lips, an aftershock shook her whole body and she moaned.

"You're incredible," he whispered, and she let out a weak, surprised laugh.

"I haven't been anything yet." She reached to his pants, felt the hard bulge through the fabric, and tried to pull him to her by the waistband, but he held steady and straightened.

"No time right now. We need to get you in the shower. And by *we* I mean *you*, because if I got in with you, we wouldn't come out for hours." He stepped across the bathroom, reached in the shower, and turned the water on, then came back and pressed a kiss to her lips.

"Are you sure?" She grabbed for his pants again, unable to imagine what could be so important that he was turning down her attention, thinking maybe she could tempt him.

"Later, you can have your way with me. Believe me, I'm going to ache every second until then, but we need to meet Giovanni in"—he took out his phone to check the time—"twenty-four minutes. Can you be ready by then?"

His words snapped her out of her post-orgasm haze. She

scooted down from the counter and crossed to the shower. "I guess we'll find out."

————

Drake had to hand it to her. Mackenzie had, in fact, made it in time, thanks to a six-minute shower, minimal makeup, and throwing her hair up in a sexy bun, and on top of it all, she looked stunning in her everyday-girl way that he couldn't get enough of.

They walked together onto the pier, him with a small bag over his shoulder, at fifteen minutes till six, the sky lightening but the sun not up yet.

Instead of the chauffeured resort boat they'd used to come and go all week, he led her to one of the covered slips, where Giovanni's personal pocket cruiser was docked. The resort owner came out from the cabin to the deck of the boat and greeted them warmly, as if it was high noon instead of predawn. They boarded, and it was a good thing Drake held her hand as she climbed onto the deck, because she stumbled in the process, making him hide a grin.

"Welcome aboard," Giovanni said warmly.

Drake shook the man's hand. The tension between them at Drake's arrival had disappeared as soon as Giovanni had conceded Monday night. He'd been nothing but cordial and friendly since, and he'd gone far above and beyond in helping Drake plan out today's surprise.

"This is yours?" Mackenzie asked, glancing around. The boat was small but classy and seemed to have everything a person needed for overnight trips on the ocean—a seating area up front that appeared to convert to a berth, a stovetop, sink, and mini refrigerator, a compact deck for enjoying the sun or fishing.

"Yes," Giovanni said. "You cannot live on an island without a trusty boat. This gets me around on my personal time."

"It's beautiful."

"Thank you. You'll probably want to sit here," Giovanni said, indicating the dinette area on the opposite side of the cockpit.

"The seats on the deck can get a lot of cool air at this time of day."

As Mackenzie slid into the dinette booth with Drake following her, she said, "So where are you taking us, Giovanni?"

The man glanced at Drake conspiratorially. "I'm not at liberty to say. It will be a short trip, however. You'll know very soon."

Drake situated himself up against Mackenzie and settled his arm around her shoulders, breathing in her fresh, feminine scent. Giovanni slid into the captain's seat and started up the engine. When he looked at his passengers again, as if to ensure they were ready, Drake gave him a silent thumbs-up.

"We're off," Giovanni said, and the engine got louder.

Mackenzie was quiet for a couple of minutes, her gaze bouncing around, taking in the inside of the boat as well as the sights outside of the windows. "Why can't you tell me where we're going?" she asked Drake, eliciting a grin from him. She was little-girl-like in handling a surprise, it seemed, as she'd peppered him with questions from the time she'd finished her shower until now.

"Because it's a surprise," he said before pressing a kiss to her temple.

"I'll be surprised right now."

"You'll be surprised in ten minutes. Stage one of the surprise."

"You're mean."

"You're impatient," he said with a low, lazy laugh.

"What's in the bag?" she asked, eyeing it as if it could reveal the secret.

He'd packed for both of them while she was in the shower, in addition to setting out appropriate clothing for her to dress in for this first stop. It was the one part of the day he was most worried about her reaction to, but Giovanni had sworn it would be worth the early wake-up. "Swimsuits, a couple of changes of clothes, a brush, a few other necessities."

"That tells me nothing." She crossed her arms over her chest as if pouting but leaned her head on his shoulder. He liked it when she put her head on his shoulder.

A handful of minutes later, Giovanni directed the boat into a covered slip similar to the one they'd left behind. On the end of the long pier was a wooden sign that said Welcome to Susulu.

Mackenzie sat up straight and read it out loud. "Okay, what's Susulu?"

"Susulu is a private island that houses my brother Pasqual's top-of-the-line health and fitness resort," Giovanni explained. "That's him approaching."

"Well, of course it's top-of-the-line. That goes without saying when it comes to the Rossi family, right? I think I've actually heard of this place," she said, sliding around the banquette table, standing, and then stepping to the back uncovered part of the boat for a better view. It wasn't very light out yet—sunrise was officially in about fifteen minutes, Drake knew—and unlike Jiva, Susulu had hills and cliffs and varied elevations beyond the strip of sand that wrapped around it, which shadowed the beach.

Once they'd docked and secured the boat, all three of them disembarked. Giovanni introduced Drake and Mackenzie to Pasqual, or Paq. Like Giovanni, Paq had dark hair and tanned olive skin and a lady-killer smile. It was easy to tell just looking at the guy he was a fitness buff, and Drake would bet he spent lots of time lifting based on his musculature.

"This is where I leave you," Giovanni said soon after, knowing they had an appointment to make.

"Thanks, man," Drake said, shaking his hand again, giving him a sincere look. "I appreciate the ride and everything else."

"Anytime, my friend. Have fun today." Giovanni aimed the last at Mackenzie, then walked back toward the pier to head to Jiva.

"We must hurry," Paq said, gesturing to an ATV with four seats parked nearby. "We'll get you up the hill quickly."

Drake let Mackenzie sit in front next to Paq and climbed into the back.

"Tell me about your resort," Mackenzie said, and though she didn't mention her job, Drake knew she was logging the information as much for business as her own curiosity.

"I'd be happy to," Paq said as he started up the engine. They lurched forward slightly when he hit the gas. "The island is almost seven square kilometers. The resort takes up less than a quarter of that, and the rest is wilderness. We have just about any type of fitness facility a person could want, from swimming pools to sports fields to tennis and racquetball courts and a state-of-the-art workout facility with weights and classes. We have multiple paths through the jungle for bicycles and running. You could do a different activity or sport every day for a month here."

"Wow. So active people all the way, huh?"

"You could also sit on the beach, but the majority of our clientele would rather be parasailing or kitesurfing or even kayaking. They are passionate about movement and fitness. We have three separate restaurants on the property, ranging from quick post-workout specialties like smoothies and protein bombs to a whole-foods sit-down dinner place where the food is the purest fuel for the body."

"Impressive. I'm afraid I might starve here," Mackenzie said. "I'm addicted to crap food."

"We have a restaurant with more standard fare as well. We offer numerous classes each day, from fitness in the gym to beginner lessons on all kinds of activities. There is always something new to learn for most."

"And what about the rooms for lodging? It looks like you don't have beachfront casitas like Bellamore."

"You are correct. Ninety percent of Susulu is perched high above the surf. We have a lodge with suites as well as individual clifftop cabins. You can hear the surf from every room and the views are magnificent, with sea vistas for miles."

"It sounds amazing. I'd love to see it all." She turned in her seat to look at Drake. "Are we doing a tour?"

To maintain his surprise a little longer, Drake said, "You're not working today," just as their climb ended and the ATV leveled out. Before them was a building with a steep thatched roof and walls made of native-looking slabs of wood and glass. There were thick, exotic-looking trees everywhere, and several similar-style buildings were visible scattered in the distance.

"This is our meditation and yoga pavilion," Paq told them.

"Come along." Drake checked the time and saw they had about two minutes to spare.

They walked inside to find a long, narrow room with shelves lining one wall stocked with supplies and equipment—exercise balls, mats of every color, blankets, yoga blocks and bolsters, and more.

"What are we doing?" Mackenzie said in a low voice to Drake, because there were voices on the other side of the wall, and it was definitely the type of building where a person was compelled to use a quiet voice.

"Grab a mat and a bolster and then follow me," Paq directed.

Drake led Mackenzie to the shelf and picked out a rolled-up mat for each of them.

"You got me up in the middle of the night to do yoga?" she whispered, confused, to Drake as they trailed behind Paq, who'd picked out his own equipment.

"More than just yoga," Drake told her, and he took her hand as they rounded the end of the equipment wall into a large open room that was obviously made for classes. The entire long side of the room was floor-to-ceiling windows and beyond them... Drake and Mackenzie stopped in their tracks at the same time, just taking in the view.

Giovanni had promised this view was astounding, but Drake couldn't have imagined.

From their elevated spot, they had a centralized view of where the sun was making its way up on the liquid horizon, already painting the sky in vivid oranges and yellows and pinks. There was a large rock jutting out of the water on the right side, not big enough to be considered an island, exactly, but its silhouette added drama to a setting that didn't need any help in the drama department. To the left, farther out, was an island with a hilly silhouette. The ocean was almost as smooth as glass and reflecting the sky like a mirror. Below them, more of Susulu was visible, with outlines of palm trees, a long stretch of sand, and the turquoise waters of a resort swimming pool.

"Wow," Mackenzie said, her eyes wide. "That's..."

"Yeah," Drake said. There were no suitable words.

"We're going outside," she said, her voice full of awe, as they followed the others toward the double glass panel that was open to the cool morning air.

"We're doing outdoor sunrise yoga with that as our view," Drake said. He wasn't a big fan of yoga himself—didn't deny the value of it, but given the choice, he'd prefer something higher impact and less gentle. But this… He would do yoga every damn morning if this was the venue.

The room had emptied out, and there were nine or ten people outside, situating their mats in silence, then standing on them, gazing reverently at the panoramic view, waiting for the class to start. Closest to the view was a single mat, that of the instructor, it appeared, and instead of creating multiple rows in front of her, people had situated their mats in a single line, so that no one's view was obstructed.

Drake led Mackenzie to the far side of the row, and they unrolled their mats side by side. As he found the center of his mat and faced the ocean, Mackenzie was suddenly right next to him. Her eyes sparkled with life as she peered up into his.

"This is incredible," she whispered, and even her whisper was filled with emotion. "You're incredible. Thank you." She went up on her toes and pressed a deliberate, heartfelt kiss on his lips that took the rest of his breath away. After lingering for an extra second over his mouth, she lowered to flat feet, looked into his eyes again, and sent him a smile of pure, enthusiastic joy.

As she went back to her own mat, Drake had the thought that he'd do just about anything to put that look on her face every day for the rest of her life. That scared the ever-loving hell out of him. He shoved it deep, determined to enjoy every second of their last day in the tropics.

CHAPTER TWENTY-FOUR

Falling in love with Drake would be the dumbest thing Mackenzie could do.

But oh, was he making it so hard to resist.

She would've bolted upright in bed the second the thought hit her had Drake not had his arm draped over her, sound asleep. Instead, she rolled over, sliding out from under him, and slipped out of bed. He made a muffled noise but didn't seem to wake up, and she was grateful for that. She needed some time alone to get her head straight.

They'd slept with the door open to the fresh sea breeze, and as it blew over her naked body now, there was a slight morning chill to it. With the dawn light filtering in, she rustled through her suitcase, pulled out thin pajama-type pants that went to her knees, and pulled them on. Then she spotted the lightweight hoodie Drake had worn for yoga yesterday, grabbed it, and pulled it over her head, knowing it would feel good against the cool air. She breathed in the scent of him that lingered in the fabric and glanced at the bed where he slept, tempted to go back and crawl in next to him, fully aware that this was her last chance before they left for home. Their boat ride to the airport was in less than two hours.

With her feet bare and her hair likely a wild tangle, she slid the screen door open and went out to the deck, then beyond, to the sand, registering the coolness of the fine grains under her feet.

The sun was up, but barely, and she would bet there was a heck of a show going on in the sky to the east—and on Susulu— judging by the streaks of pink and orange visible above her on this western-facing side of the island. Mackenzie made no move to investigate any of it. She had too much going through her mind.

She walked closer to the water and lowered herself to the sand where it was dry and powdery and soft. Glancing up and down the shore, she verified she was the only person in sight and relished the privacy. Her gaze locked on to the mellow waves lapping in a soothing rhythm.

She craved the soothing, because inside of her, a storm of disquiet was brewing.

Yesterday had been amazing, unforgettable, perfect.

After sunrise yoga, she'd figured they would head back to Jiva, but no. Yoga was only the beginning of a day jam-packed with adventure and sightseeing and fun.

Drake had gotten Giovanni to help him plan a whirlwind tour of the Rossi brothers' resorts, all six of them, which would have been awe-inspiring and interesting even if she wasn't in the travel industry. They'd shuttled between each island, either by boat or helicopter, toured each resort, and then done an extra activity or something else that went along with each resort's theme.

After yoga and a light breakfast at Paq's health and fitness resort, they'd visited Franco's water lovers' resort for a tour and a surf lesson. Next was Stefano's nature-focused resort, where they'd taken a helicopter ride to an active volcano.

For lunch, they'd met Vito at his adventure-themed resort. Afterward, Drake had let her choose their activity. They'd been heading to the shore for parasailing when Mackenzie had seen the resort's kiosk where they coordinated shark diving. She'd stopped in her tracks, an idea taking shape.

As Drake had checked out the underwater close-ups of sharks hanging on the kiosk walls, his face had lit up like a little boy with his first bicycle. She loved that about him, loved his sense of adventure and his openness to just about everything, and that's what she focused on, instead of her own fears, as she'd approached the girl at the counter, trying to hide her trepidation as she asked how dangerous it was to dive with sharks. The girl, who was about twenty and less than five feet tall, had answered countless questions from Mackenzie, explaining that they had a team of experts to ensure that it was safe.

When Mackenzie had observed Drake enthusiastically chatting with one of the divers, it was gratitude and the need to turn the tables and make a part of this day special for him that drove her to say, "Let's do this instead of parasailing."

The dive had been surreal and incredible and had pumped a crap ton of adrenaline through her, but what she'd remember even more than seeing seven types of sharks up close and personal was the way, afterward, Drake had picked her up in a full-body hug and kissed her until she couldn't remember her own name and then happily chattered about the experience for the next hour plus, reliving it, play-by-playing it, as they were taxied to island number five for the day.

Angelo's resort was a spa that centered around meditation, self-care, and pampering, and the massages Drake had scheduled couldn't have been better timed. Once they'd been blissfully scrubbed and mudded and rubbed to within an inch of their lives, all signs of the adrenaline-fest of the shark dive had been erased.

The finale of the tour was a visit to Luca's culinary resort, where they'd had a cooking lesson to prepare banana-leaf-wrapped mahi-mahi with a chili-lime sauce, a steamed dalo side dish, and honey cake for dessert. Then they'd eaten their creations at a table for two on the beach as the sun descended in the sky in another spectacular display that, along with the sunrise that morning, book-ended the day in absolute unforgettable splendor.

Mackenzie would hold on to the memories for the rest of her life. But what exceeded the awesomeness of all of that—the once-in-a-lifetime sights, the personalized activities—was that Drake had not only set out to give Mackenzie a fun, memorable day but he'd indulged her devotion to her work. He'd made sure every Rossi brother was well acquainted with Mackenzie's company and her purpose, and each resort tour they'd been on was personalized to give her information that would help her create the types of trips her clients demanded.

That Drake recognized how much value that had to Mackenzie told her he got her.

He. Got. Her.

Between that and his general thoughtfulness and consideration throughout the day, and, oh, also his charm and his wit and his warmth, Drake was, in a word, irresistible. His beautiful smile and luscious muscles and the things he could do to her with his body were just...extra.

Spending four days with him on the other side of the world had allowed her to get to know him even better than staying at his apartment in Nashville had. Here, they'd been nearly inseparable, a couple in every sense of the word except one—they had no future.

After their talk on the beach the other night, Mackenzie understood Drake better, understood that, after the trauma of his dad's death, he was afraid of losing what mattered most to him, and so he worked hard not to let any one thing—or person— matter too much. She knew now that was why he flitted from one thing to another, keeping his life full to the brim but not with any one focus.

She'd known before that he was a commitment-phobe, and now she grasped why.

It drove home even harder the plain truth—it didn't matter how close they became here on the island of Jiva. Drake wasn't a long-term kind of guy. He wouldn't get serious with Mackenzie or any other girl. He'd have fun and plan activities and be his charming self while it was new, but until he decided he wanted to get over his *issue*, he would never let himself become involved in a real, lasting relationship.

Burrowing her feet up to the ankles in the sand, Mackenzie admitted it. She wanted that relationship. She wanted the long-term. She wanted to be special to Drake even after this trip, far beyond the magical shores of Jiva.

And there was the ugly, scary, disappointing truth, staring her in the face.

She, as it turned out, was an idiot without measure, because she'd gone and done the dumbest thing possible—she'd fallen in love with Drake North.

CHAPTER TWENTY-FIVE

hough Drake barely knew what day it was, his phone assured him it was Saturday, going on five p.m. He had twelve minutes to get to his meeting with Mason, and for once in his life, he was making a point of being on time. With all the shit running through his head, the last thing he needed was a typical Mason comment about Drake's propensity for being late.

It could probably be argued that Drake wasn't in the condition to do something of this magnitude even after sleeping until midafternoon. According to the calendar, he and Mackenzie had woken up in Jiva just "yesterday," or rather, he'd woken up alone in Mackenzie's bed in Jiva just yesterday and found her on the beach in a subdued mood. The thirty-one hours of traveling they'd done since then had been twice as arduous as the trip *to* the South Pacific. The longest leg of the journey, from Fiji to LA, had not been conducive to sleep, between restless kids and a cranky baby, long patches of significant turbulence, and the tension coming off Mackenzie the whole way. She claimed it was just the getting-back-to-real-life transition, but he wasn't sure he believed her.

When he'd dropped her off at her apartment last night, just after midnight local time, he would've given anything to follow her inside and collapse in her bed with her and, honest to God, just sleep. But Mackenzie had reminded him they'd only agreed to be together for the duration of their trip, and she'd turned him down flat, even when he'd flashed her the most engaging smile he could summon, then allowed him a quick, nearly chaste kiss and gone inside alone, rolling her suitcase behind her.

Sure, they'd agreed, five days ago, to end it when the trip was over, but he didn't see the harm in letting things continue on a casual basis now that they were back in the States. They'd grown close enough that he couldn't fathom not having her in his life, at the bare minimum as friends. She was one of the only people in the universe who truly knew what this upcoming meeting meant for him. He hadn't confided just to let her disappear from his world completely.

At any rate, the journey and the day and the disappointing goodbye had left Drake sleep-deprived, jet-lagged, and, though he wouldn't admit it out loud, scared shitless of what he was about to do.

He pulled his Ducati into the North Brothers Sports headquarters parking lot, barely noticing that it was Mason's Audi he parked next to, shut his bike down, hooked his helmet on it, and headed to the main door of the bland, unassuming building.

He'd always known the cause of his commitment issue, but after talking through it with Mackenzie, he knew it was time to make a change. He wouldn't apologize for the way he'd lived his life, but once you let it out in the daylight that you were, in essence, running scared, it was tough to keep justifying it.

It didn't mean the actual pulling of the trigger was easy.

He walked past the elevator and took the stairs to the second floor. The building seemed deserted, not surprising on the weekend, as the businesses housed on the first floor were financial, insurance, and a couple of others that were likely staffed by eight-to-fivers with work-life balance and a measure of sanity. Not like Mason. But he couldn't fault his oldest brother. He was turning out to be a hell of a leader and a smart businessman, and Drake was thankful he'd taken it upon himself to steer their dad's company the way it needed in order to thrive.

The second-floor hallway was quiet, as was the NBS office once Drake went through the door and walked past the empty reception area. He didn't see or hear anyone in the endless cube farm as he beelined for the corner office.

Mason's door was closed, and as Drake got closer, he could hear his brother's voice and figured he must be on the phone. He paused outside of the door, his heart racing, palms sweating, chest tightening.

Was he really going to do this? Give up his freedom and commit to a corporate gig?

It wasn't too late to bail. He could walk in there and tell his brother he wasn't going to do it. He hadn't quit either of his jobs yet, hadn't told a soul besides Mackenzie that he was planning to take the NBS position.

And then what?

Run scared for another twenty or thirty years and hope that eventually something else as intriguing and well-suited for him someday came along?

"Not gonna happen," he muttered to himself, and then he knocked twice, swiftly, solidly on the door.

"Come in," Mason said from the other side.

It hit him at once that Mason wasn't on the phone and wasn't alone. Gabe was leaning against the side table, and Cole was sprawled in one of the guest chairs opposite Mason. All three of them pierced him with astute, analyzing gazes, as if they were trying to discern his decision before he could get in the door.

"I didn't realize you'd called in backup," Drake said with what he hoped came across as an easygoing grin.

"I didn't know whether we'd need the big guns or not," Mason said, also smiling, and that caught Drake a little off guard because he'd expected his CEO brother to be his usual uptight, all-business self. He was equally stunned that Mason wore a button-down shirt instead of a suit, Saturday or not.

"He's got you two coming in on the weekend now, huh?" Drake asked the others as he scooted the empty chair out a bit so that he could fit next to Cole without their knees bumping.

"I just got back into town," Cole said. "We're opening a store in Raleigh. Just broke ground Wednesday and I've been there ever since."

"Raleigh," Drake said. "Another state. Cool."

"Well," Mason said, "let's not beat around the bush. Tell us what you're thinking."

And there it was, CEO Mason, but Drake appreciated it. He couldn't stomach a bunch of small talk about the Cardinals' prospects or their mom's landscaping project with Lexie.

Drake sat up straighter, said a silent *what the hell* in his head, and infused confidence into his voice when he said out loud, "I'm in."

"Yesss," Gabe said victoriously, standing and holding out his fist for Drake to bump, which he did.

"Sweet," Cole said at nearly the same time, grinning widely. "Our baby brother showed up for a meeting early and accepted a full-time job all in one day. What the hell's the world coming to? Congrats, man."

"Thanks, asshole," Drake said with affection.

When he turned toward Mason, expecting to find him ready to run down the fine print, the details, maybe even whip out a contract, he was shocked to see, instead, he was lining up four glass tumblers on his desk. Then he reached down into one of his desk compartments and came up with a tall, skinny, blue wood box. He opened it and took out a bottle of Macallan 30 scotch, which Drake knew ran in the five digits for one bottle. It looked to have been opened before, but the liquid still reached two thirds of the way to the top. Mason poured a couple inches of amber liquid into each glass.

So much for the stuffy business facade.

"Ah, the special stash," Gabe said, approval in his tone.

All four of them picked up a glass without having to be told.

Mason held his glass up and nodded at Drake, and he didn't have to say a word for Drake to decipher his feelings. His pride and happiness were evident in that one glance. Drake relished it silently, for once feeling like an equal instead of the carefree, irresponsible baby in the family.

"This stuff warrants a toast," Cole said.

"Speech," Gabe bellowed and Drake shook his head at the idiot.

Mason stood, taking the request seriously, of course. He darted his gaze from one brother to the other, then said, "Here at North Brothers, we have some of the best people working for us and with us. Most of them care a great deal about this company, but none of them will ever care as much as the North family does. And now we're four strong on our side, plus the three cousins. Drake, you're going to make a hell of an addition to our team. We're thrilled to have you."

"Hear, hear," Gabe said as they all clinked their glasses together.

"Well said," Cole added.

Drake loved his brothers, and he generally got along just fine with them, but at this moment, the solidarity he felt standing among them, their support and acceptance and genuine enthusiasm overwhelmed him, and all he could think to do was take a healthy swig of the thirty-year-old scotch. The smoothness on his tongue, combined with the hint of fire and the sweet tinge of sherry, had him closing his eyes and savoring it.

"Damn," Gabe said in a tone that mimicked Drake's opinion.

"You didn't break out the good shit when I came on board," Cole said.

"If I remember right, you got cake," Mason replied, sitting back in his leather chair, one leg crossed over the other, looking mellow like Drake had never in his life seen him.

"It was damn good cake too," Gabe said.

"Not as good as this." Drake raised his glass in acknowledgment, then took another swig, smaller this time because he intended to make this stuff last.

"Not much is as good as this," Mason said.

"We talking consumables or everything?" Cole said. "Because there are a few rare non-consumables that are up there."

Drake made a whipping noise with his mouth, fully aware his brother was referring to Sierra.

"Hell," Mason said. "We're all happy you found loooove, Cole, but give it a rest."

"Jealous bastards," Cole said with a shit-eating grin.

Drake's thoughts veered to Mackenzie, because as good as

this scotch was, he tended to agree with Cole—in a non-whipped, non-pathetic way, of course. Not that he'd admit that to these lonely losers.

He had the passing thought that he was in basically the same spot as them when you got down to it. He'd likely be stuck alone tonight if Mackenzie had her way. He crushed that thought, determined not to let it ruin this celebratory moment.

"So we've got work to do," Mason said, sitting up straight and rolling his chair closer to his desk as he set the scotch on it and flipped back into business mode. "Cole and I are meeting next week to start hammering out the general layout of our first home fitness retail center. We'll have one of the branding experts involved as well, but we could use your expertise. What's your schedule like? How soon can you start?"

Drake mentally flipped through his work schedule for the next week. He intended to work two more weeks at the gym and maybe in the store if they needed him, but if this was going to be his department, he wanted in on it from the ground floor. "I'll give my notice tomorrow. I can work in some meetings when I'm not scheduled at the gym. But you need to catch me up. It sounds like you've decided where the first one's going?" The last he'd heard, they hadn't decided which of their stores to expand. There was a lot to consider, from zoning requirements to which markets had the most potential.

"We signed a deal on Thursday to build a new store here in town to replace the westside location," Mason explained. "We've been bursting at the seams for space, and now home fitness requires even more square footage."

"Market potential measures highest in that geographical area out of all the locations, even the new stores," Gabe added.

"And it'll be ideal to have it close to headquarters since it's new and you'll be right here." Mason nodded to Cole. "We've played with the idea of building for years, but now that we have Cole on board, it's a no-brainer."

"Let's do this then," Drake said.

He took out his phone and shot his gym schedule to Mason so they could coordinate times to meet. The four of them discussed the new building and the general concept of the Home Fitness Division until their glasses were empty, and then Cole headed home to Sierra while the three of them gave him hell about being stupid in love. Privately, Drake was beginning to suspect Cole was a lucky son of a bitch, and he admitted the urge to go to Mackenzie was building, even though he had no right.

When Mason suggested they order Chinese food for delivery, Drake considered for about half a second, but as revved up as he was about digging into the planning, he was antsy as hell right now and needed to get out of there. He'd taken a giant step today. Tomorrow he would tend to some details, like giving notice and stocking up on some office-appropriate clothing, since athletic pants were likely frowned upon. But tonight...

Tonight he wanted to celebrate. And there was only one person he wanted to celebrate with.

CHAPTER TWENTY-SIX

Mackenzie loved her work, but she wasn't stupid.

She'd learned, whenever she returned from a long trip, to take a full day off to recover. Saturday, in this case, was for honoring the jet lag.

Today was also about submerging herself in something she'd been anticipating for so, so long—the search for her very own home.

Before her Jiva trip, she'd asked Sierra for a mortgage banker recommendation, and she'd initiated the process of getting preapproved, scrambling to get all the necessary paperwork together prior to leaving. Now she had an approved budget to work with as well as a real estate agent—the same one Sierra and Cole were using—and an all-day appointment for Friday with that agent. Calvin Broderick had enthusiastically promised to set up as many showings as they could squeeze into the day, and Mackenzie could hardly wait.

In spite of her excitement, even though she'd been perusing listings online all day in between doing laundry and chores around the house, she was struggling hard to keep her mind off one tall, dark-haired, super-sexy man who was supposed to be a thing of the past.

She was camped out on the couch with her laptop, catching up on past episodes of Sierra's home remodeling show—her friend really did have a gift for TV—as she combed through dozens of houses in her price range, getting a better handle on which neighborhoods and what features she could afford. When the buzzer on the dryer went off, she went to the tiny laundry room on the other side of the also-small kitchen and pulled the hot, clean clothes into a basket to fold in front of the TV. She had four more episodes to catch up on and hoped to be current by the time the network ran the engagement segment. She'd heard all about it from both Sierra and Cole, more than once, but she couldn't wait to witness the romantic moment for herself.

As she made her way back to the couch, lugging the basket, there was a knock at the door, and she froze. Her heart pounded in her chest for no rational reason, except somehow she had a feeling as to who it was. She hadn't yet met any of her neighbors besides Nadine, and other than Sierra and Lexie, she hadn't had a chance to make friends. None of them were likely to drop by unannounced, which meant it was either a political canvasser or one tall, dark-haired super-sexy man who was—*sigh*—still supposed to be a thing of the past.

As far as she knew, it wasn't a big political season.

After setting the basket on the wooden trunk that served as a coffee table, she muted the sound on the TV, which had been low anyway, her instinct being to pretend like she wasn't home. Not exactly mature, but her body had shifted into something resembling fight-or-flight, shutting down reason.

She made her soundless way to the peephole, and yep. There stood the most enchanting guy on the face of the planet. He was eyeing the peephole as if he knew she was staring at him, even though she'd basically stopped breathing and there was no way he could see or hear her.

As she stared at him in indecision, his body language said he was starting to doubt whether she was there. He took half a step back, relaxed his shoulders, glanced left and right.

It could work. She could wait him out, act like no one was home, and watch him eventually walk away.

Drake stepped forward, knocked again, stepped back, turned ninety degrees, possibly looking for her car, which happened to be parallel parked on the street on the opposite side of the build-ing. He wouldn't find it unless he walked all the way around.

He did another ninety-degree pivot so that his back was to her, as if he was getting ready to give up. She was so close to pulling it off, hiding from him, saving her heart a little bit, and she…couldn't do it. Couldn't resist the pull of him.

She opened the door and he whipped around, his smile making him that much more dangerous, and she couldn't make herself care.

"Hi," she said on an exhale, belatedly realizing that, once again, she didn't look her best. With her hair an air-dried poof and her leggings and long-sleeved tee comfortable but not in the least bit flattering, she looked, well, like she'd been doing laundry all day.

"Hey, gorgeous."

"You lie," she said, smiling in spite of herself.

"Can I come in?" He advanced a step, and she wasn't sure which would be a dumber move—standing her ground and letting him get way closer or backing up and allowing him into her apartment.

Since she'd already made the first move toward recklessness, she stepped back and invited him inside. If she stopped lying to herself, she'd admit there had never been any kind of choice with Drake.

"What's up?" she asked, managing to sound casual as he came inside. "You seem…way energetic."

It was his eyes and his smile. They didn't look jet-lagged, but then why would someone like Drake North be bothered by a little thing like jet lag? The better to reel in weak souls like her, she supposed as she closed the door.

"I did it," he said, his tone dipping and his gaze becoming somehow intimate, as if he was telling her a secret.

She was drawing a blank though, fuzzy-brained as she was. "What did you do?"

"I met with my brothers. Accepted the job. You're looking at the new director of the North Brothers Sports Home Fitness Divi-sion." He stood a little straighter, and for a moment, she saw the little-boy-ness in him again, the irresistible, sometimes unsure real Drake, looking to her for approval.

She didn't make him wait, knowing exactly how much of a monster-sized step that one action was. Throwing her arms around him, she said, "Congratulations, Drake. I'm so happy for you." She meant every word.

And promptly forgot every bit of it when, as soon as she lowered her arms, he cupped her face with both hands and engulfed her in an overzealous, exhilarated kiss. He picked her up, his hands on the backs of her upper thighs, and pressed her into the door, kissing her like she'd never been kissed before. She reveled in it, the scent of him filling her nose, his rough, masculine chin abrading her skin in a delicious way, his hard body pressing into her.

When he finally ended the kiss, Mackenzie caught her breath and laughed. "That was…inspired."

He laughed too as he let her slide down his body until her feet hit the floor. "I feel like celebrating, and I wanted to celebrate with you." There was a hint of a question in his tone, as if he knew full well they weren't supposed to be close like this now that they were home.

At that moment, she couldn't be bothered with doing the smart thing. One, because Drake deserved to celebrate and bask in his moment. She knew what he'd done had been a long time coming and it hadn't been easy for him. Two, now that she'd had his body pressing into her, reigniting their combustible connection, there was no way she was letting him walk out that door. "Then let's celebrate," she said. *Naked. Please.*

In a sudden move, he wrapped his arms tightly around her again and lifted her, spun around, letting out a victory howl and then a laugh as they knocked into the kitchen counter that jutted out. When he set her down again, he gripped her waist, his fingers hitting her bare skin under her tee, then kissed the top of her head, his hips pinning her against the cabinet.

"I was thinking a fancy dinner, maybe out for drinks afterward…" he said, peering down at her with those arresting sky-blue eyes that seemed to have a hypnotic effect on her.

"I was thinking…" she started, hesitating, then giving a mental shrug and plowing forward, "sex. Maybe a frozen pizza afterward…"

"I've always liked the way you think." His voice had become rougher, his grin playful, and he lowered his mouth to hers, capturing her lips this time in a slow, sensual kiss full of promise.

He didn't break the lip-lock for some time, until he was easing her T-shirt up and was about to lift it over her head. He stopped abruptly. "My soon-to-be sister-in-law is on your TV. This feels awkward."

Mackenzie laughed and straightened as he loosened his hold on her. "Come on," she said. She took his hand and pulled him after her, paused at the coffee table to click the TV off, and led him up the stairs toward her loft-style bedroom. "Kitchen sex has its place, but tonight we're celebrating. That calls for a bed. I'm thinking slow, thorough, something to savor. It could take a while."

"Lucky thing, I have multiple whiles to take." His eyes sparked with lust as he said it.

They were barely up the last step when he turned her toward him, picked up where he'd left off with her shirt by pulling it over her head and flinging it to the floor, then skimmed his fingers down her sides to peel her leggings and underwear off, getting her naked in mere seconds. She grabbed on to the tall chest of drawers to keep from losing her balance and clumsily tumbling over.

In the low light from the living room that filtered up to them, his gaze roved over her appreciatively but not patiently, the raw desire in his eyes making her skin feel like it was on fire and only his touch could cool the burn.

In the next second, he reached back between his shoulders and whipped his own shirt off, kicked his shoes away, then unfastened and unzipped his pants and stripped them down his legs, along with his socks and his boxer briefs. He straightened and faced her in all his masculine glory, and they closed the space between them at the same time, their heated skin pressing together, lips colliding, bodies stumbling awkwardly as he half guided her, half lifted her the short distance to the bed and tumbled onto it after her.

Mackenzie pulled him to her, desperate for him to fill the ache in her. He entered her body within seconds, and slow and thorough was out of the question. And she was more than okay with that.

———

LATER, Mackenzie stirred, drowsy, sated, glowing from hours of Drake's thorough, adoring attention. And hungry. She wasn't an exercise expert the way he was, but she was certain they'd burned a few weeks' worth of calories.

She looked over at him, inches away, the living room light below still the only one on. The tips of his lips were turned upward in a slight smile as he slept, his hair tousled, his arm hugging the pillow, which gave her a choice view of the bulge of his biceps. He made a pretty picture, and she burned it to her memory. Because she knew…this was still temporary. The long-term prospects between the two of them hadn't changed.

When she rolled over to the edge of the bed to get up, he didn't stir, possibly wiped out from a sex-marathon/jet-lag combo after all. She crept to the bathroom, where she slipped on her short, silky robe and pulled her hair up into a quick messy bun, then went downstairs to the kitchen.

Making as little noise as possible, she turned the oven on to preheat and took the pizza out of the freezer. As she removed it from the box and unwrapped it, she had a niggling thought that the evening had been a bad idea. Letting Drake in, letting her guard down… She was supposed to be distancing herself from him, and there had been no distance between them whatsoever, physically or figuratively. Zero, zilch, nada. Over the past few hours, she'd opened herself up to him in ways she hadn't before, held nothing back.

As she set the pizza on a pan on the counter, waiting for the oven to heat, she made a decision. She wasn't going to regret tonight. Not a single minute of it. He was here now, and she still had the rest of the night with him if he'd stay, and she might as well enjoy it to the fullest.

She would put an end to it—to her and Drake's more-than-friends adventures—soon. Do the smart thing. But not tonight.

Once she made that conscious decision, she relaxed all the way, determined to make the most of the time she did have with Drake.

After she put the pizza into the hot oven, she picked up her laptop from the coffee table, set it on the breakfast bar, and powered up to browse through more houses while she waited. If she found any she loved, she'd let Calvin know to add them to the list of showings for Friday.

It didn't take long for her to fall through the rabbit hole of houses, clicking on one suggested property after another that popped up on the real estate site. That was how she found the perfect house—an adorable brick home full of exactly her style, with a walkout basement and a bonus room above the garage, surrounded by trees and a park, in a part of town she'd love to live in.

Naturally, it was close to two times her budget. After spending several minutes soaking up every photo of it, she cursed the website for suggesting a pipe dream to her, then hopped up to stop the beeping of the timer that signaled the pizza was ready.

Before she had it all the way out of the oven, she heard Drake coming down the stairs and smiled to herself at the cliché of food luring him out of bed.

He'd put his boxer briefs on but nothing else. Mackenzie eyed him as she straightened and set the steaming-hot pizza on the stove. That man alone had the power to make her forget the hunger in her stomach and instead become aware of a different kind of hunger that had resurged within an instant of laying eyes on him.

"You're my dream girl," he said, grinning as he came up to her in the kitchen and kissed her. "A hot girl with hot pizza. Doesn't get better than this."

"I figured frozen pizza fell into your junk-food category."

"Every once in a while, you have to throw the rules out the door and indulge."

Didn't she know it.

He kissed her again, longer, more intently this time, and she laughed.

"You're not distracting me from my much-needed dinner, mister."

"That sounds like an intriguing challenge, but luckily for you, I'm so hungry I could chew my arm off."

"Don't do anything to harm that killer body of yours," she said. She took the pizza cutter out of the drawer and sliced it up, handed him a plate, and helped herself to two heaping slices of meat lovers'. "At least there's lots of protein, right? You've got to fuel up all those muscles." She eyed his chest and arms appreciatively.

"Plus carbs for stamina," he said with a sexy eyebrow lift. He went around to one of the barstools and sat down to dig in. Mackenzie sat next to him and did the same.

"Houses," Drake said with his mouth full, pointing at her laptop. He swallowed his food. "So you're diving in now, huh?"

"Yeah. At long last. I'm going out with a Realtor on Friday. Things are getting real."

"Is this one you're going to see?"

The brick house was still on the screen and she sighed with house lust.

"Sadly, no. It's basically my dream house, but it's way over my budget. If I could find something about two-thirds the size and half the money, I'd ask to see it tomorrow."

"It's nice," he said, clicking through the photos. "Great wooded yard, lots of light inside, and that bonus room would make a good office. The whole house is you."

She couldn't argue with that, but there was no point in drooling over the listing any longer. Once he was through the photos, she reached over and went to the list of houses she'd favorited to show him some realistic contenders.

The first one was small but had a master bathroom to die for, with an enormous walk-in closet, a claw-foot soaking tub, and classy tile work. The next one was new construction and cute, maybe a little cookie-cutter, but in a neighborhood with good schools—not immediately relevant, but if she wanted to stay put for decades, schools could someday matter. The third had a pool and hot tub in the backyard but the house needed a lot of work. Since it was a lower price point, it could be feasible. She'd have to pick Sierra's brain once she'd seen it in person.

Each house on the list had so much potential, at least based on what she saw online. She was optimistic that Calvin would come up with other good possibilities as well.

As Drake went through each listing, he noticed details she hadn't. An awkward layout on one, where the master was attached to the kitchen, a fast-food restaurant practically in the backyard of another, a super-steep driveway that would be a challenge in the winter. He also noticed some positives—one had top-of-the-line appliances in the kitchen and another had window seats in all the bedrooms with what they were guessing was storage beneath.

"You should take me with you on Friday," he said when they'd devoured all of the pizza.

With a jolt, Mackenzie slid off the stool, picked up both their plates, and carried them around the counter to the sink, deliberately putting space between them. Deliberately not looking at him while she sorted through that idea.

No. She should not take him with her on Friday or anytime. Not to look at houses. There was nothing more domestic and future-oriented than looking at houses.

Attempting to keep it light, she said, "You hardly seem like a real-estate-hunting type."

"I've never done it before, but I'd do it with you."

"I've got a guy. Calvin Broderick."

"Your Realtor? Guy who's trying to sell you a six-figure something? You need someone who knows you. A neutral third party who has no stakes. I'll be your guy."

She pivoted away from him, checked to make sure the oven was off, briefly closed her eyes out of his sight. Because...damn.

She wished so much that he *could* be her guy. That he would let himself be her guy. Her life guy, not her house-hunting guy.

"I'll be your objective person so when you walk in the door and fall in love with a breakfast nook or a fireplace, you'll have someone who can look at things without emotion."

"Emotion is important when you're buying a home. It's got to feel right."

"Sure, but so is logic," he said. "It's a combination. You're putting your life savings into this purchase. You should have a second opinion."

She knew he was right about that, and she'd even considered seeing if Ezra would be available to fly in to help her out, but that seemed a little ridiculous. The search could take her weeks and dozens of listings before she found the right one. Still…she was supposed to be cutting Drake off. Not inviting him into her next chapter.

"It's going to be an all-day kind of thing," she told him, finally turning to face him as she rinsed the plates off.

He stood and came around the counter, grabbed a paper towel, and wiped down the stove, where some sauce had dripped. "What time are you going?"

"Calvin's setting our first showing for nine."

"Where are you meeting him?"

"At his office."

"Text me the address and I'll meet you there."

She shut the water off and studied him, debating internally.

"Let me help you out, Mackenzie," he said. He gently pulled her body around so she faced him. He pushed a pesky strand of her hair behind her ear, gazing down at her sincerely. "This is important to you."

"Okay," she said, telling herself it wasn't because of the way he was looking at her. It was because she did need a second opinion. She did need an objective party. "I'll send you his address and confirm the time once I hear back from him." Lifting her chin, she stretched up to him and kissed him. "Thank you."

He growled, his serious, helpful tone out the window and sexy Drake back in play as he wound his big arms around her and pulled her into him. She didn't fight it. She'd already made peace with tonight, all of tonight, and she was set on having him stay until morning.

By the time Friday came around, she'd have her defenses stronger, make the transition in her head from Drake her lover to Drake her objective third party.

Piece of cake.

CHAPTER TWENTY-SEVEN

*D*rake was going to take all kinds of shit for being late, no two ways about it. Downside of working with one's family, he supposed. They knew all your faults and weaknesses and didn't hesitate to point them out.

He gunned the Porsche the second the light turned green, swearing out loud and then laughing at himself at the realization that, for only the second time in his life, he actually cared that he was running late.

He'd underestimated Friday morning traffic, had thought with a 7:45 a.m. meeting he would be ahead of the rush, but it was 7:46 and he still had a couple of miles to go. It was nothing short of a miracle that no one had texted him yet, wondering where the hell he was and when he was going to show up. The fact that he wasn't yet officially an NBS employee didn't make a difference. In his mind, he was all in, and he didn't want to fuck this up.

One more week of shifts at the gym and then he'd be full-time at his family's company. Though he'd been willing to finish out his two weeks of retail shifts in the North Brothers store as well, Mason had intervened and informed the store manager that Drake was transferring to the corporate offices, effective immediately. His CEO brother had then kept him busy anytime he wasn't at the gym, as the new division was moving forward at a thundering pace. Fine by Drake. He liked to keep busy, and now that he'd taken that first difficult step, he wanted to be in from the ground floor up as the new division was built, literally and figuratively.

At last, he whipped into the NBS parking lot and took the first space he came to. The lot was less than half-full but that was changing by the second, as employees made their way in for the regular eight-a.m. start of the day. Drake grabbed his iPad—in its new professional leather case—and hurried to the building.

He took the stairs to the second floor and pushed through the glass NBS door, greeting Prisha, the receptionist, who looked to have just arrived at her desk, as he hurried by. The main conference room was along the back wall, on the other side from Mason's corner office, so Drake went down the hall to the right of the receptionist.

As he neared the back hall, his cousin Connor, who was VP of operations, was meandering toward the conference room from the executive offices. Connor was the oldest of their three North cousins at thirty-six. At six feet even, he was short by North standards and had a lanky build. His golden-brown hair was shaved short on the sides and longer on top, styled up and to one side.

"Morning, Drake. Look at you."

Drake did as he said, glanced down at his suit, but was preoccupied. "You're late too?" And not really in a hurry, it seemed.

Connor took his phone out of the inside pocket of his suit jacket and clicked it to see the time as they continued toward the conference room. "Nine minutes early. Relax."

"I thought it started at quarter till eight."

"You must've got your signals crossed. Eight a.m. start," Connor said as they reached the doorway.

Inside, Gabe and Logan, Connor's younger brother, sat next to each other near this end of the long table, deep in discussion.

"Hey," Gabe said when he looked up, cutting off the conversation with Logan abruptly, which made Drake think it was HR business.

All the other chairs were empty. Clearly Drake wasn't late.

"You said the meeting started at 7:45," Drake said to Gabe. He'd confirmed the time just this morning during their workout at the gym. "Is it delayed?"

Logan, who was the thirty-four-year-old VP of IT and the closest any of the Norths came to being blond, looked over at Gabe with an amused, assessing grin, and Drake began to understand what was going on.

"You lied to get me here on time," Drake said.

"It worked," Gabe said, smiling. "You're early even."

"Would've been late for a seven forty-five," Logan added.

Drake grinned, unable to get too upset, because he was legitimately relieved he hadn't missed the start of the meeting with the architects. "Thanks, asshole."

"Anytime," Gabe said, then he went back to his discussion with Logan, and yep, it sounded like one of the accounting employees had given notice the day before and they were discussing when to close down that person's access to company computers.

There was coffee at a station on the far wall, and Drake followed Connor to it to grab a cup, more just to have a beverage than out of the need to wake up. He'd been up since five, gone to the gym for a full workout, and was enthusiastic about this meeting, ready to get to work. He hadn't felt so enlivened for a long time, not professionally. Personally, Mackenzie had enlivened him and then some. Which reminded him...

"How long do you expect this to go?" Drake asked Connor as they took chairs next to Gabe and Logan, and Cole sauntered in the door. Unlike everyone else, Cole was dressed in khakis and a button-down shirt, dressy for him. The middle North brother had a complex about wearing a suit, Drake knew.

Connor blew out a breath. "I don't know but it's not going to be a short one. Probably two to three hours would be my guess."

It was the first meeting with the architects since they'd selected the firm from a pool of three, where they'd begin getting specific about the company's needs and wish list for the new store. Drake hadn't found out about it until Wednesday, as he wasn't on the company email system yet and Mason hadn't notified him until then. Luckily it coincided with one of his days off from the gym. Unluckily, it seemed Drake's real estate date with Mackenzie was in danger of being screwed up.

He pulled out his phone to warn her with a text message.

Hey, beautiful. Just found out my early meeting with the architects could run long, so I'm going to be late. Get started without me and I'll text you when I'm done and catch up with you and the real estate guy. I'm sorry and I'll make it up to you.

The dots that indicated she was typing did not appear, and he wondered what she was up to. Was she awake? Was she upset and trying to figure out how to respond—or whether to respond? Or maybe she was in the shower…naked and wet and…

There was a commotion at the door, and Drake looked up to see three people he didn't know walk in, followed by Mason, who invited the three to help themselves to coffee.

"Morning, everyone," Mason said. "Looks like we're all here, as Bill Santini isn't able to make it."

Two of the three, who Drake assumed were the architect team, took seats across the table, and the third went to the coffee station.

"You remember Gabe and Connor," Mason said to the visitors as he stood at the head of the table, "and Cole." Mason turned to Cole, who was standing near Gabe, not having committed to a place yet. They each shook hands and exchanged greetings, the male on the architect team remarking on how many Norths there were.

To Logan and Drake, Mason said, "This is Katarina Markham, senior architect and one of the partners at Martin and Baines, and her associates, Troy Greenstein and Nell Lopez."

Nell was apparently the one getting coffee, and she joined them at the table with a full steaming mug.

Mason introduced Logan and Drake, and they shook hands

and exchanged a minute or two of small talk before Mason started the meeting.

It was some time before Drake was able to see that Mackenzie had finally replied. *No worries. This is important to you. Keep me posted. I told you I can handle this on my own!*

The attitude made Drake smile to himself as the table discussed the challenges of the building site in general. Mackenzie was reasonable and used to handling things on her own—two of the things he happened to like about her. He'd reply as soon as he could.

———

As soon as he could turned out to be much later. Like, lunchtime later. Drake was surprised as hell to see it was after eleven thirty. He'd been so engrossed in what they were doing he hadn't looked at the time once. And the meeting wasn't over yet. The nine of them had gotten a lot done—preliminary decisions, priorities listed, challenges brainstormed—and they'd agreed to continue over an early lunch.

As they made their way out to their cars, Drake sent a text to Mackenzie, apologizing up, down, left, and right that it was so late and that he wasn't done yet. He slipped his phone back in his pocket as he got into his Porsche, Connor getting into the passenger side, to drive to the restaurant.

Could he have bailed and gone to meet Mackenzie? Probably. Technically, Mason couldn't do a thing to him yet, as he was on his own time and they were lucky he'd been able to make it to the meeting today at all. But Drake was into it, so deeply into it, and he didn't want to miss a second of it because this was his deal and his family's business. It was them stepping forward, into the future, paving the way for other new stores, stores that would include the Home Fitness Division. Drake's baby. As far as Mackenzie went, he knew the damage was already done and cutting out of lunch would do very little to save his ass if her understanding had run out.

He'd make it up to her tonight.

———

By the end of the day, exhaustion, emotion, and stress far outweighed the excitement of house hunting.

Mackenzie let out a big, audible sigh and pressed her head back against the headrest of the passenger seat in Calvin Broderick's Mercedes SUV as he pulled away from the ninth house of the day. It was nearing seven p.m. and the sun was well on its way to disappearing, the streetlights flickering on. They'd taken time for lunch, but it'd been hours ago, and her stomach had rumbled more than once since they'd gone in that last house.

"That one didn't stand a chance, huh?" Calvin said, and he was spot on.

"The bedrooms were tiny and the layout made it...claustrophobic."

"I agree. You've been drawn to the homes with lots of windows and light and more of an open plan. You loved the house on Muller Street from the moment you walked in. What are you thinking about it?"

She was thinking she'd never been so plagued by self-doubt in her life.

She did love that house. It felt right, and it also lined up nicely with her wish list. It was twelve years old, three bedrooms, had a fireplace, a gorgeous kitchen, and a patio with a built-in fire pit. There was plenty of space for her now, and with a full unfinished basement, there was the potential for adding lots of square footage later if she ever threw a family into the mix. For being in a subdivision with only a handful of different floor plans, the house had lots of character and was, well, adorable. The yard was on the small side but well taken care of, and it backed up to a green space.

The drawbacks were minor—one of the bedrooms was minuscule, the countertops throughout were laminate and ugly, the furnace was as old as the house, and there was more carpet than she liked, but those shouldn't be deal breakers. Based on the other houses she'd seen today, she knew she could do so much worse. It was only five thousand dollars above her budget, and she could make that work.

According to Calvin, who she'd grown to like, respect, and appreciate over the course of the long day, there were two other parties interested in the house, so if she wanted it, she should act quickly. She believed him because he hadn't been at all high-pressure and seemed to genuinely want her to make the best decision for herself.

Whatever that was.

She thought it was the Muller Street house, but she was struggling hard to give him the go-ahead.

"I like it," she finally said. "So much." She realized, as she looked out the window, they were already nearing Calvin's office and decision time. "I just don't know if I can put in an offer tonight. I might need to sleep on it."

"It's a big decision. Your first home," Calvin said empathetically.

"What if I wanted to have someone else go through it with me?"

"I'd be happy to set that up. You know with this one we're up against time and other people, but I want you to feel good about your decision. If a second opinion could help, let's do it."

Who would she even get to go through with her? Her best bet was Sierra. She trusted her as a friend and as an expert on construction. But it would have to happen tomorrow, preferably early, and she hesitated to ask. It would be an imposition and Sierra had her own house hunting to do.

Of course, there was Drake, in theory, but he'd proven today he might not follow through.

Okay, that wasn't fair of her. He'd never let her down in all the weeks she'd been back, except for today, and as she'd told him, she understood the importance of his meeting. She wouldn't have wanted him to miss that to go through houses with her.

But damn that man. He'd gotten into her head with the whole second-opinion thing.

No, that wasn't quite right. Damn herself. She'd *let* him get into her head.

Mackenzie wasn't the type to dither over decisions. She'd been on her own for so long, since she was seventeen years old and her mom had left her with a friend's family for her senior year. She'd been making big decisions ever since. Where to go to college, where to live, who to live with, whether to drop out of school, whether to move across the country… None of it slowed her down. She weighed her options and followed a combination of heart and head and plowed forward, making the best choices she could.

Was buying a home the biggest decision yet? Maybe. It was a giant one, but so was quitting college. So was moving cross-country.

What it came down to was that she'd let happen exactly what she was trying to avoid. Her involvement with Drake, no matter how unstructured and unofficial, had affected her judgment. Her emotions had swayed her life plan, or tried to. It didn't matter that she knew in her head he was temporary. She'd let her heart and her hopes override her logic on this one. She didn't need Drake's opinion on *her* house.

"You know what, Calvin?" she said. "Go ahead and draw up the contract for full price. If you could check one more time that no offers are coming in tonight, then I'd like to sleep on it, but I'll let you know for sure first thing tomorrow morning. No need to go through it again." They'd spent over an hour in the house already. "Will that work?"

"Absolutely," he said as he pulled into the lot behind his office. "I'll call the sellers' agent and let you know yet this evening if we need to expedite things."

There were only a few cars in the lot, and as Calvin drove into a spot close to the building and down the row from her car, Mackenzie's heart lurched.

There was an orange Porsche next to hers. Drake sat in the driver's seat. He looked in her direction, and she felt a reaction in every cell of her body. She bit on the inside of her lip and turned away, back to Calvin as he killed the engine.

"Thank you, Calvin. For everything. You've been amazing all day, just like Sierra said." She offered her hand across the front seat, and they shook awkwardly in the small space. "I'll talk you in the morning at the latest."

"Have a good evening, Mackenzie."

She got out of his SUV, shut the door, and took in a fortifying breath.

It was time for her to look out for herself. Time for her to make a change.

CHAPTER TWENTY-EIGHT

*D*rake tried to read Mackenzie's mood as she made her way across the parking lot toward him with unrushed, measured steps. She wasn't smiling, but she wasn't frowning either. She looked confident and determined and so damn pretty. Her hair was down and being rustled by the breeze, and she wore skinny jeans, a long shirt, and a fuzzy vest, along with ankle boots and lots of jewelry. She'd turn his head even if he didn't know her.

He'd texted her the second the meeting with the architects had finished, but unfortunately, that hadn't been until after two p.m.—a marathon meeting that could not have gone better. Mackenzie hadn't replied. He knew she'd been busy, in and out of houses with her "guy"—who he reassured himself now was mid to late forties and way too old for Mackenzie—and probably wrapped up in discussions and decisions as well, so Drake refused to jump to the conclusion that she was mad at him. But he wasn't going to assume anything. And she wasn't giving him a single clue.

Mason had wanted to meet with him and Melody, who'd been charged with branding the new division, after the architects left, so when Mackenzie hadn't answered, Drake had joined his brother and the marketing VP. They'd finished that meeting around four thirty, and Drake had come directly here, to the real estate office, determined to show Mackenzie he was sorry and to spend the evening—and the night, if he was lucky—making it up to her.

He'd mistakenly assumed she and the Realtor would be done close to five. He'd spent the past two and a half hours in his car jotting down notes after the day's work, his mind spinning on two tracks, home fitness and Mackenzie. It was a relief to have work to focus on instead of giving in to trying to figure out what he was doing here, waiting for so long. It wasn't his way. He'd never done anything like this. It went into the same category as chasing her around the world, maybe not quite as drastic, but for him to sit in a small sports car for hours on end…

Instead of walking to his driver's-side window as he'd expected, Mackenzie went around to the passenger's side, opened the door, and dropped into the seat next to him.

"Hello," he said, still waiting for any kind of cue to cross her face. "How did it go?"

"I found my house, so I'd say really well." She smiled then, but the smile was off, not deep enough, more of a surface thing, and Drake's early-alert system sounded in his head.

"That's exciting," he said, genuinely happy for her—if she was, in fact, happy. "You don't sound excited."

"Oh, I am. I'm going to sleep on it, but the house feels good. It's a short drive from here. Near Weston and Muller. A two-story with three bedrooms and an unfinished basement."

That wasn't far from his mom's house, but in a newer neighborhood, he knew. A family neighborhood. One of those that brought to mind kids playing basketball in the driveway and dogs running around a fenced-in backyard. The thought of Mackenzie there sent an uneasy ripple through him that he couldn't quite define. Wasn't sure he wanted to define.

"Maybe you can show me sometime," he said. "I'm game as long as I can get away from work. Mackenzie, I'm sorry about today." His instinct was to grasp her hand, but she had both of hers wrapped tightly around her clutch wallet.

"I told you I understand and I meant it. Drake…" She was sitting so rigidly, and she absently stuck one finger in the loop of the wallet's wrist strap and started circling that finger around and around, twisting the strap.

Drake tensed and waited, then prompted, "What's up, Mackenzie?"

The looping motion stopped abruptly, and she turned slightly in the bucket seat and looked him in the eyes. "This isn't working for me."

He felt his mouth open as his brain floundered and tried to catch up. Before he could, she continued.

"I knew going into it that you don't do long-term relationships. I knew what I was getting into. None of this is your fault. It's mine, but I can't do it anymore."

He swallowed, feeling like a deer must feel when it leaped onto the road and landed smack up against a moving car. He wasn't dead, but he was panicked and stunned into stupidity and having trouble plucking out a coherent thought to voice. Mackenzie had looked back at her wallet as he mentally stumbled around. Finally, he managed, "Can't do what?"

She sucked in an audible breath. "I can't be with you casually. I can't do day-to-day part-time. Not with you. I let you talk me into being together in Jiva because, well, I'd like to say it was because you traveled so far for it, but it was more than that. It's because I couldn't resist you. And then, when you came over last weekend with your good news, again, I couldn't resist you."

That seemed like a good thing to him, not a bad one, but the look on her face said the opposite. And then she stunned the breath right out of him.

"I've done the dumbest thing I could ever do and that's"—she closed her eyes and inhaled—"fall in love with you."

He closed his eyes too, as if maybe that could stop the clusterfuck of feelings that hit him in that moment.

The silence in the car was so loud his ears were ringing as he processed. Shit. Damn. Fuck. She wasn't supposed to fall in love. They were supposed to be two adults enjoying the hell out of each other. They had a good thing going just the way it was. He was fully aware he was emotionally stunted—she knew it as well —but the *L* word had never been part of the deal.

Of course, he'd been the numb nuts who'd chased her around the damn world, literally. He was all kinds of fucking idiot and all wrong for her. How he could want to pull her into him and tell her it would be okay at the same time he wanted to rant at her was beyond him.

It likely wouldn't be okay. She'd picked the wrong guy.

"Annnnd your silence confirms exactly what I needed to know," Mackenzie said quietly.

"I'm sorry, Mackenzie," he said, because he heard the hurt in her voice, and if there was one thing he was crystal clear on, it was that he never wanted to hurt her.

"Me too." She shook her head, as if at a loss as to how it'd come to this. "Having you in my life as a friend, with or without benefits, jacks with my head. And my heart. I have to stop it. I'm looking to the future, buying a house, building up the Nashville branch of To the Stars. And I want the rest of the package, Drake. I do. I want to get married someday, want to have a family. And I know that you don't."

"I might someday," he started, reflexively, almost defensively, because yeah, the thought of being alone for the rest of his life… That suddenly seemed like a cold, lonely existence. It hadn't before, but as he peered at Mackenzie's profile and imagined not being able to see her whenever he wanted to… He clamped down on that line of thoughts right quick.

"I understand why you can't," she said softly, and he knew she was talking about his dad's death and the way that had fucked him up good. "If I was a different person, maybe I could wait around for you to sort things out. Maybe I could do halfway, but I can't. That's not me. So I need to stop. I need to say goodbye."

He felt that like a physical blow, and the need to lash out boiled up in him. He couldn't believe she was just going to walk away. "So I get no say in this? You're just done?"

With her clutch sitting on her legs now, she ran her hands over her face, pausing with her fingers covering her eyes. When she dropped them, she said, her voice rough and emotional, "What do you want between us, Drake?"

He knew what the "right" answer was, knew she wanted him to want a commitment, exclusivity, to be her boyfriend, to love her back. But right now, the thought of saying any of that made his chest go ice-cold with fear.

He wasn't a commitment guy. He didn't know if he could ever let himself love a woman the way Mackenzie needed—deserved—to be loved. Over the years, content to be carefree and single, he'd questioned whether he was actually capable of that kind of love. In spite of the charming, happy, friendly face he put forth to the world, he was selfish and stunted and fucked up inside and he knew it.

It didn't matter how much he wished he could tell her what she wanted to hear. He couldn't lie to her. Couldn't risk hurting her even more in the end.

"I like having you in my life. I care about you, Mackenzie. I respect you, I admire you, I like hanging out with you. I like the way things are." That she didn't made him want to yell and punch things.

Gazing at her lap, she nodded sadly, slowly, repeatedly, as if lost in thought. "I wish I could settle for that, Drake."

Before he could say anything else, Mackenzie leaned across the console, cupped his cheek, and kissed him. She didn't open to him, didn't take it physically deeper, but he could feel the depth of her emotion behind it as she lingered for an extra second. As soon as he put his hand on her waist to pull her closer, she cut him off. Ended the kiss. Looking into his eyes, she said, "Unfortunately, I love you, and that changes everything."

She pulled away, picked up her wallet, which had slid to the floor, opened the door, and sent him a sad smile before climbing out and walking away.

He watched her, a painful wad of emotions jamming up his throat, as she got in her car, started it up, and, without another look in his direction, drove away.

CHAPTER TWENTY-NINE

*I*n all the years of upheaval and moving around and roommates, it seemed the one thing Mackenzie had rarely been was alone. It was taking some getting used to in her apartment, and it would take even more adjustment in her home. Her two-story, three-bedroom home.

Her home.

"I'm moving to Muller Street," she said to herself with a partial smile as she maneuvered into a parallel parking spot on Hale, on the other side of the street from Sierra's apartment, right in front of the recording studio.

The joy at receiving the call from Calvin a couple of hours ago was tempered by the heaviness that still sat like a lead weight in her self-inflicted broken heart, but she was determined to stifle the sadness and savor her news. Thank God for Sierra's insistence that they celebrate.

Mackenzie made a solemn promise to herself, as she killed the engine, to leave the Drake-related sadness in the car. She climbed out, determined to enjoy the night.

It was Wednesday evening, a little after seven o'clock, and though the retail businesses on Hale seemed to be closed, the street was alive with activity. Between Frank's Diner and Clayborne's and the restaurant within the Wentworth, the air was filled with tempting food aromas, and she thought she even caught a whiff of sweet baked goods from Sugar Babies. There were quite a few people about, coming and going and window-shopping. Lights were on in the studio, shining out onto the brick sidewalk in front, and Mackenzie glanced in, wondering which musicians were working and whether she'd recognize them if she saw them. They were apparently tucked inside the recording rooms though, out of sight.

Next door, Henry Interiors caught her eye, even though it was obviously not open, the display windows dimly lit and showcasing a rustic farm table made of three wide planks of dark-stained wood. It was beautiful and unique, and the place settings of simple white and blue coordinated with a sprawling spring floral centerpiece of white and green with a few blue-violet blooms as accents.

She needed a dining table. Most of the places she'd lived in the past few years had had breakfast bars and stools and little to no room for a full table, but now she had a dining room to fill. Walking closer to the door, she noted the store's hours and promised herself she'd come back. She shoved down the thought that she'd either be eating at that table alone or standing at the kitchen counter.

After a cursory glance at the other display window of Henry Interiors, she darted across the street toward the spa, following Sierra's directions to get to her second-floor apartment at the end. Once she'd knocked, she put a smile on her face and didn't have to fake it much, because this was exactly what she needed. Girl time, even if she didn't yet know Hayden, Sierra's friend who was joining them.

The door opened, and Sierra welcomed her in with a warm hug. "Hello. Congratulations! I cannot believe you found something so fast."

"Thank you. One day of searching! I figured it would take me a month to find a house," Mackenzie said, her melancholy taking a backseat to gratitude and affection even as she forced down the thought that what had brought this friendship about —the North family—was now less a part of her life. The important thing was, her ties to Drake had introduced her to Sierra, who was fast becoming one of her closest friends in Nashville. "And you guys found one too. Calvin's having a very good week."

"God's truth," Sierra said. "He's more than earned his money with me." She laughed. She'd texted Mackenzie last night when the offer she and Cole had put on a fully renovated ninety-two-year-old farmhouse-style home had been accepted.

"Come meet Hayden," Sierra said, gesturing to the kitchen, which was open to the entry and living area.

At the kitchen island stood a cute brunette with a warm smile and a bottle of wine in her hand. She was dressed in cream-colored pants, a classy leopard-print blouse, a black jacket, and bare feet. Mackenzie could tell in an instant she was going to like her.

"It's nice to meet you, Mackenzie," Hayden said. "We've got a Shiraz open. Can I pour you a glass?"

"Absolutely," Mackenzie said, walking toward her. "Good to meet you. Thanks for letting me crash your evening."

"You're not crashing at all," Hayden said as she filled another glass and held it out. "I just got done with work across the street and didn't think I could make it all the way home without a glass of wine."

"Or a couple of bottles," Sierra said as she made her way to the counter, where a carryout bag sat. "I just picked up pretzel bites, fried mushrooms, mozzarella sticks, and fries from Clayborne's. Hope you girls are feeling snackish." She unloaded multiple takeout boxes and took down three appetizer-sized plates.

"Health food at its finest," Hayden said, which of course made Mackenzie think of Drake. Stupid man and his stupid health fetish. He would wholeheartedly disapprove of Sierra's offerings, and Mackenzie was going to savor every drop of greasy goodness. "Bring it on. Where's Cole tonight?"

"He and Gabe are installing their mom's new appliances. Her refrigerator stopped working and she decided to go with a new top-of-the-line one in black. Everything else is stainless and ten years old, so the guys convinced her to upgrade everything."

"Good for her," Mackenzie said, setting her glass on the counter in hopes of avoiding a spill.

"Cracks me up that she probably spent a small fortune on appliances but didn't spring for the store to install them." Hayden opened a drawer and took out serving spoons, obviously at home here.

"Are you kidding me?" Sierra said. "Cole wouldn't allow it. He said half the time those guys don't know what they're doing anyway, and he's right. So he's taking care of his mama." Her affection for him oozed through her tone and her smile.

"You've got yourself a good guy. What can I do to help?" Mackenzie asked, sidling up next to Sierra at the counter. As Sierra opened the boxes, steam came off the fresh-looking bar food.

"Sit yourself down and tell us all about your new home," Sierra said.

Mackenzie's stomach growled, and she realized she hadn't eaten since an early lunch. "I'd love to," she said to Sierra.

She and Hayden went around to the stool side of the island and settled in.

"Ahh. I've been waiting hours to get off my feet," Hayden said.

"Do you work in retail?" Mackenzie asked, guessing from the aching feet and the *across the street* comment.

Hayden nodded as she swallowed a sip of wine and set her glass on the granite counter. "At Henry Interiors."

"Oh!" Mackenzie said, perking up.

"What Hayden doesn't mention is that she *owns* Henry Interiors and is a designer," Sierra said. "A very good one."

"*Oh,*" Mackenzie said again. "That's awesome. The store looks amazing from the window. I just fell in love with the farm table on my way here."

"The one in the window?" Hayden said, her eyes sparkling. "Isn't it gorgeous?"

"It's beautiful, and so is the way you set it up. Is it bunches and bunches of dollars? Because I might need it."

Hayden laughed. "I like this girl so much," she said to Sierra.

"I have pieces in the bunches-and-bunches range, but that isn't one of them. I found it in an estate sale in not-so-great condition and refinished it myself."

"You did that?" Mackenzie asked.

"She has a serious knack," Sierra said as she slid three plates of fried goodness onto the island and then set out various bowls of condiments and sauces.

"All it needed was some TLC," Hayden said modestly. "Anyway, come in sometime and you can see it up close. And if I drink wine with you in an intimate setting, you're automatically qualified for the girlfriend discount."

"I for sure will," Mackenzie said, lifting her glass. "To drinking wine in an intimate setting…and girlfriends."

Hayden and Sierra made sounds of agreement and clinked their glasses to hers.

"So tell us all about it," Sierra said, coming around to their side. She scooted one of the four stools around the corner and sat at a right angle to them. "Isn't Calvin amazing? How many houses did you go through to find the one?"

"Calvin is a godsend. He took me through nine houses on Friday. It was the third one we saw that I fell in love with. I knew the second I walked in the door," Mackenzie said. "It *felt* right, even before I saw everything, if that makes any sense at all."

"I get it," Sierra said. "My crew thinks I'm crazy, but I believe buildings have a soul. It's something you sense rather than see, and if a house doesn't feel right, you're not going to be happy there."

"To heck with what your crew thinks," Hayden said affectionately. "You gotta do you."

"I do me better than anyone else." Sierra laughed. "So what's the house like?"

Mackenzie described it in minute detail, thanks to their genuine enthusiasm and interest, and lost herself in the excitement the milestone called for.

"It sounds perfect for you," Sierra said. "I assume Drake went through it with you?"

"Ahh…um, no," Mackenzie said, and her surface happiness

drained away, as if someone had released the stopper from a bathtub. Because she hadn't told Sierra, hadn't told anyone about her short, intense, and now *over* adventures with Drake, not since he'd showed up in Jiva. She hadn't had a chance until now. It wasn't something you discussed over text.

She'd apparently not shoved that ball of sadness down nearly deep enough, because just the mention of his name had her throat closing up.

"Oh, hon." Sierra clutched Mackenzie's wrist intuitively, her smile disappearing. "You guys... He went on your trip with you, didn't he? I just thought..."

"Yeah," Mackenzie managed before her breath was stolen by a wave of emotion.

"Who is Drake?" Hayden asked. "Cole's Drake? And do I need to hunt him down with a baseball bat?"

There was so much feeling in Hayden's voice, so much support and sisterhood in that one sentence that tears instantly welled in Mackenzie's eyes.

"I have a Louisville Slugger by my bed," Hayden continued, and that did it. Mackenzie laughed at the same time the tears poured over the rims of her eyes.

"Oh, hon," Sierra said again and put her arm around Mackenzie. "The sad thing is, Hayden means it." She shook her head as if Hayden was beyond help. "Yes, Cole's Drake. You have to get over your man anger."

"No anger. Just being supportive," Hayden said with a half grin. "Want to talk about it?" she asked Mackenzie.

Mackenzie covered her face with both hands, a little embarrassed to bawl like a baby in front of this girl she'd just met. But when Hayden moved her stool closer and leaned up against Mackenzie's other side, she felt these women's support with every fiber of her being and knew it was okay. They weren't going to judge her.

Sucking in a deep, shaky breath, Mackenzie nodded and launched into a summary of her time with Drake, starting back on the night she'd flown into Nashville, for Hayden's sake. Sierra added in parts she knew, and when Mackenzie told them how

Drake had shown up unexpectedly at the romantic resort on the island of Jiva, both of them gasped.

"I had no idea it wasn't planned and he wasn't invited by you," Sierra said.

"Oh, my God," Hayden said. "That's…" She shook her head. "Even considering that the money factor was not blink worthy for a North brother, that is incredible. I thought Drake was the one who rarely goes out with a girl more than once."

"None of them really do relationships, from what I understand," Sierra said, "but yeah, Drake goes out all the time but rarely with the same person twice. Until now, apparently." She raised her brows with a knowing look at Mackenzie.

"For a guy like that to travel all the way to the other side of the world to surprise you?" Hayden shook her head. "That's quite a statement."

Mackenzie gaped at Hayden, because it was true, and hearing it from someone else somehow made it sink in.

"Whatever happened between you two," Sierra said, "because I sense there's not a happy ending to this story, there isn't a doubt in my mind that he cares deeply about you."

Mackenzie swallowed, the tears not slowing at all.

Hayden spooned several fried mushrooms onto her plate. "He put himself out there. It was a grand, romantic-as-hell gesture. How were you supposed to *not* fall for that boy? I've met him. I know what he looks like," she added.

Mackenzie laughed through the tears again and then said, mournfully, "He's so damn good-looking."

"Damn him," Hayden agreed.

"So your trip once he got there…was it good?" Sierra picked at a fry from her plate, dragging it through the excess salt before sticking it in her mouth.

"So good." Mackenzie told them about their final day and the customized tour of the islands.

"Wow. I did *not* know he had that in him," Sierra said quietly. "You didn't stand a chance, did you?"

These girls… Mackenzie didn't know them well yet, but she knew she would, because they so got it. She felt a strong bond developing already and was so glad she'd texted Sierra her house news first, even before Ezra and her boss and friend, Cora.

"Our agreement to spend time together was just for the duration of our trip," Mackenzie told them, her voice sounding thick and off. "And then he showed up at my apartment last Saturday night to celebrate his new job."

Sierra explained the job details to Hayden and said, "Thank God he was smart enough to take it. You know…that was a big, giant step for Drake."

"Taking a job with his family's business?" Hayden asked.

Both Sierra and Mackenzie nodded.

"He's never committed to a career-type job," Sierra said. "He's the baby of the family, and Cole says it's been a long time coming for Drake to take some steps toward growing up."

"Heading up a brand-new division of a big company seems like a pretty big leap," Hayden said. "Good for him."

As Sierra told Hayden more about Drake's history of splitting his time between various part-time gigs, Mackenzie stopped hearing her as her mind spun.

They were both so right with their observations—Hayden's that it was a big step for Drake to fly around the world to spend time with Mackenzie and Sierra's that taking that job was monumental. Mackenzie knew all too well how monumental—probably better than anyone else did, because Drake had confided in her.

Crap. She stared at her half-empty plate without really seeing it as a bad feeling took hold in her chest.

Drake had dropped everything and surprised her in Jiva. He'd planned and executed an unforgettable day tailored perfectly for Mackenzie. He'd opened up to her about his deepest issues regarding loss and fear and how they had affected him so profoundly. Then he'd taken the big step of accepting Mason's job offer.

And she had walked away from him because she "knew" what kind of person he was and that he wasn't going to try any kind of relationship with her. Scratch that. She hadn't walked away. She'd run away scared.

What had she done?

"So you two aren't together anymore?" Hayden asked and then took a bite of a gooey mozzarella stick.

Mackenzie's eyes fluttered closed and she sucked in a shaky breath, then dove into a play-by-play of the scene in his Porsche last Friday.

"I think…" Mackenzie's voice gave out, and she sniffled deeply, then forced out the rest of her thought. "What if I made a mistake?"

"Ooh." Hayden wrapped an arm around Mackenzie and pulled her close, then added her other arm in a full-fledged hug.

Sierra scooted closer and added a gentle hand to Mackenzie's back. "There's no right or wrong in this," she said, "but you can always change your mind."

Mackenzie cried harder at that, ducking her face into Hayden's hair, because she could change her mind till pigs flew, but that didn't mean Drake would ever give her a long-term chance. She'd done nothing but turn him away and decide *for* him that he couldn't be what she wanted. The worst part about it? She wasn't looking for him to propose or anything like that. That would be super fast and sort of crazy, and she wouldn't even expect that from a non-commitment-phobic guy. All she really wanted from Drake was the chance for something deeper to develop.

After another big inhale, she sat up straighter, nodding. "I think I want to talk to him. See if he wants to… I don't know. Not break up but not get married. Something in the middle." She laughed and wiped her eyes.

"That sounds fair," Sierra said, smiling.

"What if he says no?"

"Then he's an idiot," Hayden said, "and the bat offer still stands."

Mackenzie's next big inhale was steadier as she thought it through. "I'm leaving for LA at the butt crack of dawn tomorrow. I've got meetings for the next two days, then an event Saturday evening. I'll give myself the trip to think about everything and figure out what to say to him."

"That sounds like a wise plan," Sierra said. "You're upset and full of emotions tonight. It never hurts to sleep on things. Or so I've been told."

"Says the most impulsive woman in the world," Hayden said, laughing. "I'm a big fan of planning. When will you be home from your trip?"

"Sunday afternoon," Mackenzie said, her mind whirling over her plans and whether she should alter them to talk to Drake.

"You can talk to him Sunday then," Hayden said authoritatively, and Mackenzie nodded, suddenly so tired.

"Thank you. Both of you," Mackenzie said. "For letting me cry on you and snot in front of you and generally break down. I wasn't going to do that."

"Sometimes you've got to break down before you can build yourself back up again," Sierra said.

Hayden nodded and added, "We're here for you, no matter what happens with Drake."

With an indelicate sniff, Mackenzie nodded and breathed and said, "Yeah. You girls are the best. And we should get back to the celebration that I totally derailed."

"Let's blame Drake," Hayden said with a devilish grin.

They all laughed, and even though Mackenzie's future was up in the air and she felt almost as much unsureness as she used to the night before her mom moved them to a new apartment, new suburb, new neighborhood, she swallowed it down and reached across the counter for the wine bottle to top off all three of their glasses. For the rest of the evening, she was going to try to lay her doubts aside and revel in the fact that, in one month, she would be living in her very own home.

And she knew, she felt it in her heart that if it didn't go well with Drake on Sunday, these two would be there for her, with wine, junk food, a bat, and plenty of hugs.

CHAPTER THIRTY

There was nothing springlike or gentle about the rain coming down. The Saturday-morning spring "shower" was closer to biblical proportions, cold, and miserable.

As Drake sat on the screened-in porch of the house Cole and Sierra were buying, he stared out at the rotten weather, feeling the gloom in his soul.

Cole had brought him along to take some measurements and get some other info for the minor repairs and projects he planned to do before they moved in. He'd also been excited to show Drake the house, excited in a way Drake would never have guessed his brother would be—at least not until he'd met Sierra.

Funny how the right woman could change things.

The house was nice. Better than nice, really. It'd be a great home for Cole and Sierra and a few rug rats. It was no surprise that Sierra had pushed for a farmhouse-style home that was close to a century old, recently restored—and restored *right*, according to both of them—so she and Cole wouldn't have to do the major work themselves, and set on a two-acre wooded lot that was at the edge of the city limits. Actually, it fit Cole too, and Drake didn't figure Sierra had had to push much at all. Those two seemed in tune with each other on a lot of things.

As well as it fit his brother and his wife-to-be, the house probably wouldn't be Drake's first choice for himself, but to each his own.

It was weird to even think about houses, but think about them he had been, maybe because both Mackenzie and Cole were in the buying process. Or maybe because he was tired and the thought of moving into another apartment in a few weeks as he'd always planned wore him out.

Of course, he didn't have to move. He could sign another lease, stay put for another year or two. He'd never put too much thought into a place regarding the long-term though, knowing he would only spend a year or two there before he found something new and different. Though he lived in a luxury apartment, there were some elements he didn't love.

He was starting to think maybe it wouldn't be so bad to buy a house. Financially, of course, it would be smarter, but he'd never worried too much about that, more concerned about his lifestyle.

It seemed his lifestyle was changing.

After Mackenzie had walked out of his life a week and a day ago, Drake had sat there in his car, a little stunned, a lot crushed like a bug. And then he'd raced off and reverted to his old ways, stopping at his apartment to change out of his suit and then hitting the bars. It hadn't taken him long to catch up with some people he knew—even though he hadn't been out and about much in weeks, his bar friends were creatures of habit and hadn't altered their routines.

He, on the other hand… Nothing was the same with him or in him.

He'd spent the rest of Friday night and early Saturday morning fighting that fact to an extreme. First, he'd only lasted till ten p.m. at the bars, the people and the scene wearing on him quickly. Second, he'd gone home and curled up with a bottle of scotch, thinking that was the only way to get Mackenzie out of his mind.

Although he was a social guy who had always loved parties and nights out, he'd never been a heavy drinker. Knew too well what that shit did to the body in large quantities. But that had slipped his mind Friday night.

He'd woken up on his couch late Saturday morning to only the dregs of the bottle left on the coffee table, an empty pizza delivery box, and a hangover to end all motherfucking hangovers.

As much damage as the bender had done physically—he'd felt like hell for a full thirty-six hours as he tried to detox—it had screwed him up even more mentally. Because he didn't drink to drown his sorrows. He didn't lose his mind and his self-control because of a woman. He didn't let himself be bothered by anything for too long.

The joke was on him, apparently.

More than a little shell-shocked by his reaction to Mackenzie's goodbye, he'd veered to the opposite extreme by Monday morning and thrown himself into work—both the new job and the old one. There was barely a moment between seven a.m. and midnight this past week when he hadn't been working one or the other.

He'd finished out his last four shifts at the gym, hung out for a full hour at the goodbye party they'd thrown him, and fully moved into the office Mason had had emptied for him at NBS. He'd spent hours enmeshed in plans for the new division, hammering out everything from the physical setup of the space to the nuances of the branding. Not only did it allow him to avoid downtime at home, by himself, but he was also genuinely that absorbed in the project itself.

Last night at 9:27 p.m., Gabe had come into Drake's office and told him, in a kind but firm tone, to get the hell out, reminding him he wouldn't be an official employee until Monday morning. He'd said he didn't want Drake burning out before he even started and had gone so far as to ban him from coming into the office this weekend. Mason had backed the fucker up on it.

So here he was, with an entire weekend looming. No shifts at the gym, not allowed into the NBS offices, not in the mood to go out and be social. When Cole had texted him this morning, asking for help at the house, he'd easily said yes. When they'd finished measuring, Cole and his agent, Calvin Broderick, had gotten wrapped up in a conversation, and Drake had excused himself and escaped out here.

The door behind him squeaked open and Cole came out. He sat next to Drake on the rudimentary wood-plank bench the previous owners had left behind.

"Hey," Cole said. "So what do you think of the place?"

Drake dragged his mind back to the house. "It's impressive. It fits you and Sierra. I'm guessing it must have a 'good soul' for her to have fallen in love with it?"

Cole laughed. "You got it." He shook his head, half a goofy grin still on his face. "I never would've pictured myself in something this big and striking, but it feels right."

Striking was a good word for it. Striking in that the historical details were intact, just the way Sierra loved, and it made quite a showpiece while still being homey and livable. There were lots of rooms and lots of space, but to Drake, it felt a little closed off and segmented, the way older houses did. He would choose something more modern, full of openness and light.

"Major upgrade from your dumpy apartment," Drake said.

"My apartment's not dumpy. You've never been inside of it."

"I've seen the outside. That's enough."

"I've remodeled the inside, asshole." Cole let out a half scoff, half laugh. "Not nearly as nice as this place though. Don't know what we're going to do with so much square footage."

"Make some babies, I believe is how it goes," Drake said.

"Never pictured myself doing that either, but now I can't imagine not."

"Sad." Drake was giving him shit. He himself would love to be an uncle and have little nieces and nephews running around who he could rough-house with and tickle and spoil.

Cole ignored his dig and said, "The yard is good for kids. Trees to climb, grass to roll in, space to run."

"Lots of all of it," Drake agreed. He personally would want a little less lawn to mow and more of an intimate entertainment area. Maybe a barbecue area, a couple of tables, loungers, lots of trees…

It hit him like a sledge hammer that the yard he was imagining and the house he'd envisioned with openness and light and a more modern appeal were…Mackenzie's dream home. The one she'd showed him online that was double her budget. The one with the beautiful wood floors throughout the main level, the crisp white trim and gas-log fireplace, the roomy master bedroom, the perfect-for-Mackenzie's-home-office bonus room above the garage. He'd only browsed through it for a few minutes at Mackenzie's kitchen counter, but he'd liked what he'd seen. Apparently a lot.

Clearing his throat, he asked, "Where's the Realtor?"

"He got a call from another client. Took it to his car for privacy. Told us to take our time."

"Are you done with everything you needed to do?"

"Yep."

Neither one of them moved; both just sat there on that uncomfortable bench, watching the low spots in the yard puddle up. Drake's mind was on anything but mud and water though. He was thinking about Cole, his antisocial, formerly grumpy-as-hell brother. Thinking about all the changes he'd made. Wondering if he ever had moments of doubt.

"How hard was it for you to let yourself fall for Sierra?" Drake asked him.

Cole scowled at him as if trying to figure out where that came from. "Falling wasn't hard. Admitting it to myself was."

"Why?"

Another glare. "Because I was an asshole who didn't like people. I'd ask you why so many questions, but Sierra said you fucked it up hard with Mackenzie."

"There was nothing to fuck up," he said, irritation ringing in his voice. Technically, wouldn't he have to have an actual relationship in order to fuck anything up?

Technically.

"That's not what I heard."

Drake hesitated, because he wasn't sure he could handle the answer, but finally, he asked, "What did you hear?"

"Just that Mackenzie came over a few days ago and was nursing a broken heart, direct quote."

He felt the sting of that in his chest, an actual physical sensation. Fucking hell.

A gust of wind came through out of nowhere and blew rain in through the screen, getting both of them wet, but it wasn't enough to pull Drake all the way out of his dark thoughts.

"You ever worry about losing it all? With Sierra, I mean?"

Cole turned to look at him again, at first with a frown, but then he gawked and looked thoughtful. It made Drake antsy, and he fought the urge to jump up and pace or maybe punch his assessing brother.

"No, man. You can't do that. You'll make yourself crazy. It's like worrying that someone's going to get in a car wreck. It could happen any damn day, but if you let yourself think that way, you're going to lose your mind."

A car wreck was something they were all way too familiar with as that's what had taken their dad away from them. Drake had worried, for months afterward, whenever his mom got in a car.

"I'm talking more about something like you screw things up and she leaves you. Or she finds someone she likes better and she leaves you. Or—"

"No," Cole said. "I mean, I did. Before I decided to go all in. I held back because why the hell would a woman like Sierra want to be stuck with me?"

"I've wondered the same damn thing," Drake said, grinning, lightening the tension in the air just a little.

"Jackass." Cole didn't say more on the topic, just left Drake to his thoughts once again, which wasn't a comfortable place.

Drake leaned forward and rested his elbows on his knees, barely registering the wood flooring of the porch. "I've been keeping people at arm's length for years because I didn't want to get too attached. Didn't want to get hurt."

"Nobody wants to get hurt," Cole said. "We Norths seem to be particularly screwed up though."

Because of their dad's death—at least in part. No one had to say it out loud.

"Kind of stupid when you think about it," Drake continued, "because by trying to avoid losing her, I've already lost her."

Cole exhaled a sort-of laugh through his nose. "Kind of true and kind of stupid. Not gonna lie, it's scary as hell to put your whole life into someone else's hands by choice."

"Yeah," Drake said and pushed out a breath full of stress.

"Know what's scarier?"

"What?"

"Thinking about some other guy giving her everything she wants, getting everything she's got to give."

"Shit." Drake's stomach literally turned, and a wave of nausea and panic swept through him.

"Yep."

Drake lifted his head as the rain lightened in intensity, gazed out at the yard. He imagined for a moment…himself…with a fat plastic baseball and a fat plastic bat and a chubby-cheeked little boy standing a few feet away from him as he lobbed the ball in a gentle pitch. Imagined the giggle when the toddler made the bat connect with the ball.

His reverie switched to a little girl with two pigtails sticking out of her head like antlers, her eyes big and brown and irresistible just like…Mackenzie's.

It wasn't this house he imagined, but it didn't matter. It was a home filled with love, with a mini Mackenzie and a mini him and a white fireplace and a rambunctious puppy and… Hell.

He not only wanted that future, he wasn't sure he could survive without it.

"Well," Cole said nonchalantly, "you about ready to head out?"

Still staring at the sopping acreage but seeing a sunny backyard with a play area instead, with his heart suddenly racing, Drake stood. "Yeah. I'm ready."

As they made their way out to Cole's truck, Drake began to formulate a plan as to how he could possibly win over Mackenzie.

CHAPTER THIRTY-ONE

A few hours later, Drake rode the elevator up to the twenty-second floor in Ezra's condo building. Though it was, according to the pilot on his flight, a beautiful spring evening in Houston and a temperate seventy-two degrees, Drake was sweating his balls off.

His entire future depended on the next half hour. Bottom of the ninth, bases loaded, batter up. He had to hit it out of the stands.

For the hundredth time, he checked the Find My Friends app on his phone to make sure Ez was still here, that his own device showed as nearly on top of his friend's. It'd been a joke of sorts when they'd given each other access to their whereabouts, one that came about when Drake was giving Ez shit about never knowing which continent he was on from one night to the next, but thank God they had. He was hoping the element of surprise would work in his favor.

The doors dinged open, Drake muttered a nervous curse to himself, and he exited. The walk to Ezra's unit, where he'd been plenty of times before, was short. And then he stood there facing the door, heart racing, like a goddamn pussy, going over all his talking points in his mind as if it was a presentation for the NBS board.

"Fuck it," he said, and he knocked on the door.

It took a while, but just as he was about to beat on the door again, he heard movement inside, and then the door opened and Ezra stood in front of him, eyes narrowed, brows dipping down.

"What the hell are you doing here?" Ez said, his tone chilled but more confused than outwardly hostile. He wore plaid pajama pants and a plain white T-shirt and his hair was mussed, as if he'd been in bed or something, but Drake didn't ask. Didn't care. He was going to force this conversation regardless.

"Can I come in?"

Their eyes locked for a moment in a stare down, a visual game of chicken to see who would back down first, and then without a verbal reply, Ezra stepped back and let Drake inside.

Drake shut the door behind him, turned around, and found Ez leaning against the wall of the entryway, arms crossed over his chest, waiting.

Ezra's condo was similar in layout to Drake's apartment, but with three bedrooms instead of two and a lot more square footage. To the left of the foyer they were in was the guest room, where Drake had stayed in the past, and Ez's office. The only light in the place besides the one over their heads filtered out from the office, and Drake realized Ez had been working. No surprise there, even though it was nearly nine on a Saturday night.

"You want to do this right here?" Drake said when Ezra made no motion toward the kitchen or living room or even the office.

"Do what, exactly?"

Okay, then. Here it was. "I came to talk to you about Mackenzie."

"Is she okay?" Ez said, alarmed.

"She's fine, as far as I know." He didn't mention he hadn't spoken to her or seen her for over a week.

Ezra dropped his arms to his sides and turned and walked down the short hall toward the kitchen. Drake followed and stepped into the kitchen area, delineated by tile floor instead of hardwood, and leaned his left shoulder against the pantry while Ezra continued to the fridge.

"Beer?" Ez said as he opened the door and took one out.

"Sure."

Just like old times. Friendly and all. Not.

Ezra opened a second bottle and handed it over. He leaned against the oven, facing out over the sink and the breakfast bar and into the darkened living area. Taking a swig of beer, he waited without looking at Drake, his intent to not make this easy clear as fucking day.

So Drake straightened away from the pantry and dove into the deep end.

"I love your sister." He blew out some extra air. That was the first time he'd said the words out loud—to anyone. Mackenzie should've been first, but he'd screwed the situation up enough that this was how it was.

He waited for Ezra's response—a swear word, a punch, a scowl. What Ez did was the last thing he expected.

Ez let out an amused half laugh, half scoff. "I was wondering when you were going to figure that out."

Drake was the one who scowled. "What do you mean?" He himself had only figured it out in the past few hours, after leaving Cole's new house.

Ezra took his time answering, raising his bottle for another swallow, expelling a slow breath before he spoke. "I knew as soon as I found out you followed her to some obscure island on the other side of the globe."

"How could you know that? I didn't even know."

"I'm not as dense as you, I guess," Ez said smugly.

Drake ignored the barb and understood, belatedly, Ezra's point. He'd known at the time it was unheard of for him to do that, but he hadn't equated it to *love*. If he was honest with himself, he couldn't have handled that truth at that time.

"Question is," Ezra said, "what are you going to do about it? When I talked to her on Thursday, she said you two were through for good."

"I'm hoping to convince her we're not."

"How are you going to do that? Seems to me, in the month and a half since she moved to Nashville, you two have been on and off more times than a cheerleader's uniform."

With a curt laugh, Drake said, "Like you said, I'm a little dense. I know I haven't been good at handling responsibility. I've sucked at commitment. I'm making some changes."

"Such as?"

"You're looking at the new director of the Home Fitness Division of North Brothers Sports."

Ezra's brows rose toward his hairline. "You committed to a full-time job?"

"Got the new custom-suit wardrobe to prove it."

Ezra studied him with narrowed eyes for several seconds. "You've told Mason?"

Drake laughed. "Two weeks ago. Official start date is Monday but I've been deeply enmeshed for the past week and a half. Done deal."

Ezra continued to stare at him as if he was still absorbing such a shock.

"Here's the thing," Drake said, setting his beer down on the counter but not removing his hand from it. "We've been friends since middle school. You know me better than just about anyone. You, Zane, and I were inseparable back then, and when our dad died, you were there, not acting weird about it, not making us talk about it, but you were there."

Ezra nodded once in acknowledgment.

"You were there again when Zane blindsided me with his decision to go the military route instead of with you and me to Memphis. You've seen me at my worst and you've seen me at my best, and the one thing you better fucking know about me is that, while I don't commit to much, *if and when I do,* I follow through. I'm ready to commit one hundred percent to your sister. And I'd prefer to do it with your blessing."

"Does Mackenzie know you're here?"

"Mackenzie doesn't know any of this yet, except that I took the job. As you mentioned, I'm a little slow, and it took losing her to realize I don't want to be without her. When I tell her, I'm going to have a ring."

"Holy shit." Ezra set his bottle down and straightened. Took a step closer to Drake, scrutinizing him hard, head cocked slightly.

"I wasn't sure I'd ever see the day." He extended his hand as if to shake. "Congratulations, man."

Drake looked into his friend's eyes, seeing nothing but sincerity, then glanced down at his offered hand and finally took it.

As they shook, Ezra said, "Screw that," and pulled him into a man hug with enough back pounding to avoid awkwardness. "Welcome to the family, Drake."

Drake stepped back, his mind more than a little blown, and said, "Really?"

Ezra let out a genuine laugh and said, "Hell yes. As long as you're getting your shit straight, there's nothing that could make me happier than you and Mackenzie being together."

"Well, then Merry fucking Christmas, a few months early," Drake said, laughing. "Have to admit I was sweating hard. Your jab hurts like a son of a bitch."

"North boys always were a bunch of wusses."

"You wish."

"One more thing," Ezra said, sobering up. "If you ever hurt my sister again, I swear to God I'll do more than a single punch."

"I know that. I'm smarter than I look." He looked his friend in the eye, stood straighter. "I love her. I want to spend my days making her happy if she'll have me. That, of course, remains to be seen."

With a grin, Ezra said, "That's your problem. God knows that girl doesn't listen to me."

"She knows what she wants, doesn't she? I just hope she hasn't given up on me."

"I guess we'll see. You going to stay here tonight or what?"

Drake shrugged. He'd left his bag down with the guy at the lobby desk, not knowing what was going to happen. "I'll fly back tomorrow. Don't have a ticket yet. This whole trip was spur-of-the-moment."

"The North Suite has clean sheets."

"My lucky day," Drake said, smiling. "If it's not too late for you, Grandpa Ezra, put some clothes on and I'll take you out for a drink."

"Only if it's top-shelf." Ezra started toward the master

bedroom but stopped as he hit the hallway and turned back. "If you want, before you leave tomorrow, we can hit the jewelry store. If you want some moral support."

"Damn straight I do."

As Ezra went into his bedroom and closed the door, Drake leaned his back against the pantry and breathed fully for the first time in several hours.

Step one, done. Only thing left was to get Mackenzie on board.

CHAPTER THIRTY-TWO

*S*unday was not going according to plan at all for Mackenzie.

Both legs of her flight home from LA had been delayed. She'd hoped to do a little follow-up work from the party last night—where she'd gotten two new leads—on the plane, but somehow her laptop had not charged overnight and it was down for the count. And now, there was a wreck on the interstate in Nashville, the one she was on, trying to get to Drake's. Traffic was down to one lane and barely moving, but moving enough she couldn't search for an early exit and an alternate route on her navigation system.

With a glance in the visor mirror at herself, she verified that she really should head to her own place and freshen up before she went to plead her case to Drake, but that wasn't going to happen. She'd been waiting too long to be able to talk to him, had too much time to think about what she would say and how she would persuade him to give them a chance at a pace that wouldn't scare him away.

He was going to get the travel-grungy, day-after-a-Holly-wood-party, jet-lagged-once-again version of Mackenzie and either like that version enough to hear her out and say yes or...not.

She didn't want to think about if it was a *not*.

By the time she hit her exit, she was pretty sure she'd aged significantly and had let in all kinds of new doubts about what she was going to say to Drake.

What if he wasn't home? She hadn't texted, hadn't wanted to give him any kind of heads-up, because she wasn't sure he'd want to see her.

Or worse, what if he had company? What if he'd already moved on and had gone out last night and met an irresistible floozy and they'd spent the day in bed and he was only just getting ready to kick her out at—she glanced at the dashboard clock—5:29 p.m.?

"He'd kick her out before noon," she said, shaking her head at herself, not feeling at all reassured by the truth of that statement.

By the time she pulled into a visitor's space at his building, her nerves were rioting. She pulled her brush out of her glove compartment and ran it through her hair, checked for any mascara smudges under her eyes and found none, and glossed her lips with a barely there light pink. "Good as it's going to get," she told her reflection.

Without letting herself think any more, she launched out of the car and hurried inside. Before she could freak out further, she was at Drake's door.

She knocked and waited and fretted and went over the first thing she was going to say yet again, and then she realized it was taking too long for him to answer. There were no sounds from behind his door, but she knocked again anyway, thinking maybe he was asleep, knowing he didn't take naps or slow down enough to sleep during the day.

After the third knock, as she was strongly considering parking her tired butt on the carpeted hallway floor and waiting, she heard the ding of the elevator around the corner and could tell someone got out. Before she could decide what to do next, Drake came around the corner, saw her, and smiled.

At her.

That beautiful, charming, so familiar smile that she never

wanted to be without. Behind it, she saw a moment of surprise on his part.

"There's nothing like coming home to find a beautiful girl at my door. Even if she did dump me and break my heart."

"I didn't dump you," she said, frowning. "You can't officially dump someone if you're not officially together."

He stopped right in front of her, close, close enough she caught a hint of his scent, and peered into her eyes, assessing. "What are you doing here, Mackenzie?"

"I need to talk to you."

She expected him to make a joke about the dreaded T word, but he merely unlocked his door and let her precede him inside.

With her nerves stretched taut, she headed toward the kitchen, only giving the guest room, where they'd first been together, a passing glance, not wanting to think about how that night had ended. She knew Ezra still wasn't on board with her and Drake being a couple, but she couldn't let that bother her now. They could cross that bridge if and when they got to it.

Drake came in behind her, flipping the kitchen lights on. "Drink?"

Mackenzie shook her head.

"Let's sit." He went into the living room and lowered himself to one end of the couch, sitting on the edge, not relaxing, and it was the first sign she'd seen that he wasn't totally at ease.

She followed him and chose to sit on the chair adjacent to the couch. Close but where she could face him. She swallowed hard as he waited expectantly.

"Is everything okay?" he asked.

"Yeah. I mean, yes and no. I've been thinking a lot this past week, ever since the Friday when I found my house. I... I screwed up, Drake." She let out a self-conscious, nervous laugh sort of thing and was pretty sure she sounded like an idiot. "I said I couldn't be with you because you aren't a commitment kind of guy, but that wasn't fair."

There was the slightest twitch of his brows, and she wasn't sure how to interpret that, so she barreled on. "I like being with you."

Which was an understatement, but she was trying to keep *love* out of this for now. Because she didn't think that was necessarily a selling point. "Jiva with you was magical, and sure, that place would be pretty incredible even if I was by myself, but the Drake factor made it extra and exponential, whether we were hanging out together while I worked or hiking to a waterfall or sitting on the beach."

"The Drake factor," he repeated, obviously pleased and letting the phrase go to his head.

"Stop it," she said, trying not to grin, just wanting to get everything out. "I liked being with you even before the night we first slept together, when I was staying with you."

Drake sat back on the couch and seemed to relax, which was the opposite of what she'd expected.

"My point is, I think I jumped the gun. Because I miss you," she said.

"Yeah?" His expression turned downright cocky, and annoyance jabbed at her. She was trying to pour her heart out to him and he was almost…smug?

"Can you try not to let it inflate your ego for a minute?"

He schooled his expression to something more serious and said, "Sorry. Go on."

She let out a breath, her irritation fading. "I understand why you have issues with committing. After everything you told me that night on the beach, I get it on an intellectual level. It's just that, when it came to an emotional level and *my* emotions were involved, I was seeing it as black and white. Commit to me or get lost. And that was wrong." Regret and fear and hope and all the emotions got globbed up in her throat and had her stopping to suck in a deep, steadying breath. "Because even if you can't promise me more than right now, I want that. I want to be with you. We can do no strings for as long as you want, if you want, and we can see if we might have a future together eventually."

His eyes took on a sort of gleam, and she didn't want to say it was mischievous, but…yeah. It was. Which was standard flirty Drake, she supposed, and part of why she loved him. And she wanted to tell him that, was bursting with the words and the emotions, but she held back, because she didn't want to scare him away.

"So what you're saying is you'll wait for me to get my head unfucked?" he said, one corner of his lips twitching upward in a self-deprecating grin.

"Well…" She smiled back at him, because he was irresistible, damn him. "That sounds like pressure. Waiting for you. But yeah, I guess what I'm saying is if you aren't up for committing right now, that's fine. I just want to spend time together and see where it goes."

He just sat there, staring at her, with a strange, pensive half grin, and Mackenzie started to get a little concerned. Was he going to tell her she'd blown it and he'd moved on and he was fine without her?

The tension inside her crept up when she'd thought it couldn't go any higher. She moved even closer to the edge of the chair, on the verge of jumping up just to expend some nervous energy. "Just say it, Drake."

"Say what?"

"Whatever's putting that look on your face."

"What look is on my face?" he said, again going serious.

"I don't know…smug or amused or—"

"Relieved as fuck? Happy? Surprised at my luck?"

Still studying his face, Mackenzie scooted back in the chair, feeling lighter but still not sure she understood. It sounded like a good sign. "You're going to have to elaborate on that."

———

Drake was nothing if not spontaneous.

He slid to the edge of the couch again and reached for Mackenzie's hand, his insides humming with so much relief and love and, well, downright terror.

Here I go, he thought. *Into the deep end.* As he took in her pretty, familiar features, her chocolate-brown eyes that were deep and assessing and sparkling with both confusion and hope, he held back from kissing her the way he wanted to and instead dove in with a full-hearted, love-filled cannonball.

If you were going to do it, might as well do it with fanfare.

He held on to her hand with his left one as he went to the floor in front of her, kneeling on both knees, his abdomen bushing against her legs.

"Mackenzie," he said, and his voice came out gravelly. He swallowed and grabbed on to the courage he needed. "You're right. I have issues. I'm one screwed-up guy. I've never claimed any differently, and I was always fine with that…until you. You came along and penetrated my thick, selfish skull and my deep-buried, wussy heart."

She let out a quiet laugh, the sound warming said heart, and she said, "It's a good heart."

"Good but chickenshit." He flashed her a sheepish smile. "But hopefully it's not too late to change my ways. I'm working on it."

"I know." She grasped his hand that was still holding on to her other one and squeezed. "I know how big of a thing it was to take that job."

He nodded, her words sending another wave of emotion through him that had him clearing his throat so he could say more. "Yesterday I went to Cole and Sierra's new house, and though I think it's been building for some time, everything just hit me like an aluminum bat to the head. I've been miserable without you the past week and a half. I think about you all the time, miss being with you, miss waking up next to you… I miss hearing about your latest work details and watching you negotiate on a client's behalf on the phone like a badass and arguing with you about your penchant for junk food. Something happens to me during the day, and it's you I want to share it with. Something shakes my confidence while I'm at work, and it's your encouragement I long for. You make me want to be a better man. You make me want things I've never wanted before. You make me want a future, a stable—to use your word—*settled* future, with a full-time job, a full-time house, and a full-time partner who will help me handle all the hiccups that life will inevitably throw at us."

Her eyes were wide and filled with moisture, and Drake couldn't be sure, but he thought his were watering too. He plowed on anyway. "I flew to Houston yesterday to make peace with your brother."

"You went to see Ez?"

"Do you have other brothers I don't know about?"

"If I do, I don't know about them either."

"I love you, Mackenzie, and I told him that."

She inhaled on a sniffle and pressed her lips together, staring into his eyes. "What did he say?"

"Something like, my best friend and my sister, I can't think of anything I'd want more, but if you ever hurt her, I'll string you up by your balls. Paraphrasing there."

She sniffled loudly as she smiled.

"I want all of that stuff and more with you," he continued. "The house, the jobs, the weekends and nights and every other spare minute together, the partnership. Someday, the kids and the dog and the yard. I'm a work in progress, but…" He shifted so that he was on one knee and the other was bent in front of him as he rustled through the pocket of his athletic pants and grasped the little box. He let go of her hand long enough to fumble with the box and open it, then took her hand again as he held up the box, where the ring was nestled in velvet. He gazed into her eyes as they veered down to the ring. "Will you marry me, Mackenzie?"

She squeezed his hand as her mouth fell open and her eyes got even bigger. And she laughed or cried or both at once, letting a bunch of pent-up something out, staring at him for another never-ending, excruciating few seconds as he began to wonder if he'd dived in too soon.

He lifted his brows in question, and she lurched forward and threw her arms around his neck and laugh-cried and said, "Yes. To all of it. Yes."

He laughed too and managed to stand without untangling their bodies, letting the ring and the box fall to the chair. He picked her up, her legs swinging around his middle, and he spun her around, holding her close, trying to convey that he would never let her go.

Intoxicated with happiness, he spun until he started to get dizzy, and then he took her to the couch and collapsed down on it with her straddling his lap. "So I did a thing," he said.

"It sounds like you did a lot of things."

He laughed again. "That's true. But today when I got home from Houston, I called the Realtor of that home you said was your dream home."

"The one that's double my budget?" she asked.

"That's the one. On Cranberry Street. Hear me out," he said in a rush, not wanting to say this wrong or ruin anything for her. "I know your offer was accepted on the one you found, and I would be perfectly happy to make that our home if you want."

"You haven't even seen it."

"I don't need to. I would live in a barn or an igloo with you if that's what you wanted."

"I don't."

He laughed. "I thought that was a safe bet." Sobering, he said, "I don't want to buy you a house, Mackenzie. I know how you feel about being in control of that, and I understand why and I respect it. But I wanted to throw out a second option to you."

Her fingers were playing with his hair as she studied him, eagerly waiting for him to go on.

"The house on Cranberry is incredible. I think you would love it. I love it. So while I meant what I said about being absolutely willing to move to the house you already found once we're married, I'm wondering if you'd like to go through the one on Cranberry and see what you think. Because if you wanted, *we* could buy it together."

"The bonus room above the garage is good?" she asked.

"You'd have room for a big, badass, girly desk and a couch and a worktable and whatever else you wanted to put in the Nashville To the Stars office."

"Is the backyard as nice as it looks in the pictures?"

"Even better. It's full of spring blooms right now and has

room for a swimming pool and a barbecue area and still would allow for a good game of catch. If we were ever to have kids."

"Do you want kids?" she asked, running her finger over his jawline now.

"I love kids. Though I'm not quite ready yet, I definitely want kids with you. If you want them."

"Someday. Yes." With her eyes big and sparkling, she nodded.

"So what do you say? Do you want to look at the house to see what you think?"

"Maybe," she said, drawing the word out. "But first, I want my ring."

He laughed and stretched his arm to the chair to grab it where it'd fallen. He clutched the box and brought it over and held it out in the scant space between them.

Mackenzie took the ring out with a squeal, held it up and admired it, then extended her hand for him to slide it on. He let out a breath when he saw that it fit perfectly.

"I love it, Drake." As soon as she tore her eyes from the bling on her finger, she leaned in to kiss him, her ringed finger sliding over his cheek and her other hand burrowing into his hair, urging him into her, ensuring he wouldn't pull away. Apparently not understanding that there was zero chance of that.

"Second," she said between kisses, "I want you. Naked. I don't care where. For the rest of the night. The house can wait until tomorrow."

He lifted her with him as he stood, locking their lips together for several more seconds. "I couldn't agree more," he managed in a husky voice as he carried her off to his bedroom.

EPILOGUE

*T*he air in the lofted upper level of Clayborne's vibrated with laughter and good feelings. Glasses and tumblers overflowed with spirits. A long table by the wall brimmed with scrumptious appetizers as well as cupcakes and pastries galore, supplied by Sugar Babies. With Drake by her side and his ring on her finger, Mackenzie was the luckiest girl at Sierra and Cole's engagement party.

"Are you having fun?" Drake asked as they walked away from his mom, Aunt Liz, and Geraldine, who sat with Hunter Clayborne's parents at a table in the corner.

"So much fun," she said honestly. Sierra and Cole were adorably blissful and in love, and it was impossible to see them, be with them without being happy for them.

"See anyone else you'd like to be introduced to?" he asked, his hand possessively at her waist.

Mackenzie glanced around at the people she'd started getting to know in the past few weeks, many of them Sierra's ties who lived or worked on Hale Street—Kennedy and Hunter, who were hosting the party, Sierra's parents, who'd flown in from Arizona,

Sloan and Micah, Gin and Tucker, Asia and Jackson, and a couple dozen more of their closest friends, plus, of course, all the Norths, brothers, cousins, and moms, except for Zane. She realized she knew most of the people present and didn't feel like an outsider. She felt...like she belonged, in a way she hadn't ever before. Sure, she'd had people in LA, a social group she was a part of, who she liked, who accepted her, but this group seemed more cohesive, more intimate, more genuine somehow. It fit her better. She fit it better.

"I'm good," she finally replied, meaning it in every sense.

Ezra was in Toronto, but they'd talked multiple times, and now that Drake had made his commitment to Mackenzie known, her brother was on board, verging on enthusiastic. He'd promised to make a stop in Nashville soon to take them out for a celebratory dinner.

"Hey, pretty girl. Do you need another drink?" Hayden sidled up to Mackenzie on the opposite side from Drake and spoke close to her ear to be heard over the steady roar of the party, holding her own glass of wine in front of her.

"That depends," Mackenzie said, winding her free arm through Hayden's. "Are there party games?"

Hayden laughed and shook her head. "It was one of Sierra's conditions. No games. She and Cole just wanted to bring all their friends together to eat, drink, and celebrate. Low-key."

"I approve. This is perfect."

"So no games at your own party?" Hayden asked with a wicked grin. "Because I know some good ones."

"I can't decide whether to be intrigued or scared."

"Intrigued for sure. Can you imagine watching all these big, tough North brothers on a plastic ring hunt or designing fabric squares for a couple's quilt?"

Mackenzie laughed. "Tempting. I don't know if we're having a party. We haven't talked about it."

"You," Hayden said emphatically, "are having a party. Sierra and I will plan it if no one else is. And I bet Sloan would help."

The dark-haired entertainment manager for Clayborne's was

smiling as she and Micah walked up to them, even though she couldn't have heard what Hayden had just volunteered her for.

"Sloan what?"

Hayden filled her in as Mackenzie greeted Micah.

"Oh, yes, definitely!" Sloan practically bounced on her toes. "We have to celebrate all the good things. I'm in. It's official. You're having a party. It's good to see you both again." She brought Drake into the conversation.

"You too," Drake said. He shook hands with Micah, and the two men started their own conversation as Hayden and Sloan threw out ideas for an engagement party, making Mackenzie laugh again.

"You two are serious," she said, unable to keep in the widest grin ever. She was overwhelmed by their kindness and enthusiasm. With a nudge to Drake's side to include him, she said to the girls, "Would it be improper to have it at our house? If all goes well, Drake and I will close in two weeks. I'm moving in right away. He's not until after the wedding, but it will be ours in every sense of the word, and it seems fitting to have our first get-together in our home be our engagement party. Yes?" She looked up at Drake to get his take.

"Hell yes," he said, then pressed a quick kiss to her lips.

"Screw improper," Hayden said. "If that's what you want, that's what you shall have. I can't wait to see the house."

They'd gone with the "dream" house on Cranberry. It hadn't been a hard decision. Once they'd gone through it together, Mackenzie had jumped on board easily because it felt, well, perfect for them. Like, long-term perfect. Her only regret had been pulling out of the original deal, and she'd lost a chunk of money doing it, but it was too big of a purchase not to go with her heart—and Drake's.

Hayden and Sloan jumped right into planning as Mackenzie listened, her own enthusiasm growing. She couldn't wait to fill Drake in later, afterwards, when they were back at his place alone. He'd returned to his conversation with Micah, and then Gabe, Lexie, and her fiancé, Raleigh, joined them. Mackenzie tried to make eye contact with Lexie to get her to join the girl talk, but Lexie kept her gaze to the floor, and it seemed like she and her soon-to-be husband might be the only two in attendance who weren't in a celebratory mood. Mackenzie made a mental note to pull her aside to see if everything was okay.

A few minutes later, Drake squeezed her hand, and she dragged her attention away from Hayden and Sloan.

"I think it's about time," he said.

"Gift time?" Mackenzie asked.

"Just need to find Mason and Mom."

As she started to skim her gaze over the room, her attention was pulled across the way, to the top of the stairs, where Lexie and Raleigh now stood face-to-face, glaring at each other, and then Raleigh said one last thing, some cutting comment judging by his body language, and took off down the stairs.

"What do you think's going on?" Drake asked, and Mackenzie realized he and Gabe had witnessed Raleigh's exit as well, as they both stared in the same direction. Mason walked up to them then, also glancing toward Lexie, as if trying to figure out what they were gaping at.

"Shit," Gabe said. "He's been an ass all night. He couldn't have made it more obvious he didn't want to be here."

"I didn't think Lexie looked happy," Mackenzie said. As she spoke, Lexie looked in their direction, saw them all staring with expressions varying from confusion to concern.

Lexie did her best to force a grin on her face, but it wasn't convincing. She mouthed the words *Be right back* and darted down the stairs, and before Mackenzie could decide what to do, Gabe swore again.

"I've tried to like that guy, but he makes it impossible. I don't have a good feeling about them at all." Without another word, Gabe headed off after her.

"Gabe to the rescue," Mason said with a hint of a smirk. "Again."

Drake pulled Mackenzie into his side as they seemed to be thinking the same thing—that Lexie's wedding was less than a month away.

"He's not going to go after Raleigh, is he?" Drake asked. "Do we need to follow him?"

Mason shook his head. "He's all about making sure Lexie's okay. Always has been." The last he sort of mumbled, but Mackenzie was close enough to hear.

There was a world of meaning in the statement, one that she'd have to think about later, but just then, Faye, her future mother-in-law, came up to her other side.

"Earl Clayborne rounded us up a mike," Faye said to all of them. "He says we can do this whenever we're ready. I'm ready anytime."

"Are you doing okay, Mom?" Drake asked with enough concern that Mackenzie was fully prepared for the reaction from Faye.

"I'm doing fine, Drake," she replied with conviction and a good dose of built-in scolding. "I've been waiting for weeks for this. Years. Maybe even decades."

"As soon as Gabe comes back, we'll do it," Mason said, taking the helm as Mackenzie had noticed he so often did.

Gabe rejoined them within a couple of minutes, without Lexie, who he said was in the restroom, had insisted he go back to the party, and would be up momentarily.

The five of them made their way to the corner with the microphone, and as Mason tapped it to see if it was on, Sierra and Cole, who were nearby, talking to an older woman named Winona and her significant other, exchanged a confused look and then shot a questioning glance—at the same time—to Mason, who merely grinned.

"Hello," he said into the mike. "May I have your attention?"

When Mackenzie looked again at Sierra, Sierra made eye contact and mouthed, *What's going on?*

Mackenzie merely laughed and shrugged.

"For those who don't know me, I'm Mason, Cole's oldest brother. Thanks for coming out tonight to help us celebrate Cole and his prettier half, Sierra."

There was a round of laughter, cheering, and approval. Cole's loving expression as he looked at Sierra said he definitely agreed.

"I believe, on the invitations, it said this party was no gifts, but we Norths don't always follow the rules, and the six of us—including Zane, our mom, and Mackenzie, who is another soon-to-be North—have a little something for the lovebirds."

Cole frowned in confusion and Sierra tilted her head.

"Why don't you two join me over here so we can embarrass you thoroughly," Mason continued, and the crowd parted to allow the couple of the hour through. As they made their way forward, Mason continued, "As some of you know, Mackenzie runs the Nashville branch of a company called To the Stars, which is a honeymoon planning company. After hearing about the trips Mackenzie plans, and knowing how busy Cole and TV star Sierra are"—Sierra, who now stood beside him, nudged him at that—"my brothers and mom and I decided to go in together and take care of the honeymoon of your dreams, whatever that entails." The last he aimed at Cole and Sierra.

Sierra's mouth gaped open, and she whipped both hands up to cover it, but her wide eyes continued to give away a mix of emotions. Cole had narrowed his eyes at Mason as if he didn't quite believe him and was waiting for the punch line.

"You're serious?" Cole said.

Mason smiled, seeming to enjoy Cole's reaction, and he held up a folder with the printouts of the formal presentation Mackenzie had put together. "It's all here, in black and white… and full color. Your beloved at one point said the word *beach*, and we ran with that. Mackenzie has put together three detailed beach options for you—one in Malta in the Mediterranean, one in Jiva in the South Pacific, and one in the Seychelles off the coast of Africa."

"Oh, my God. Best surprise ever," Sierra said, and Cole threw his head back and laughed in what looked like pure joy.

"I guess the rest of us are off the hook for gifts since there's no way to match that," Hunter called out from the crowd, generating a round of laughs and a light punch in the arm from Kennedy.

"You two deserve it," Winona hollered to Cole and Sierra in her deep smoker's voice.

"Mackenzie will sit down with you whenever you're ready and go over everything in detail," Mason said.

"Thank you," Sierra said as she pulled Mason into a hug that Mackenzie would swear surprised him and maybe even embarrassed him slightly, which was perfect and made her laugh. "All of you," Sierra continued, moving on to Faye, who held her for several long seconds, speaking quietly into her ear, then Gabe and Drake and finally Mackenzie. "You little secret keeper! I love it. I love you. You're amazing."

Mackenzie laughed and hugged her tightly, and as Sierra ended the hug, Cole pulled Mackenzie in for another, the whole family hug happy and full of tangible love.

"Side note to anyone who's in the market for a dream honeymoon," Mason said into the microphone again, "Mackenzie will hook you up. Talk to her."

"I second that," Jackson Lowell yelled out, and Mackenzie laughed gratefully, with warmth and acceptance infusing every cell.

And then Drake came up to her and pulled her into him and kissed her in such a manner that she normally reserved for private, but tonight she didn't care. Nobody cared. Everyone was too busy celebrating, laughing, congratulating to notice the heat between her and the man she was going to marry.

"I'm so fucking glad you decided to move back to Nashville," Drake said into her ear when he finally ended the kiss.

Glad didn't begin to cover it, she thought. "Me too. Second-best decision I've ever made." She sent him a heated, flirty grin, their faces still just inches apart.

"Oh, yeah?" he said in his smug, knowing tone. "And what's the best?"

"You know exactly what it is."

"White wine instead of red?"

She laughed. Hard. This man knew her so well, and still, he loved her. "The best decision I ever made was you, and you know it, and one of the many things I love about you is that you know it."

"Best decision I ever made was you, and you know it," he

repeated, going serious. "I love you, Mackenzie Shaw, and I can't wait to make you a North."

"I love you too," she said, her voice going rough, and she thought she might honest-to-God melt into a puddle from all the goodness and love and hope surrounding her, filling her.

245

NOTE FROM THE AUTHOR

Thanks for reading *True Colors*! I hope you loved Drake and Mackenzie's story.

Watch for Gabe and Lexie's story coming soon. She's his best friend and she just got jilted on her wedding day...of course he's going to help her through the fallout. Watch my newsletter or Facebook page for more info on *True Blue*.

True North, Cole and Sierra's story, is available now in case you missed it! Find out what happens when Mr. Socially Awkward spontaneously volunteers to be his beautiful boss's fake date.

I love to hear from readers! Please drop me a line at amy@amyknupp.com or on my Facebook author page at facebook.com/AuthorAmyKnupp.

ACKNOWLEDGMENTS

I often say in my acknowledgments that writing is not a solo journey. It's practically a cliché, but every cliché originates from a truth, and this is mine.

I've been writing for publication for a lot of years, and when I think about the people who have helped me on my path of learning to tell my stories, the list is mind-boggling. From early critique groups to editors to fellow authors to my own editing clients to my husband to my core group of writing friends and soul sisters, each has helped form me into the writer I am today, with my foibles and insecurities and strengths and published book list.

I would not be the same writer without them. Every single one of them.

This book, this beloved story of Drake and Mackenzie, it tested me hard. For reasons unknown, it was one of the most difficult books for me to write, whether because of story blocks or life happenings or a hundred other possibilities. And a core group of people deserves my thank you—for listening to me vent, for helping me plot, for reminding me of my abilities, for boosting me when I was down, for believing in me.

Thank you, from the very center of my heart, to Justin Knupp, Colton Knupp, Camden Knupp, Natasha Lake, Emily Leigh, Sue Campbell, Meshanna Burno, Rachel Childers, Lisa Guertin, Edie LaReau, and Kathy Paltan. I'm so very grateful to have each of you in my life and on my side.

ALSO BY AMY KNUPP

<u>Henry Brothers Series</u>

Untold (prequel)

Unraveled

Unsung

Undone

<u>North Brothers Series</u>

True North

True Colors

True Blue

True Harmony

True Hero

North Brothers Box Sets:

North Brothers Books 1-3

North Brothers Books 4-5

North Brothers: The Complete Series

<u>Hale Street Series</u>:

Sweet Spot

Sweet Dreams

Soft Spot

One and Only

Last First Kiss

Heartstrings

<u>Hale Street Box Sets:</u>

Meet Me at Clayborne's

Clayborne's After Hours

It Happened on Hale Street

<u>Island Fire Series</u>:

Playing with Fire

Heat of the Night

Fully Involved

Firestorm

Afterburn

Up in Flames

Flash Point

Fire Within

Impulse

Slow Burn

Island Fire Box Sets:

Sparked (books 1-3)

Ignited (books 4-6)

Enflamed (books 7-10)

OR

Island Fire: The Complete Series

Themed Box Sets:

Friends to Forever (Friends to Lovers Romance)

Working It (Workplace Romance)

ABOUT THE AUTHOR

Amy Knupp is a *USA Today* Best-Selling Author of contemporary romance and a copy editor for Blue Otter Editing. She loves words and grammar and meaty, engrossing stories with complex characters.

Amy lives in Wisconsin with her husband and has two sons, four cats, and two box turtles. She graduated from the University of Kansas with degrees in French and journalism. In her spare time, she enjoys traveling, breaking up cat fights, watching college hoops, and annoying her family by correcting their grammar.

For more information:
www.amyknuppbooks.com

If you'd like to know when her next book is available, you can sign up for her newsletter, follow her on BookBub and / or follow her on the social media below.